A DANGEROUS HISTORY

A DANGEROUS HISTORY

G T MORRIS

For Terry,

who gave me the space to write my story.

*It is in vast spaces that certain men are fated to
meet and understand each other.*
GIUSEPPE VERDI

Chapter One

November 5th 1999

'Penny for the Guy.' Cassie glanced down at the forlorn Guy Fawkes propped up against the shop window.

'Worzel Gummidge it isn't boys,' she laughed, rummaging in her handbag for change. 'But a good effort all the same,' she added, crossing the road, her sights firmly on the estate agents opposite.

Normally she would not be in this area of Bristol, but a rearranged dental appointment had made it necessary for her to come here, plus of course the promise of a holiday Mark had asked her to book after they had discussed it earlier.

'Thank God the Casper contracts are finalised. Roger put his signature to the papers yesterday, and you my darling wife,' he reached out and encircled her waist, 'will be able to book that holiday you threatened every time I came home too tired to eat.'

'But what about …' Mark placed a finger against her lips.

'I promise we will concentrate on finding that perfect plot to build a house as soon as we get back. Seriously, though Cass, it might be a good idea to go to Jamaica. You have always wanted to see your adopted family's country.'

'As long as we haven't got Sabrina in tow, but it would be nice.'

'What about you?'

'I imagine one Caribbean island is very much like another.' He winked at her, picking up his briefcase.

'Dangerous ground, Mark Campbell. I shouldn't let Sab hear you say that!'

She smiled, thinking about the bargain holiday in Port Antonio she had just booked. Feeling she was on a roll, Cassie looked beyond the glossy photographs of luxurious harbour side apartments gracing the city skyline and instead, scoured the window for building plots. On impulse, she went in. A blast of wind caught hold of the door as she entered, slamming it shut.

'I've had better welcomes,' she joked, feeling slightly uncomfortable.

The young man looked up and eyed her with approval.

'I'm enquiring about building plots in the area.' Thinking perhaps she had been a little hasty, she began to waffle. 'I know it's highly unlikely but …'

'They rarely come up, in fact; I can't remember the last time I sold one.'

The man that spoke came out of a back room and stood in front of her. He was of mixed race and smartly dressed, obviously the manager. He glanced at the young man to confirm.

'There is that plot on the coast.'

'Too late, the auction is next week! Anyway, Mrs …?'

'Campbell, Cassie Campbell.'

'What I will do, Mrs Campbell, is put you on our database. That way, we can ring you as soon as anything comes up. Spring is a good time: daffodils, tulips, get my drift?' He began shuffling papers on his desk. 'Now if you will excuse me.'

Humiliated by his patronising tone, Cassie made a hurried exit.

'Mrs Campbell.' The young man walked over and handed her a set of particulars.

'It's OK; I'll call again when I have more time.' She

waved the particulars in the air. 'Thanks for these, though.'

The manager turned on the agent, banging his desk with such force that his coffee cup shattered against the computer screen. The young man looked on in horror, at his manager's face, contorted with rage.

'Why did you go against me? Why?' With extraordinary energy, he swept his arm across his desk scattering everything onto the floor. He moved menacingly towards him.

'I'm sorry, I didn't think …' He grabbed his jacket and made for the door.

'You didn't think?' he sneered, thanks to you, the succession of hundreds of years is now in serious jeopardy!'

The noise of the traffic grew loud in the young man's ears. Holding his head, he stepped on the zebra crossing. Feeling the hysteria overwhelming him, he began to panic as he looked back towards the shop and saw the sardonic face of the manager, a slow evil grin spread across his face. He held out his hand and a small girl joined him, laughing up at him, her golden curls bouncing. In his confused mind, he wondered where she had come from.

Suddenly, she fixed her gaze on him. Totally disoriented, he stared at her, unable to move from the crossing. The girl's cruel laugh reached him and he felt his head would explode; her angelic face had changed into a malevolent snarl. Her laugh reached a crescendo piercing his ears, causing him to bend double. The sound reverberated around the street, isolating him from the day. He saw a white van coming towards him and he knew it had no intention of stopping. The laugh turned into a blood-curdling wail, drowning out his screams, as the van ploughed into him.

Chapter Two

By the time Cassie reached Leigh Woods, the weather had already begun to close in; the November gloom bringing its inevitable drizzle. Pulling up at the traffic lights, she switched on the defunct wipers and absently watched them disintegrate. Damn, Mark promised he would sort it. Her thoughts went beyond the blurred windscreen to visualising the plot.

The driver behind her hit his horn, making her jump. She scowled at him in the wing mirror, unable to see his face because of the murky weather. He wound down his window, shouting obscenities, his breath spilling into the cold afternoon.

Flustered, she crashed the gears as the white van overtook her at speed, almost forcing her off the road. Shaken, Cassie pulled over.

'What was that all about?' she said, getting out of the car, reaching for her mobile and punching Mark's number.

'Cass, what's up? You okay?'

'Apart from some maniac trying to run me off the road, yes. Listen darling, can you meet me?'

'Meet you where?'

'Mark, I need you to be open-minded about this. I know we said we would look for our plot after the holiday, but I think I might have found it.'

'Cass, what are you talking about?'

'Sorry, I know I'm not making much sense.' She adjusted her mobile, tucking it under her chin as she held the sale particulars.

'It's off Sandy Way according to this. If you look for the auction sign at the top of the road …'

'Whoa, whoa, Cass, what auctions sign?'

'Mark, please!'

'OK, but there is one small problem: you have the car. Besides, I haven't a clue where this Sandy whatever is?' He heard her laugh.

'It's the other side of Warren Point, on the coast road.'

'All right, I'll get Roger's friend to drop me off, he lives on that stretch of the road.

'Anyway Cass, what am I looking at?'

'I told you, it's a surprise.'

'Well, it's going to cost you, Mrs Campbell.' She heard his sharp intake of breath.

'At the very least, a takeaway.'

'I love you, Mark Campbell. Give me a ring when you get there.'

Standing outside the car, she glanced up at the crows circling above her head, the bleak sound of flapping wings unsettling her as they noisily regrouped in the trees.

Pulling out on to the busy road Cassie listened to the haunting strains of 'The Hebrew Slaves Chorus' from the opera *Nabbuco*. Concentrating on the traffic leaving the city, she drove to the plot.

Mark sat back in his chair, reflecting on his conversation with his wife. He thought the surprise had been the holiday they talked about, but as always, she proved him wrong.

He admitted to being disappointed; oh to be somewhere with half-decent weather.

Mark got up and went over to the window, looking forward to a quiet night in with Cass, before Sabrina's and Roger's dinner party. According to Roger, Mark's old university friend and business partner, Sabrina, had put everything into it, even inviting a distinguished lecturer on

Bristol history. Of course, there was the matter of Cassie's surprise, and from experience, he knew to go along with her. But to choose today of all days and get caught up with everything that goes with November fifth … Resigned, he reached for his coat and left a message for Roger to ring Bowden Plant. Leaving the office, he crossed the road and waited for his lift.

His thoughts switched to their forthcoming wedding anniversary. Her dearest wish would be to start a family, and there wasn't any reason why they shouldn't, especially now that the contract had ended. He wanted to wait, arguing that the city would not be the ideal environment, but the memory of her turning her back and walking away had been all too real.

Of course, it would be a wrench to leave Bristol. He loved the city, with its rich history and culture; they valued their many friends and were respected in the business community. Yes, life had been kind and he didn't want anything to change.

He waved to his lift as it pulled up alongside; perhaps this property was a good thing. At least it would put an end to the never-ending search for the right place.

Reaching the outskirts of the small town, Cassie dropped her speed to thirty miles per hour and referred once again to the particulars. Continue straight ahead at the roundabout, to the top of the hill and turn right after the Seagull pub to the coast road, and right again into Sandy way, where the property can be found. Ignoring the town centre sign, she crawled up the hill behind a builder's lorry, and saw the pub in the distance.

She drove down the neat tarmac road with a sense of disappointment. The endless rows of bungalows with their tidy borders certainly did not lend itself to the image she had in mind. Turning, by mistake, into a dead end, she reversed, and went back the way she had come, passing children putting the finishing touches to their bonfire.

This time she took the correct turn and found herself in a secluded cul-de-sac. She parked and got out of the car. She shivered, her thin mac inadequate against the keen wind. In the distance she could see the outline of Wales.

Amongst the bungalows behind, she spotted a track sandwiched between a broken fence and derelict wasteland. Cautiously, she lifted the branches of a fractured elder tree that obscured the entrance. She was careful not to tread on the auction sign embedded in the mud.

The track, although narrow, seemed well used. Someone had taken the trouble to beat back the brambles that threatened to take over the path. Carefully disentangling a thorn from her sleeve, Cassie took a deep breath and began the climb.

Following the steep track had not been as easy as she first thought. Stopping several times to look around at the older bungalows, she noticed that they had all seen better days. The path followed a yew hedge that bordered one of them, until it disappeared, only to be replaced by old railings. She looked behind, in awe at the view below. Even from where she stood, the sound of waves could be heard lapping in the distance.

The hedge on her left had given way to a fence bleached by so many years in the sun, buckled and disintegrated by the sheer force of the weather.

Cassie pulled out the details: tall, timbered gate in need of repair. Despairing, she noted the path continued farther up out of view, she knew that unless there was access from the road above, there was no way Mark would even consider it.

Nothing could have prepared her for what she saw. Shocked, she took a step backwards, stinging her ankles on a clump of nettles. Before her stood the remains of a modern split-level house, now completely gutted and so charred that it contrasted starkly against the November sky. She glanced at the particulars for any reference to fire but found none.

Unable to comprehend what had happened, Cassie walked towards the building, slipping on the patio. The stench of old ashes met her and made her feel sick. An out-of-control Russian vine wove through the lattice breezeblocks of a seventies wall. It covered broken terracotta pots that lay strewn alongside a beaten-up rotary line that added to the desolation of the day. Bulbous heads of dead hydrangeas scraped against her legs as she stepped off the patio. The whole area had a feeling of neglect.

The building loomed ever closer as Cassie walked towards it. She could sense hostility with every step, as if the remaining walls held a secret. She found herself before a large open space to the right of the building, which had obviously been a used as a garage or storeroom. Charred remains of various tools were still visible: an intact saw blackened by the fire hung on a wall. To her left, without a doubt, had been a kitchen that had also suffered the same fate, stools lay restless against a scorched table. An Aga stood nearby against the wall, and above hung kitchen appliances, bleak, abandoned and twisted with heat. In the centre of the building steel girders rose up, supporting the first floor.

Cassie went up the concrete steps and stood on the threshold, staring into the blackness, the silence eerie. Her heart began pounding at a sudden clanging on the concrete floor somewhere at the back of the buildings.

Frightened, she distanced herself from the building and found a path that led to a terrace of matured plants.

The clouds had lifted, enabling her to see the garden sloping gently towards the channel. Her view was dominated finally by an old and very large willow tree that obliterated the view towards the Welsh coastline. Cassie reasoned that the garden ran parallel to the same track she had followed earlier.

Walking towards the willow, she saw the trunk shrouded in mist. Mesmerised, she stood in front of it. The shrill sound of her mobile phone echoed around the plot, making her jump.

'Cass, I'm going to be later than planned. We're still in Bristol; we're on the move now but …'

'OK. In the meantime, I'll see if I can find any more information about this place.'

'What's it like?'

Cassie turned and looked back up at the garden and at the building in shadow.

'Different … Mark, the daylight isn't the best up here and if you can get …'

'I'll get there as soon as possible, darling. Speak to you later.'

She went back down the track to the car; she had a sinking feeling. It would be a hard job convincing Mark that they could make a home here.

Chapter Three

Joseph Morgan put down the phone, pushed back his chair, and went over to the window. The high street was busy at this time of day with weekend shoppers. He spotted a middle-aged woman choosing vegetables with great care and wished his own life could be that simple. He began thinking about the conversation he had had with the auctioneer. The forthcoming auction had given him more grief than he cared to remember, especially the plot off Sandy Way. He turned his thoughts to the set of golf clubs he had bought and, weather permitting, he hoped to get a round in tomorrow. With retirement imminent, he wanted as much practise as possible. He took out a number-one wood, and began to practise his swing.

'Mrs Campbell to see you, Mr Morgan. I'm sorry, I did knock …'

'I wasn't aware I had any more appointments?'

'No, you haven't. She has come here on the off-chance that you might be able to give her some information.'

'About what?'

'The Sandy Way plot.'

Here we go again, he thought. What was he supposed to tell these people? This had been his precise argument to the auctioneers 'Meridian Properties', but Ross Meridian hadn't seen it as a problem.

'Tell them anything, flesh out the positives. Christ, Joseph, you've been in this game long enough, you know the score.'

'That's all very well Ross, but you don't have to deal with these people on a day-to-day basis. Ever since you featured the plot in the local paper, it's been manic. The phone never stops ringing.'

'Has anyone been up there?'

'Not from this office, but I think a few people have made the effort. I tell you, Ross, I'll be glad when it's sold.'

'Mr Morgan?'

'Sorry, I was miles away. I'll be right out.' Wearily, he picked up the file and went into the conference room.

'Thank you for seeing me, Mr Morgan. I really appreciate it.'

Joseph flung the file on the highly polished table, and indicated a chair she smiled at him, and he found himself smiling back.

'There's not a lot I can tell you, Mrs Campbell, other than it's due to be auctioned next week along with several other lots.'

'Yes, I know that, and I also noticed it has a price guide of five to six thousand pounds.'

'That's because planning approval to rebuild the property had been turned down.'

He leaned forward. 'There is a lot of interest in this particular lot, mainly from developers who are willing to sit on it until they eventually get planning again.'

'But it's obvious some people have tried to climb up there,' Cassie added.

'Very few and I have to admit I haven't been able to get up there myself.' He paused, fiddling with his pen. 'You know there's been a small fire in the house, don't you?'

'A small fire? It is a charred mess; it's horrific, Mr Morgan. You have to see it to believe it. What happened up there? Did anyone lose their life?'

'All I can say, Mrs Campbell, is that I have been told the fire has left some structural damage, but I believe everything else is in order. The relevant searches have been found to be satisfactory. However, as to any history of the place, the auctioneer would be the one to ask.' He took off his spectacles, indicating the end of the meeting and placing them carefully in the case.

'Can I ask where you got those sales particulars, Mrs Campbell? My understanding is that the auction deadline had closed.'

'A helpful young man in the estate agents gave them to me.'

'Well, all I can say is the property has a lot of potential and with those views towards the channel, it's a smart investment.' They got up and he walked her back to reception. 'Good luck,' he added, shaking her hand.

Cassie went back to her car with mixed feelings; she felt either he knew nothing about the property, or he knew more than he had told her. Disheartened, she watched a family with boxes of fireworks walking on the pavement. Looking up at the sky, she noticed clouds gathering, making the afternoon even gloomier. Please don't let it rain, she thought, as she drove back to the plot to meet Mark.

Chapter Four

Mark watched his driver disappear into the distance. Crossing the road, he made his way down the steep cul-de-sac, already disillusioned with the numerous identical bungalows. He hurried, annoyed at himself for allowing Cassie to talk him into coming here.

The breeze caught the back of his neck as he approached the channel. With the Welsh coastline barely visible, he could just make out one or two twinkling lights, promising to increase as they embraced the late afternoon. He swung around, startled, as Cassie came up behind him.

'You've won the first round; I like the area, not too sure about coming down through the bungalows though, and I'm slightly concerned about the sea wall. Where is it?' he said, looking around. Cassie laughed, linking her arm with his; she knew he would like it.

'Come on, let me show you before the light fades.'

They took the same track Cassie had taken earlier, but this time it seemed sinister.

Mark followed, stumbling on some loose stones.

'Cass, you can't be serious about this. Where the hell are you taking me?'

Knowing she should have told him or at least something about the plot, she pushed the gate open.

'Well, what do you think?'

'The truth was Mark didn't know what to think. At that moment, his first concern was his suit and the mud splashed on his trousers. Walking towards the half building, he stared at it, horrified.

'My God, Cass, I expected a level site. We can't make anything of this! Look at the work involved in demolishing the rest of it, and where's the access road to get machinery in?' He looked at her accusingly. 'At least you could have told me, instead of luring me here on false pretences. What the hell happened here anyway?' He began brushing mud off his sleeve.

'Mark, Mr Morgan seems to think the owners wanted to off-load it because they couldn't get planning permission to rebuild it, and for the record, I did not lure you here. I wanted to surprise you, and I knew that if you …'

'If I knew this,' he pointed towards the building, 'you know what, Cass? You were right. I wouldn't have given it the time of day.' Mark turned to leave. 'Now if you don't mind, I'm tired and hungry. Are you coming?'

Cassie leaned towards him and held his arm, indicating the building.

'Darling, I'm sorry. I know I should have told you, but we're here now. Surely it makes sense to look at it before it gets dark. You are the far-sighted one Mark; with your vision we could take our time to rebuild it. The situation is ideal; just look at all the natural light we would get up here. What more could we want?'

'Not that for a start,' he said, nodding to the building.

'Please, Mark, I can't think of a better place to settle down and bring up a family. Go and look it over – it might not be as much work as you imagined. I'm going down to look at the garden again.'

He watched her as she disappeared. Shaking his head and thrusting his hands into his pockets, Mark walked towards the gutted shell. A strange silence descended as he got nearer. Rain that had earlier held off came in on a sudden strong breeze. Carefully sidestepping a mangled rotary line and other debris, he confronted the building. Bracing himself, he went up the concrete steps into the main building, wondering what kind of builder would use such a cold element for a staircase, reminding him of a stairwell in a high-rise block of flats. Even in the shadows he was stunned to see the devastation the fire had caused. The bittersweet smell of dead ashes reached his nostrils as he kicked through the traces from the aftermath of the fire.

Mark stood rigid, spooked by the silence and the constant drip, drip of water from one of the steel girders above his head. He felt the urge to shout out, convinced someone would answer. Shuddering, he looked up, tasting the rust in the water falling on his lips. Indignant, he wiped his mouth on his sleeve.

Sodden waste squelched under his feet as he entered what seemed to be a child's room. His foot came into contact with a humming top, and he inadvertently kicked it, causing it to spin bizarrely amongst the rubbish before shooting off into a corner and resting against a doll's pram. Mark watched it with an overpowering sense of sadness. In the half light, he noticed a chest that had somehow escaped the fire next to the charred remains of a small bed. For no reason, Mark opened it. He took a backward step, recoiling in horror. Piles of children's clothes, neatly folded, that now were stained and sodden in the waterlogged drawer. Mark, nauseated at the stench, slammed it shut.

Feeling uneasy, he crossed the room, leaving behind the harrowing destitution, only to find the lounge opposite had suffered the same fate. Moving to the back of the building, he found the bathroom. Unable to move, he stopped in the doorway. A distinct chill made his skin crawl as he peered into the shadows.

The bath extended the length of one wall, the white porcelain at odds with the charcoal surroundings. In the corner, a glass shelf balanced dangerously on a fitting that had been wrenched from the wall. Shards of glass pointed toward him, reminiscent of a medieval trap. Wet towels slung casually over the bath now hung, embedded, with splinters of glistening glass.

Beads of perspiration broke out on his forehead, and he accidently caught hold of a bathrobe next to him. Distancing himself, he edged over to the other side of the bathroom, all the time aware of the drips of water that had multiplied with the onset of the rain. Drawn back to the bath, he noticed shifting images floating around it. They were becoming stronger, and Mark watched them drifting outwards into the room. The atmosphere had suddenly changed, and he backed off, wanting to get out of there. The wind moaned through the building, bouncing off the girders and sweeping through every room, stopping abruptly behind him. Seriously spooked, Mark stood petrified, and felt the slime that clung to his fingers from the bathrobe. The hair on the back of his neck bristled at the nearness of a presence. Without warning, the bath taps turned full on, steam filling the room. He watched, terrified.

A scream pierced the building, bringing him back to the present. The wind had withdrawn, recoiling into the walls, and the images vanished. He knew beyond doubt it was Cass. He ran, leaving the harrowing building.

Delayed by the unfamiliar layout of the garden, he shouted out to her, unsure which way to go, but the strength of the wind and violent weather made it impossible. Side-stepping the patio, he tripped on the rotary line, and fell on the concrete slabs. He felt the line tightening around his legs, gripping him. An excruciating pain coursed through his body.

The building loomed up in front of him, silent and threatening, as he tried to free his legs. He heard Cass scream. It was even more gut-wrenching, and his pain turned to anger.

'Oh, I get it, you don't want us here, but you better get

used to it because I'm personally going to take you apart, brick-by-fucking brick.' He felt the wire slacken. A surge came from the building and, turning his back on it, Mark rushed down the garden to Cassie.

Taking another path, Cassie found it led to a rockery. Larger-than-usual boulders were home to ice plants and various other small succulents growing out of gaping crevasses. The willow had a strange aura that she hadn't noticed earlier. Mesmerised, she watched the branches whipping up into a frenzy caused by the storm coming in from the channel. The sound of fireworks peppered the night air, intensified by the rolling seas far below.

Gripped by the willow's sudden unrest, she stood looking up at it; the whole tree had a life of its own. Disoriented, she stumbled and fell on to the rockery, feeling the raw earth against her face. She cried out.

In the near darkness, she saw them. Disturbed by her fall, they were everywhere, their cold slimy flesh scrambling over her arms and feet as she tried to raise herself. Her scream tore through the storm. Hysterical and unable to move, she looked down at toads tumbling over themselves trying to climb her ankles. The feeling of mucous already congealed on her skin

'Mark! For the love of God, help me!' The rain beat down on her and with the sickening stench of disrupted earth, she felt herself sink down into the rockery.

The willow began thrashing uncontrollably, and with an effort, Cassie turned to look. The branches were reaching out towards her. Her scream was agonizing as once again she called for Mark.

'Cass, dear God, what's happened?' She clung to him as he held her close.

'Mark, there are toads in there.' She pointed to the rockery.

'Come on, let's go and see.' He led her back to the

rockery. 'Cass, there's nothing.'

'I know what I saw, Mark, they were crawling all over me.'

'It's all right, darling, I believe you. Here, take my coat, you're freezing.'

Clinging to each other, they looked up at the willow.

'Come on, let's get back while we can, otherwise we'll have hundreds of years come crashing down on us.'

They hurried back up the garden. A firework lit up their way; it was followed by a loud bang.

'Mark? What happened to you?' Cassie noticed his clothes in the light.

'I had a fight with a rotary line.' He steered her towards the gate, glancing briefly at the building. 'Anyway, I've got the gist of this place.'

Cassie, surprised at the bitterness in his voice, went through the gate, pausing to look at the plot. The building had merged into the darkness adding to her disquiet.

The storm raged through the garden; only the willow seemed immune. It stood, silent and spent. She stared, remembering how ferocious the tree had been. Unsettled, she hastily followed Mark down the track.

The persistent rain had almost obliterated the path. Wincing with pain, Cassie struggled to locate her shoe that had succumbed to the mud. The skyline was lit up with bonfires not yet extinguished by the storm. Treading carefully, they eventually reached the bottom.

'That's strange; I don't remember that bonfire being there earlier!' Cassie shouted over the storm, as the bonfire, burning brightly ahead, confronted them.

Mark grabbed her hand, dodging the sparks as they side stepped it.

'Me neither, but it won't be there much longer. This is the worst storm in years. You should get in the car, Cass.'

'There's something else, Mark. Look! No one is standing around the fire. Don't you think that's strange?'

'Oh, come on, Cass, you are reading too much into it.' He opened his door, glancing back at the bonfire burning intensely.

'Like the toads you mean?' But her sarcasm was lost on the storm.

'It's dangerously near the entrance of the plot and those brambles over there,' Mark said, looking at the bundle of clothes passing, vaguely, as a Guy. He moved closer. 'If I didn't know better, I would think he was guarding it. Hang on a minute, since when has the traditional Guy Fawkes been replaced?'

Cassie followed to where he pointed, wiping the rain from her face.

'Look in the centre, Mark. What is that?'

The bonfire had taken on another dimension; it began crackling fiercely with a life of its own. Immune to the storm, the flames reached higher and higher. Cassie stared at the bizarre scene and found herself walking towards it. Sparks began flying, creating pools of fire where they fell.

Staring into the core of the bonfire, the face of a little girl smiled out at her. Drawn, Cassie stepped towards the wall of heat; it felt comforting and warm like a soft blanket. The girl held out her arms, her golden hair framed by a white light of intense heat that only added to the vision.

'Cass! What are you doing?'

She turned and saw Mark's horrified expression; the spell was broken. Shocked at the scene she had witnessed, she ran back to him, and he wrenched the door open for her. Cassie looked back at the bonfire and the child's fading image, appalled to see the change in her features, a sneer obviously meant for her. Shaking, she reached over towards Mark.

'Whatever possessed you? I thought you were going to

step into that goddam inferno. What did you see anyway?'

'An illusion, nothing more.' Cassie sank back in to the passenger seat and closed her eyes, now totally convinced the plot was definitely bad news.

Chapter Five

Shivering, and not only from the cold, Cassie stared at the windscreen, trying to make sense of everything. Mark, noticing her mood, placed his hand on hers. She smiled at him, finding it comforting.

'Still want to do this?' he asked casually.

'What about you?' Cassie looked straight ahead.

'I'm asking you, Cass.'

She sucked in her breath. 'If you had asked me that question an hour ago, I would have had no hesitation; you know how passionate I was about it, but …'

'But?' he prompted.

She looked at him, listening to the grinding of the wipers dealing with the onslaught.

'I wish I knew. It's not the shock of seeing the building gutted by fire, or the toads. It's the slow trickle of uncertainty that comes with it. I don't think I am emotionally able to deal with it, Mark. I felt on such a high when I picked up the details from the estate agent but now … Oh I don't know, it's all these weird things that are happening around us, and I have to ask myself, do I really need this? I already feel guilty about bringing you here, and perhaps, with hindsight, I should have thought about it more.'

'Cass, my darling, you know I would not want you any other way, but if it's any consolation I feel the same. Like you, I became seriously spooked, especially inside the building. It got to the point where I actually thought I was seeing things.'

'You sensed it too.'

'Cass, who is the solicitor?'

'Mr Morgan, of Morgan, Watson and Prewitt.'

'Can't say I've had any dealings with them. What about the auctioneer, did he mention them?'

'No, but his secretary did, Meridian Properties.'

'Not Ross Meridian? Well, well.'

'Do you know him?'

'Yes, my darling, you could say that, and I wouldn't trust him any farther than I could throw him.'

***

'Christ, Cass, these wipers are bloody useless.'

She bit her lip, reminding him he had said he would renew them would only aggravate the situation. They left the coast road for their own safety taking the back road until a welcome glow of streetlights came into view and with it a sense of security. Her thoughts turned to the weekend.

'Did Roger say anything about tomorrow night?'

'Yes, I said we would be over at eight.'

'We'll have to be on time, Mark; you know how Sab is for punctuality.'

Mark glanced over at her and grinned. 'That's local government officers for you. I really don't know why she doesn't lighten up sometimes.'

'Because she wouldn't know how.'

They fell into silence, passing through avenues of trees that had a life of their own. Torn branches swept before them and debris, coiled like tumbleweed, bounced on the side of the verge. Cassie began laughing uncontrollably, staring out at the road.

'Cass?'

'I'm sorry, Mark, it's the situation, it's surreal. It's as if we're watching a film.' She began laughing again. 'I can't believe everything that is happening to us.'

'Well, you better believe this, my darling, apart from that white van on the other side of the road, I haven't seen another vehicle.' Cassie sat bolt upright.

'Did you say a white van?'

'Yes, why?'

'A white van almost ran me off the road, in fact; we are nearing the very place it happened!'

Trees swayed in the inky blackness behind a curtain of rain, angry, as if holding a secret. She shuddered as they passed, half expecting to see the van in the wood.

Mark changed gear as they approached the suspension bridge. The bridge lurched, buffeting the car violently, sweeping the storm through the gantry. He pulled into one of the filter lanes.

'Something's happened – there are flashing lights ahead. I'm getting out having a look. Cass, you stay here.' He went before she could answer.

Suddenly, a crack shook the car. She screamed as a tree almost came down on top of her. Beside herself, she began scrambling to get out.

'Mark, it's coming after us! It wants me!' Mark turned back to their car,

'It's OK, Cass. Are you all right?' he asked, wrenching open the door, and holding her close. 'Now what were you saying?' dabbing her eyes with a tissue.

'Nothing, I'm tired and overreacting. What about the car?

'Stay here, Cass.' He saw her hesitation. 'I'm only going around the back, you'll be safe here.'

He reappeared, drenched, with the rain penetrating his clothes.

'We can't reverse out of here that's for sure. How that tree missed the car I'll never know, talk about divine intervention. Listen, I'll try and get the barrier to work. We have to cross that bridge somehow, incident or no incident.'

Shaking with cold, Cassie saw the cables swinging perilously. She could also hear branches scraping against the rear window like arthritic fingers trying to gain access. The thought of it caused her to scream – it sounded hollow as the storm raged outside. Wrapping her arms around her body, she began rocking, tears falling into her lap.

Mark banged on the window, making her jump causing the window to drop. The full force of the rain impacted in her face.

'The barrier is jammed!'

Disoriented, the contents of her handbag spilled into the foot well. She recoiled, appalled, at the coldness of his touch as she handed him the coin. She realised he had reached breaking point. His usually immaculate clothes hung wet and useless. Racked with guilt, she watched him thumping the machine in frustration, the deluge almost knocking him sideways.

'Goddamn it,' he said, fighting his way back to her side of the car. 'We're going to have to abandon the car!' he shouted over the cyclone.

'It's getting worse. I say we walk to Rownham Hill, and try, to get down to the Portway and catch a taxi.' Cassie wasn't listening: her mind was focused on the bridge.

'Mark! Look behind you – all the lights are out on the bridge! My God, we are trapped. We're going nowhere. It won't let us!' Mark saw the terror in her eyes.

His voice sounded deadly calm. 'I'm not listening to this!'

Cassie shouted after him as he disappeared out of sight.

***

Mark almost welcomed the vicious onslaught from the mouth of the River Avon. The bridge swayed uncontrollably and

32

with it, a fog that came from nowhere. His emotions were in turmoil as he stared out towards the channel. Barely able to stand, he gripped the rail, angry with himself for leaving her.

Feeling isolated, Cassie stood terrified, and the panic was overwhelming her. Then she saw him. A black male standing in front of her appeared agitated and furtive. Even in the eye of the storm, she noticed blood from facial wounds mingling with the torrential rain. He lunged towards the car; his arms outstretched.

Cassie opened her mouth to scream, but nothing happened. His frightened eyes darted from side to side. A flash of lightning lit the bridge like daylight, and for a split second, his eyes locked with hers. Powerless before him, she felt an overwhelming compassion.

'Don't be frightened. I understand you, believe me, I feel your need. You have to help me – I can't do this on my own.' Her words must have reached him because he raised his arms upwards towards the sky, letting out the most excruciating cry.

Drained, she leant forward and closed her eyes, determined not to give in to the torrent of emotion.

'Cass.'

'Mark, thank God! Did you see him? You must have seen him – he stood over there.' She pointed into space.

'Who, Cass?'

He wrapped his arms around her, trying to give warmth to her freezing body 'Anyway, who would be out on a night like this?'

'You don't understand – I saw a man here, a black man, by our car.' Mark felt exhausted. Besides, he had little appetite for confrontation.

'Cass, darling, I don't see anyone here now. Come on, let's try, and get out of here.'

She pulled away, looking up at him. 'Mark, what I am

going to say is important. Forget everything I said earlier about not wanting to buy the plot. Somehow, and don't ask me how, it's linked to this man. We must buy it! Don't you see he is willing us, Mark …?

'Cass, Cass, hang on a minute. You were dead against it earlier, and you really can't expect me to believe some far-fetched story about a black …' He sighed at the expression on her face.

'Come on! At this moment I'll believe anything, even this nightmare of standing on the suspension bridge in the dark, in one of the worst storms in living memory.' Catching hold of her arm, he got her back into the car. 'Anyway, whoever it is has long gone,' he added.

'Look – the barrier is working and the lights are on.' She watched the shimmer of lights trailing the drawbridge at the entrance of the bridge.

Driving with care, they reached the other side, where a police officer flagged them down.

'What's happening? We were in complete darkness back there.'

'Yes, and it could happen again, that's why we're closing the bridge. We're in the process of clearing the earlier accident – an impatient driver trying to overtake, can you believe it on this bridge!'

Cassie leaned over. 'Was it a white van?'

'No idea, but I'd get home if I were you.'

'Just a minute, Sergeant.'

'It's Constable, Constable Palmer.'

'I think you should know we had other problems. A tree is down near the barrier, it narrowly missed our car and naturally my wife is badly shaken.'

'There is someone injured on the bridge,' Cassie added. 'Please, he's distressed.'

'I'll make a point of getting over there and checking it

out. This storm wasn't forecast so it's possible some people were taken by surprise. Quarter past six. My shift finishes soon, thank God. Don't worry I'll get across somehow. Where are you two heading?'

'Cotham.' They both answered.

A feeling of security surrounded them as they drove through Clifton towards Cotham.

Chapter Six

Morning light streamed through the bedroom window. Cassie groaned at the intrusion, turned over and pulled the duvet over her head, drifting back into that halfway state between sleep and consciousness. Did that really happen last night? The thought slipped into her mind and left it again as she dozed.

Mark, already up, contemplated his reflection in the bathroom mirror, carefully negotiating the dark stubble with his razor and thought about the events of the last twenty-four hours. In the cold light of day as always, things looked entirely different. Nevertheless, he couldn't shake off the strange atmosphere he'd felt at the plot. The phone rang, causing him to cut himself.

'Damn! Cass, can you get that?' he shouted. Hearing no reply, he flung down the towel and went to answer it.

'Mark?'

'Oh, hi Sab.'

'Are you all right? Mark?'

'A heavy night, Sab. I expect you want to talk to Cass. I think she's awake.'

'It's OK, don't disturb her, I only rang to confirm tonight.'

'Roger said eight.'

'Couldn't make it earlier, Mark? You know Cass and I like to have a natter. Oh, and I've invited our new neighbours from Devon, or was it Somerset? A nice couple relocating here. And Lorna's bringing her new date; he's an eminent historian who's taken up a post at the university.'

If nothing else, it will give our little soirée a touch of

class.' Mark ended the call and grinned to himself. The last time they attended one of Sabrina's dinner parties, Lorna's escort on that occasion was a middle-aged man who turned out to be married. Lorna responded by getting drunk and flirting with every male at the party.

He went into the kitchen to make toast, noticing the slight movement of the telegraph lines in the aftermath of the storm. But it was an uneasy calm. Reaching for a plate, he switched on the radio in time for the local news.

'The suspension bridge gave cause for concern last night. It seems a freak storm and a minor accident led to the bridge closure at five o'clock. Traffic had to be diverted to other routes. A police spokesman said they were unable to establish the failure of the lights on the bridge, and it took several minutes before they were restored. In a tragic twist …'

Mark went into the bedroom. 'Cass?'

'Please leave me, Mark. After last night, I could sleep for a week.' She rolled over.

'What time were we on the bridge?' He persisted.

'How do you expect me to remember?'

'It's important.'

'We left the plot at about five-thirty.'

'And?' He prompted.

'What's all this about?' Cassie raised herself on her elbow, now fully awake. 'Look I remember the police officer saying it was quarter past six, because he said he was waiting to go off duty.'

'Thank goodness.' He sat down on the bed.

'Mark, what is it?'

'The suspension bridge. According to the radio bulletin it closed at five o'clock.'

'But that's impossible. They've made a mistake.'

'That's why I wanted to establish the time we were there.'

Cassie pushed back the duvet; her lie-in forgotten. 'Who

was on the phone?' she asked changing the subject.

'Sabrina, she wants us to go over before her other guests arrive. She has invited her new neighbours that have relocated from Somerset. Oh, and your favourite person Lorna.'

'Oh no,' she groaned, pulling a face at her reflection in the mirror.

'Apparently, she wants to show off her date.'

'That's even worse, does he know what to expect? Should be an interesting evening,' she added looking for her other slipper. She will eat that poor man for hors d'oeuvre and then start on you and Roger for the main.' She found the other slipper and thrust her foot into it.

'Cass, I don't like her either, but she is a friend of Sabrina's and let's face it, she's never harmed us. In fact, Roger says she thinks we are a lovely couple.'

'You always have a way of making me look bad, Mark Campbell.'

'That's because you are bad, Mrs Campbell.' He took off her slipper.

'By the way, Mark, I've booked that holiday we talked about. Jamaica as you suggested.'

'Sounds good to me.'

Cassie giggled. Yesterday's events momentarily forgotten.

***

By mid-afternoon, Sabrina Henderson had made the final touches to her meringue. She stood back to admire her creation, before placing it carefully in the fridge.

Passing the casement window, she saw her husband, Roger, spearing his garden fork into the bonfire. He leant forward on the handle, watching smoke from damp leaves curl upwards. He caught sight of her and waved. Sabrina noticed branches from her beloved monkey tree had taken the brunt of the storm. Roger gathered them up and threw them on the fire, prompting thick smoke to fill the garden. With a sigh, she went back into the kitchen.

She had been expecting a call from Cassie but for whatever reason, she hadn't rung. With an uneasy feeling, she picked up a duster.

Her thoughts turned to the past, and the tragic day that Cassie's parents lost their lives in a car accident. Without any relatives and at the age of twelve, Sabrina's family had adopted Cassie.

They had become friends at an early age and, both being only children, they naturally formed a special bond. In the words of Sabrina's mother, it made perfect sense. Passing the duster over the ornate mirror above the mantle, she looked at her reflection. She had inherited most of her features from her Jamaican father; her English mother's genes were much more subtle, resulting in a poise and elegance that typified her beauty. She picked up a photograph of Cassie and herself taken at their graduation, remembering the occasion clearly, especially her mother's pride that day. Wiping away a tear, she picked up the silver frame next to it. The four of them on holiday in Wales. How could they have possibly known how ill she would become? Her mother died the following year, never discussing her cancer with either of them. Her father never got over it, blaming himself for not recognising the signs. He left his position as a senior oncologist and took a posting overseas.

Cassie met Mark at Leeds University, and his declaration of love came when she least expected it.

'I can't believe it, Sab; I didn't think he was the least bit interested in me.'

'Well, you should have asked me, Cass. I could have told you. It was obvious – everyone in our circle knew.' She smiled, rubbing the silver sugar bowl and holding it up to the light. It was uncanny how everything had fallen into place.

Sabrina met Roger the day of Cassie's and Mark's wedding. Mark had made his friend best man. When Mark relocated his business to Bristol, where he and Cass bought a flat, he took Roger with him, setting up a partnership in the city. She jumped as Roger came behind her and kissed her neck.

'And what are you thinking about?'

'The past and how much we owe Mark and Cass for bringing us together.'

He crossed the room and poured them both a drink.

'I'll drink to that.' He handed her a glass. 'I never for one moment regretted meeting you, Sabrina, or moving to Bristol, even though you fought against me,' he said, winking.

'That's out of order, Rog. I only wanted to make a career for myself, and I needed to get to know you properly.'

'Can't argue with that,' he said, watching her short hair curling tantalising close to her ears as she concentrated on the place settings.

'Any information on this guy Lorna's bringing?'

'Only that she used to be his temp, and that he is well respected at the university.'

'Are you okay, Sab?'

'It's Cass. I can't get hold of her, Rog.'

'Perhaps she's shopping,' he offered, stacking logs on the hearth.

'On Saturday? I doubt it.'

Throwing a match on the fire, they both watched it burst into life.

Chapter Seven

Cassie arranged the three-strand pearl necklace carefully around her neck, the lustrous hue enhancing her skin tone. The evocative strains of the Slaves Chorus played in the background. She walked over to the full-length mirror, leaning forward to put on her matching earrings. She chose to wear black tonight – it matched her mood. If only she could shake off this melancholy feeling, she thought, spraying on perfume.

It had been Mark's idea to take time out and relax at home; they needed to be calm and reflect on the last twenty-four hours.

She laughed as he came up behind her, struggling with his bow tie. 'Here, Campbell, let me do it.' She turned to face him.

'It's ridiculous having to dress up like this. It's only a dinner after all,' he muttered, poking around with it.

'You know what Sab's like, she'll be out to impress.'

'Oh, you mean Lorna's lecturer? That figures.' He stood back, running a forefinger underneath his collar. 'You haven't seen my cufflinks, Cass?' She went to get them.

'Mark, you don't suppose I should ring Sab?'

'There's no time. Anyway, you will be seeing her in ten minutes.'

Rain clouds scudded across the night sky, and the wind had begun gathering pace again. A gust caught the cerise tissue wrapped around a bottle of wine, tossing it into the night before it fluttered down into the gutter.

'Clifton, please, driver,' Mark said as the taxi drove away.

***

The hall radiated light through the open door.

'Cass, thank God, I've been out of my mind! Where have you been?' Cassie hugged her.

'We were exhausted,' Mark answered for her, shutting the door behind him. 'Where's Rog?'

'In the lounge. Come, I want you to meet our new neighbours.' Mark laid a casual arm around Sabrina's shoulder as she led him through. Cassie had never seen her so animated; Sabrina's brown eyes glowed as she made her entrance, she introduced them to a couple standing by the window.

Cassie immediately sensed the man's unease. Sabrina's magnificent chandelier cruelly highlighted the beads of perspiration shining down on his smooth head. His wife seemed tiny by comparison but pretty in an old-fashioned way. Her ageing hair was already escaping from under a dark red hairband that Cassie found strangely endearing.

'Sabrina tells me you're a builder, Don?' Mark said, offering him nuts from a nearby table.

'That's not strictly true. I'm a developer actually. My wife, Anne, and I have moved here to expand the business further,' he smiled. Relaxing, Mark began discussing opportunities in the area and Cassie turned her attention to Anne who listened politely to Cassie's small talk.

At that moment, Sabrina breezed in with a tray of nibbles. Excusing herself, Cassie went over to her, only to be waylaid by Roger.

'Don't know where you were today, but Sab's been fretting.'

'Oh, come on, Rog,' she chided. 'I don't have to explain.' She saw his amused expression as he winked over at Lorna.

'It had better be good, 'he added, mischievously.

Slightly rattled, Cassie turned her attention to Lorna.

'And how are you, Lorna?' she asked, diverting her eyes from Lorna's exquisite cleavage to the man leaning against the mantelpiece. He smiled at her. Lorna, following Cassie's gaze, held out her hand and drew him into the circle, introducing him as Felix.

She listened to Lorna's inane banter, before excusing herself and going in search of Sabrina.

'What's going on, Cass?' she said, opening a bottle of wine over the kitchen sink.

'I suppose you've been talking to Mark?'

'Only briefly when you were chatting to Roger.'

'Did he tell you anything?'

'Only that you had a surreal experience, and not in a good way … are you going to tell me, Cass?'

They sat down together at the table. Cassie sipped her wine and listened to the faint splatter of rain against the window. She stared at Sabrina, her expression serious.

'Everything started out normally yesterday. I went shopping in Bedminster and …'

'Bedminster? You never shop in Bedminster!'

'Sab, listen. My dentist sent me there. Anyway, on the off-chance, I went into the estate agents and came out with details on a plot of land.'

Sabrina topped up their glasses. 'Go on.'

'Well, I went to view it.' She noticed Sabrina's surprised expression. 'I had to, Sab. It's going to auction next week. The situation is perfect, overlooking the Bristol Channel. Anyway, I rang Mark, and Roger's friend, what's his name?'

'Chris.'

'Yes, he dropped him off.' Cassie took a deep breath. 'Mark took some persuading and that's still on-going. The access isn't great and he wasn't keen on the approach through the bungalows that overlooked the channel.'

'Don't tell me, you twisted him around your little finger.' Sab laughed.

Cassie didn't laugh. Instead, she got up and walked across the kitchen, her arms folded.

'Sab, although it has a lot going for it,' she absently kicked a bottle cork along the floor.' There is a dark side.'

'A dark side, Cass? Whatever do you mean?'

'The whole area is devastated by fire, including most of the house. Frankly, it's a complete mess.'

Sabrina sat back in the chair, incredulous. 'It sounds horrendous. What are you going to do?'

'The more we stayed at the plot, the more it unnerved us. And when the storm came in with a vengeance, it all became too much, so we decided against it.'

Sabrina stared ahead, lost in thought.

'Then circumstances happened on the suspension bridge that caused me to change my mind.' Sabrina snapped out of her thoughts and stared at her.

'In that storm? Were you mad?' She listened as Cassie described the incident on the bridge.

'My God, Cass, it takes some believing. You must have been terrified. Don't take this the wrong way but are you sure you saw this man?'

'I know, I've been over this myself. If I'm honest, I don't think Mark believed me, although oddly, we didn't discuss it today, probably because of what we had been through.'

'I felt an empathy with him, Sab, almost as if our fates were interlinked. For a split second, I felt in another time zone. His broken spirit reminded me of a …'

'Slave?' Sabrina offered. A sudden gust rattled the window.

'Cass, remember that day when we were children and Mum took us to Weston-Super-Mare?' Sabrina got up and opened the oven door, stabbing the turkey with a skewer.

'And we came across that Romany on the beach and she said you had a sixth sense. She insisted you had a destiny to fulfil, and only you had the key, and we all laughed because mum told her that any key you had you would lose.'

'Yes, I remember, and we hadn't any silver to cross her palm because we spent it in the arcade. And she spat in the sand, and we all thought she would put a curse on us,' Sabrina finished.

'Come on Cass,' she said, linking arms with her. 'Let's drink the rest of this bottle with our guests.' Laughing, they went to join the others.

***

Don Berry cast his eyes around the magnificent drawing room. So, this is how the other half live, he thought. It was their first invitation since moving to Clifton and he hoped it would be the first of many. Always ambitious, he imagined the business contacts he could make, especially with the Campbell Henderson partnership. They were held in high esteem throughout the southwest, and to get to know them socially would be a coup indeed. What a stroke of luck that he and Anne happened to buy the house next door to Roger and Sabrina Henderson; he intended to use it to his advantage. He realised Mark was talking.

'Sorry, Mark, I was miles away.'

'Oh, I see – our Lorna. I agree she can be a distraction, Don, particularly when she knows she can create havoc on us mere males,' Mark said, watching Lorna with Felix. 'Has Sabrina introduced you?' he added.

'No, I was about to when you and Cass arrived,' Sabrina interrupted, holding a tray of canapés. 'Roger, darling, you're neglecting your duties again,' she whispered in his ear.

Roger introduced the couple to Lorna, who held out a

languid hand.

'I understand you're the new neighbours.' The intimidation in her voice alarmed Anne.

'Somerset, isn't it? I've never been there, but I'm sure it's very green,' she added sweetly, aware that she had everyone's attention. 'And what do you think of our great city, Anne? You will have many more work opportunities here in Bristol.'

'I don't intend to work, I prefer to stay at home and look after Don, and of course there is the garden to attend.' Anne smiled, trying to sound interesting.

Lorna laughed. 'Oh my God, Anne, you're priceless!' She tapped Don on the arm. 'I hope you appreciate the little wife looking after your every need, Don.'

Don, choking on his wine, uttered a garble response, tearing his eyes from the red satin dress that fitted Lorna like a second-skin.

'I admire you, Anne, for not having aspirations. It's commendable in this day and age,' Roger said, kindly.

'Sab and I will show you how we do it in Bristol, Anne. I take it you have a credit card, Don?' Lorna said seductively.

'Platinum, actually.' Don beamed.

'There we are then; we'll start by hammering that.'

Mark roared with laughter, and Don watched, fascinated.

Anne, humiliated at Don's response, gave him a scathing glance, and moved towards a large painting that had caught her eye earlier.

'Do you like it? Roger asked, from behind her.

'Yes, it's very unusual.' Anne tilted her head to one side. 'I don't know Bristol very well, but it seems to me it's painted from an unfamiliar viewpoint.'

Surprised, he said, 'that's very perceptive of you, Anne. It's painted from St Vincent's Rock, from the original drawing by William West. Sabrina bought it for my birthday.

Notice the chain bridge, it's one of the many design ideas put forward at the time.'

'Well, I'm glad they chose the Brunel design. It certainly makes life easier coming from the West Country.'

'You have a point there,' Roger acknowledged.

'Are we all ready to eat?' Sabrina waved a decanter of wine towards the dining room with one hand and steered Felix with the other. Lorna followed, linking arms with Don.

'Don't let Lorna get to you, Anne. I know she's out of order, but the secret is to ignore her,' Roger whispered, guiding her towards the dining room. She smiled up at him, feeling more confident.

A warm ambience settled on the dining room as they took their places. A sudden gust rattled the casement windows and Sabrina got up, closing them firmly. Unnerved, Cassie glanced at Mark who was seated at the other end of the table. Felix listened to Anne's description of rural life, all the time watching Lorna flirting outrageously. Lorna picked up a serviette and blew it softly into Mark's face, who was sitting beside her.

'I know the feeling, people can disappoint,' Anne said, following his gaze. Felix smiled at her as if he was seeing her for the first time. He shrugged his shoulders and listened once more to the benefits of making one's jam.

Sabrina had good reason to feel satisfied. Everything appeared to be going to plan. Animated conversation filled the room with the arrival of the first course. Smiling with satisfaction, she took a seat next to Mark, watching Roger chattering to Cassie. At one point Cassie laughed at something that Roger had said, her auburn hair falling forward in a natural wave as she chided him. Mark also observed the scene.

'She told you what happened.' He cut into her thoughts.

'You must know that she would. Do you think it's likely someone would have been on the bridge?' Sabrina chose her words carefully, playing with the stem of her wine glass, her long fingers playing with the intricate design. Mark stared into the middle distance.

'I didn't see anyone, but that's not to say … Sab, something kept us on that bridge last night – we were completely immobilised! The incident with the car, and then the accident on the bridge with the lights failing.' He paused. 'And then the worst storm, certainly in my lifetime. Christ, Sab, I found myself pinned to the rail. The surge of the sea came rushing in from the channel on a dangerously high tide into the gorge. To say I feared for my life is an understatement and on top of all that, I had no idea where Cass was. And then the wailing started, becoming louder as the sound travelled on the tide, bouncing off the rocks before stopping abruptly on the bridge.' Mark could feel Sabrina observing him. 'Sab, I was left with this overwhelming sense of …'

'Of what?' she pressed.

'Lost souls,' he whispered.

'My God, Mark, Cassie never mentioned this!'

'That's because I haven't told her. I don't know why I'm telling you, Sab. Don't they call it being in denial?' Mark smiled into his glass.

'So, what next?' She sensed he wanted to move on.

'I'm finding out more on Monday. Apparently, there is very little information on the place. It's ironic because we had already decided not to buy it.'

'But from talking to her, I think she's changed her mind.'

'Yes, I know, she now believes we are meant to buy the plot, and nothing will persuade her otherwise. I personally think the plot and bridge incidents are not connected but Cass is adamant they are.'

'Well, perhaps if you decide to buy it and build a home, she will feel more settled. Cass said the auction is next week, which doesn't leave much time.'

'What auction?' Lorna switched her attention to Mark. 'What are you up to now, Mark darling?' She pouted and Mark laughed, glad of the diversion.

Lorna had become bored with Don and his tedious empire – as if she cared. He even offered to take her sailing in his yacht.

'With the wife of course – all above board, eh?' he said, laughing at his own joke.

Mark got up to make a toast. 'Fellow guests, I would like to toast my wife, Cass, for finding the perfect plot to build our dream house. Please raise your glasses to Cass.'

All eyes turned towards her, and she felt herself blush at the unwanted attention. She looked up the table at Mark, surprised at his words, and wondered what had prompted him to drink so heavily.

'All that remains is to secure the property at the auction next week,' he added.

'That's fantastic, Mark. Who's handling the sale?' Roger queried.

'Ross Meridian.'

'Not Meridian Properties? Be careful, you know what a slippery customer he can be.'

'This all very intriguing, Cassandra, do tell all,' Lorna said, resting her chin in her hand.

'There's nothing to tell really, Mark has said it all. Although I have to say the views over the channel are something else.'

'It's not Bristol then?' Roger said, surprised.

'No, it's farther down the coast.'

'I don't know of any level building sites on that coastline.' Roger looked at Mark for confirmation.

'That's because it's not level, Rog,' Cassie cut in. 'For a start, the plot is on a steep incline with part of a building still intact.'

'What do you mean, part of a building still intact?'

Cassie stared at her, unable to hide her dislike. 'I mean, Lorna, there had been a fire at the property and …'

'And the place had been left in a hurry. Anyway, that's what we think happened,' Mark finished.

'Oh, how creepy. Give me good old central Bristol any day. Bars, bright lights, a cash-point on every corner.' Lorna wagged a manicured nail at Don. 'Oh no, you won't bury me deep in the country.'

Don laughed, relieved to be given another chance.

'It's hardly deep in the country, Lorna.' Felix's voice was measured, his arm slung casually behind the back of a chair. Lorna glared at him, both knowing their relationship had already run its course.

'I'll help with bulldozing the rest of it,' Don offered. 'My equipment will soon sort it out – clean as a whistle in no time.' He grinned, looking at the other guests for approval.

'Thanks, Don, I may well take you up on that. It would certainly help to level the site while we are on holiday. That's if we buy it,' Mark said, looking down the table at Cass.

Anne glanced at her husband, surprised at his offer, but looked away quickly at his frown.

The conversation turned to Mark and Cassie's holiday destination. Sabrina seized the opportunity to clear the plates, only to return with the meringue.

'Piece de resistance,' Sabrina declared, placing the dessert in the middle of the table.

Roger got up and carefully balanced a large apple log on the dying embers. It crackled, and then exploded, the flames throwing a warm glow into the room.

'Cass, I received a letter from Dad. He's decided to return to Kingston.'

'I'm so glad he's decided to settle down at last. I had a feeling he was not happy in Durban. At least he'll be true to his roots.'

'Okay, who's for a slice of dessert?' Sabrina said brightly. 'I'm sure you don't want to hear all our family history do you, Felix?'

'On the contrary, I'm most interested. Any connections, be it first or second-generation Jamaicans in Bristol, are intriguing.

'Of course, you and Rog could holiday with us Sab. That way you would both be able to meet up with Winston,' Mark suggested.

'And who's going to look after the business if we all go?'

'Good point.' Mark laughed, listening to Lorna.

'What a coincidence, choosing Jamaica as a destination, Cass,' Roger said

'Yes, it was, although Mark suggested it. I would settle for anywhere as long as it's hot, and this was the best deal on offer. It's not the usual tourist area, though. It's on the other side of the island in the mountains, hence the realistic price, I guess.'

'Sounds interesting and it will get him out of my hair for a couple of weeks,' Roger said, pointing his wine glass in Mark's direction.

'But seriously Rog, surely you and Sab could take time off and come with us to the auction?'

'Where is it held?'

'Chippenham. We could take in a pub lunch in one of those pretty places by the river. The auction doesn't start until the evening.'

'What are you two gossiping about down there?'

'You, actually. I suggested that you both came to the auction with us.'

'It depends which day. I have a finance meeting sometime next week.' She noticed Cassie's disappointment. 'Don't worry we'll be there.'

'Don't get too carried away, Cass. I have to speak to

Ross Meridian first,' Mark warned.

'Sabrina is a development co-ordinator within Social Services,' Roger whispered to Anne.

'Whatever he is telling you, Anne, it's probably true. It means endless meetings, all very tedious. Ask Roger how many times I have come home drained, because of my job.'

Anne smiled thinly, wishing she could be that confident and self-assured.

An awkward silence fell over the room, and Anne looked down at her lap. Sabrina got up and cleared the plates, and Cassie helped her.

Chapter Eight

'Felix, you're very quiet. I have it on good authority that you've many a good tale to tell,' Roger said, steering the conversation in another direction

'Someone's been telling you about my Egyptian mummy theory,' he said with amusement.

'That was in my archaeology era, but changing the subject, I'm very interested in your plot, Cassie. I don't think it is generally known how important the channel has become over the years. Bristol was known for its trade links at that time. It is fascinating to think of all the ships that sailed through that stretch of water.' Felix paused. 'Your plot must be near that same coastline, Cass. It narrows dramatically as it winds towards the mouth of the Avon and consequently into Bristol.'

'I have a feeling there is a story in the offing here. Who's for more coffee?'

As Sabrina left the room again, Roger took the opportunity to dim the lights, rendering the heavy curtains a deep burgundy. The earlier wind had subsided, bringing a welcome calm.

Cassie relaxed for the first time since the incident on the bridge. Looking up at Sabrina, she took the coffee cup she was offered, and teased the cream into a swirling pattern.

'I think you're referring to the slave trade, Felix,' she said. The room fell silent.

'I have to say it's one area that some Bristolians find difficult to come to terms with. At least that's my understanding.' Felix considered her, surprised at her remarks.

'Swept under the carpet no doubt,' Lorna stated.

'You know, you have a point there, Lorna.' For the first

time, Felix felt a glimmer of respect. 'Very few people mention it, and yet it's an important part of Bristol's history.'

He glanced around the table; the silence almost tangible. 'I'm sorry; I didn't mean to bore anybody. It's just a particular hobby-horse of mine.'

'No, please, Felix, carry on. I'm sure I speak for all of us.' Mark waved a coffee spoon in the direction of the other guests. The candle in front of him flickered, causing wax to slide down the outside of the holder.

'By the mid-eighteenth century Bristol had become one of Britain's premier slave ports; there were a staggering five hundred and eighty-eight ships by 1786.'

Roger gave a low whistle. 'I for one didn't realise this city played such a big part in the trade.'

'That's because there's hardly anything recorded on the subject.' Felix sat forward, commanding everyone's attention. 'Very few black slaves came here to Bristol. Any that did were possibly either kept as personal slaves or exploited to other subordinate roles in the households of wealthy merchant ventures.' The bitter tone in his voice was not lost on the other guests. Felix sat back, watching their faces in the candlelight.

It was the first time since arriving in Bristol that he had been able to relax and meet others socially. 'You know about the triangle, I presume.' His measured gaze fell on Lorna, willing her to answer.

'Tell us,' she challenged, looking at him through the side of her wine glass.

'I know it involved trade links with Africa,' Mark said.

'It went further than that, Mark. It's well documented that manufactured goods were made in local foundries, such as brass guns, hardware and, in particular, cookware, and were loaded on to outgoing vessels that left Bristol for the African coast and traded for healthy tribal people who were rounded up from remote villages. They also relied on the African traders to target the 'best' from the various tribes, mainly from Angola or the Gold coast, or Ghana, as we now know it. Journeys could take up to a year in some regions, depending how far inland they went.' Felix paused, watching the faces behind the candlelight. 'A whole tribe would be shackled with neck chains and forced into line by a rope.'

'But that is inhuman!' Anne shrieked, looking around the table.

Don shuffled uncomfortably. 'What happened then, Felix?'

'They were left in stockades before being loaded on ships for the squalid middle passage across the Atlantic. The voyage could easily take up to twelve weeks, sometimes even longer. The captives were kept chained below deck, shoulder to shoulder.' Felix removed a piece of meringue from his cuff, aware of the silence that had settled on the room. 'Many became sick, weakened by the vomit and excrement that surrounded them. Others died – suicide was common. The ones that looked like they would make it were given the best attention – even oiled to look healthy – with a view to get the best price when they reached the West Indies.' A draught from the kitchen caused the candles to waver and Sabrina got up and closed the door.

'It's too ghastly for words,' Lorna protested loudly. 'Can't we change the subject for goodness' sake?' She looked around the table for support.

'It's possible that the slaves were ancestors of mine. I remember my father, who rarely spoke of such matters, told me that many of the men were skilled tradesmen,' Sabrina said, handing out liqueurs.

'Yes, they were very much in demand. And then of course the human traffic enabled them to purchase commodities such as molasses, rum and sugar for the third and final trip back to Bristol.'

'Hence the triangle,' Roger said.

'There were other tales of cruelty such as tar and feathering on board ships for instance,' Felix added, declining liquor for a brandy.

'It must have been tricky coming up through the channel though,' Don said, holding out his brandy glass towards Roger.

'Yes, that last stretch would be the most hazardous. It has more dangerous sandbanks than perhaps any other waterway in the country. Even today, the phenomenal tidal range causes a build-up of sand and mud, not to mention the prevailing wind that would have intensified over the two thousand miles from the Newfoundland coast, with virtually nothing to stop it.'

'Surely it couldn't be that risky. What about the lighthouses, for instance?' asked Roger, helping himself to more cheese.

'Believe it or not, there were only two, in the mid-eighteenth century. Flat Holm, and later, Mumbles Head. In fact, people used to light bonfires to guide the ships up the channel.'

Don looked at Felix, also helping himself to cheese. 'I had a boat moored up on the North Devon coast and …'

'Don't you mean down, Don? Devon is south of Bristol.' Lorna smiled sweetly at him, seductively biting into a mint crisp.

He glared at her. 'Apparently, the priests kept a wood fire burning on Lantern Hill.'

'Whereabouts on the coast Don.' Sabrina asked.

'Ilfracombe.' Anne answered for him. She looked up the table at Lorna.

'Actually, from where we lived before moving here, Ilfracombe would have been up.' Lorna shrugged her shoulders and began talking to Sabrina. Don caught Anne's eye and winked at her, and as always, it made her heart jump.

'Getting back to what you were first saying Felix, would it have been possible that ships from the West Indies could have fallen foul of the channel?' Roger asked, handing out his special Havana cigars.

'I know where you're coming from.' Felix reflected. 'To my knowledge I only recall one that supposedly sank out there, a direct trader from Africa, apparently it capsized somewhere between Clevedon and the mouth of the Avon, but I don't remember the name of the vessel.' He leaned forward conspiratorially.

'More significantly, on board were Coromantee slaves. These men were very sought after because of their strength. The story goes that because of an imminent storm, all hands were needed on deck. The captain gave the order to unshackle the slaves.' Felix paused; he could have reached out and touched the silence. The smoke from Mark's cigar drifted towards him and hung in the air just above his eye level.

'So, what do you think happened?' Sabrina broke the silence.

'Apparently, it started with a northwest gale, which increased as they came up through the channel. The heavy seas pulled the vessel into the tides, and because the channel narrows dramatically, it's safe to say it would have tossed the frigate like a cork. It seems the high winds brought the main mast crashing down causing it to capsize, throwing everyone on board into the pitching seas.'

Felix sat back in his chair; the candle close to him trembled, throwing up the last of the light, illuminating the faces in the shadows. 'And no, I don't know what became of the Coromantee slaves? Hearsay has it that they might have reached the coast, but my feeling is they drowned along with the captain and other members of the crew. Some say that once the fate of the ship was known, the majority rule of the day sent out a search party to find the slaves, but that's only hearsay.' Felix paused. 'I only wish I could remember the name of the ship, and then I could finish the story.'

As Felix told his story, Mark watched Cassie with increasing

concern.

'*Silas Hunt*' There was a stunned silence. 'The ship's name was '*Silas Hunt.*' Cassie's voice shook as she glanced up at Mark, and he knew his earlier instincts were justified.

'Cass?' Sabrina pushed back her chair to go to her. Mark put a reassuring hand on her arm holding her back.

'But how do you know, Cass?' Mark asked.

She stared at him; her eyes distant in her pale face. 'I don't know, Mark, really I don't. It must have been something I learnt many years ago at school.' She gestured with her hands. 'Please everyone, don't make a fuss.' The other guests looked relieved as they began discussing Felix's story.

Cassie felt detached from the conversation. The cold that had gradually inched up her legs had a chilling effect, almost dragging. She bit her lip to stop herself from crying out at a searing pain tearing into her left thigh. I am out of control she thought, horrified at the sight of her hands digging claw-like into her freezing body. She felt something clinging to her right leg. It began aching; pulling at her. Anne offered her a glass of water and she drank it gratefully. She didn't dare look up the table; she already knew Mark was watching her. She heard Don's dulcet tones, and the clatter of plates as Sabrina cleared them. A log perched precariously on the fire chose the moment to topple, falling into the hearth. Everything seemed to be happening in slow motion.

Rog, do something Sabrina demanded slamming the plates back on the table. The flames intensified, casting instant light into the room.

Scooping up the log with a pair of tongs, he placed it

back on the fire.

'Okay folks, panic over,' he said reassuringly.

'You're shivering, Cass, are you all right?' Cassie looked up from the newspaper headlines she had retrieved from the fire. Looking at it, she said.

'Sab read the story on the front page.' Sabrina turned up the dimmer lights and read aloud. 'A police officer lost his life last night while on duty on the Bristol suspension bridge. It transpired he left the scene of the accident and for some unknown reason, made his way across to the other side of the bridge …' Mark took the newspaper from Sabrina, the image of the police officer's face in front of him. 'There's also a small piece about a fatality in Bedminster on Friday: a young man run over on a crossing, not named until the next of kin are informed. That's the day you were over there, Cass!'

Cassie looked at Sabrina, her eyes drooping with tiredness, shaking her head.

'It must have happened in another area. I didn't see anything. Is there any more on the lead story, Sab?'

'No,' she said, taking the paper from Mark and handing it back to Roger.

'There was a discussion about it on the local news,' Roger said, putting the paper in the log basket. 'They interviewed one of his colleagues who spoke highly of him. He went on to say that there would be no way that he would have left the scene of an accident.'

'I can't think of a worse place to be. Thankfully, I was at a girlie reunion; much more civilised, I can tell you,' Lorna said, winking at Don.

Felix looked at her with pity. Her carefully applied black mascara had smudged, leaving dark rings around her eyes, contrasting harshly against her spiky peroxide hair.

Felix turned to talk to Anne.

'Mark and Cassie were caught up in it,' Sabrina said,

looking at Mark, wondering if she should have broached the subject.

'Really!' Felix broke off his conversation with Anne and looked up the table at Mark. 'How interesting!'

Mark glanced at Cassie, noticing her pallor. 'Yes. It felt like a full-scale hurricane, but we survived,' Mark said, trying to make light of it.

'So, you didn't see the accident on the bridge, then?' Felix continued to probe.

Mark gazed into the middle distance, choosing not to reply. Eventually he looked directly at him. 'We did see something, but to be honest, Felix, we want to put it behind us.'

'That sounds a bit cryptic, Mark.' Felix smiled.

'You're quite right.' Don's voice woke everyone up. 'I've been in a force-nine and that is scary. I thought I would never see land again, let alone my dear Anne.' He grinned at her.

'There was talk of it being a force-twelve, but I don't think that's official,' Roger added.

Don stared at him. 'Christ, that's a hurricane; nothing could stand up to that. We're talking revolving storms of at least seventy to eighty miles an hour that are well known in the Caribbean and Africa. The seas are very white. But whether a storm like that came through the gorge, I must say I have my doubts.' Don tilted his brandy glass, smiling at Lorna.

'Well, if it happened, it wasn't reported in the evening paper,' Roger added.

'Probably because of the main story of the accident on the bridge,' Sabrina said.

Felix nodded. 'When you're in the eye of the storm like that, what feels like minutes is in reality only seconds. Cassie, I'm sorry, you were there, you must know more than any of us.'

'Don, you were right when you described a storm of that magnitude. It was surreal. Mark and I were completely immobilised by the strength of the winds. And to answer your question, the sea surged into the gorge under a mass of white foam.'

The silence in the room was broken only by Don's low whistle, and the conversation turned to the possibility of Bristol being in the grip of a tropical storm.

'How did the police officer lose his life?' Her voice sounded unnatural even to her own ears.

'I thought you knew,' Roger said. 'An enormous tree was uprooted in the storm and crashed down on top of him. His colleague made the point that if he had stayed where he was, it would never have happened.'

Cassie no longer listened. The drone of Roger's voice melted into the background. She felt perspiration, cold and damp against her body. How was it possible, she reasoned? They had not met the police officer until they crossed the bridge – after the tree had come down behind their car.

'Did they mention the time he died?' Mark asked.

'Sometime between five-thirty and six o'clock, apparently.'

Cassie pushed back her chair and stood up. She felt herself choking, her heart pounding. The image of the slave on the bridge flashed before her. She tried to focus, but the last thing she remembered was Mark catching her in his arms.

Chapter Nine

'How is she?' Roger asked, rolling up a set of plans. Mark flung his briefcase on the chair and poured himself a cup of coffee.

'Exhausted.'

'Don't take this the wrong way, Mark, but do you really want this plot? I mean, it seems to be giving you a hell of a lot of grief already. Why not walk away from it?'

'You won't talk her out of it, Rog, especially now, after the bridge incident.'

'Bridge incident?'

'Talk to Sab, she'll fill you in. Is this all the mail?' he asked, opening it. 'Cass is convinced there is a purpose to this plot and for all we know, she could be right. You know how psychic she can be. Besides, if it comes at the right price, it will be a snip of an investment; we could even sell it on eventually.' Mark handed him the mail. 'Sorry we broke up the party, Rog.'

'Not your fault, we were all ready to call it a night anyway. Oh, and Don's rung – he's very keen to go up there and see what's involved.'

'Already? Well, he hasn't lost any time. I suppose he's up to it, Rog, not some one-man band, is he?'

'Now you're being a snob.' Roger laughed, sorting out the invoices into a filing cabinet.

'We don't know anything about his work, or what he's capable of.'

'He employs a couple of workers.'

'Subcontractors, I expect,' Mark said absently, already dialling the number for Ross Meridian.

'I need to get to the bottom of this once and for all.'

'Be careful, that's all. You know his reputation for off-loading.'

'You're getting cynical,' Mark teased.

'That's because I've been at this game a long time,' he quipped, going down the stairs.

***

Ross Meridian was already regretting appointing Joseph Morgan, of Morgan Watson & Prewitt. The estate agent in South Bristol had put closure on the auction, but not Joseph, oh no, if he wasn't ringing every five minutes, he was hassling his secretary.

'Bloody small-town solicitor!' He screwed up the paper and aimed it at the wastepaper bin.

The phone rang and he answered it. 'How are you, Mark? Heard the Casper deal was a big success. You and Roger are the talk of the town, you lucky bastards.'

'It's hard out there, Ross. Come on, give us some credit.' He laughed.

'Anyway, how can I help?'

'It's about the auction off Sandy Way, at the end of the week. I wondered what your thoughts are. My wife and I had a quick look over it and because of the damage on the place I thought you might be able to tell us more.'

'And how did she find out about it, Mark?'

'An estate agent in Bedminster, I think. Why, is it important?'

'No of course not. Joseph Morgan is the solicitor on this one.'

'Cass has already been to see him. Apparently, he's not able to help with the history on the place.'

'Look, Mark, how interested are you?'

'Put it this way, Ross: my wife wants this property.'

'I think we'd better meet. What about the Market Bar off Corn Street? I'll tell you what I know. Noon suit you?'

'Perfect, see you tomorrow.'

***

The old clock chimed midday as Mark made his way towards Corn Street. An apologetic sun made a brief appearance, causing him to squint.

He found Ross in a seat by the window. 'What can I get you to drink, Mark?'

He beckoned to a nearby waiter and ordered two beers. 'I don't fancy fighting my way up there,' he indicated the bar, knee-deep in students. Mark looked over at a noisy group in the corner, agreeing with him.

'First of all, do you understand that you may not be able to get planning permission to rebuild? Local planning is not happy …'

'Leave that to me, I have a few contacts in planning. It's the history on the place that I am concerned with, Ross.'

'Okay, I'll tell you what I know, but I want your word that it will remain confidential, at least until after the auction. I stand to lose a lot of money if this story gets out. You're a businessman, Mark; you know what I'm saying.'

'Obviously I will have to tell my wife.'

Ross sucked in his breath. 'The house burnt down in April this year. Apparently, a fire started in one of the rooms.' He stopped talking while the waiter set down their beers. 'The owners bought the property two years ago and as far as I am aware, everything seemed normal. It happened on the night of a violent storm. The parents were in the lounge, and it seems that the couple's small daughter, who was woken by the storm, went in search of her parents. When you went up there, you probably noticed stone steps divide the building into two halves. The story goes that the parents settled the little girl back in her bed, but at some point, during the night the fire started, possibly in her bedroom. The girl's parents fought their way to her room and managed to grab their daughter but by that time, the fire had almost surrounded them. The kitchen was already well alight, crackling beneath them. The only refuge they found was the one place the fire was not able to penetrate – the bathroom. Mark's hand shook as he drank the last of his beer.

'Another one, Ross?' Mark returned with the drinks looking around for a beer mat before he set them down.

'It's said that the family crouched in terror, watching the fire sweep through the building,' he continued. 'It appears that the child made a dash for the door, screaming for her friend. The father went after her, but it was too late.' Ross drank deeply. 'Now you can see why I am reluctant to make this public knowledge.

'But how do you know it happened that way?'

'The mother, although badly burnt, was able to give a statement. They had to coax her from the corner, severely injured and in shock. It's all very tragic.'

'Did you say there was another child in the building?'

Ross looked puzzled. 'I found it slightly sinister but according to the mother's statement, her daughter had an imaginary friend – a little girl, the same age.'

'Did the mother survive?'

'No, she died shortly after.'

Mark sat back, taking stock. He knew he had stood on that very spot in the bathroom. He had sensed tragedy in both those rooms.

'Are you okay, Mark?'

'Any idea how the fire started, Ross?'

'No – it's a complete mystery. Apparently, it's not the

first time.' Ross saw his bewildered expression. 'Look, I'm only repeating what I've been told.'

'So, you're telling me this has happened before?'

'I don't know how reliable the information is, but the house has burned down on at least one other occasion.'

'I wonder if there's any way of finding out for sure,' he pondered.

'Look, Mark, my advice is to take the property as it is. That's if you're still interested, of course.'

***

Mark had intended to go back the office but with the latest revelations, but decided against it. God knows how Cass would take it.

The flat appeared unusually quiet. Sorting through the mail and binning the junk, he went into the lounge and poured himself a scotch, knowing there would not be an easy way to tell her.

Hearing her footsteps in the hall, he called out to her.

'I didn't expect you home this soon?' she said, hanging up her coat.

'Roger can manage. We're not that busy at the moment. How are you feeling?'

'Much better. Mrs Lethbridge rang and asked me to price two rooms. I had a walk across the Downs – I even looked over at the suspension bridge. It was as busy as it always is. I think it was the motivation I needed to get me out.' She smiled at him, accepting a glass of wine. 'Oh, and I had several phone calls: Sab, of course and Anne, bless her.'

'I suspect Don was behind that.'

'Don't be so cynical – a bit early for this isn't it?' She looked at him.

'I think you might need it. I had a very productive

meeting with Ross Meridian.'

'How bad is it?'

'As bad as it gets. We were right to feel uneasy about it.' He walked over to the window, watching parents collecting their children from school. 'The fire claimed the lives of an entire family.'

'My God, I felt the sadness there, but I didn't realise … How many?'

'Three, the parents, and their small daughter.'

Cassie listened as he told her everything Ross had told him. She closed her eyes, her mind in turmoil.

'The point is, Cass, the auction is this week, and you know my views on it. I think we are putting unnecessary stress and pressure on ourselves at a time when we don't need to. Roger and I have sorted the Casper job and you have booked this holiday. I want to relax and chill for a bit.' He waited for her response, aware that it was unlikely she would agree.

She took a deep breath. 'Mark, we have been through so much emotion on this place, we owe …'

'Cass! Have you listened to a word I have said?'

'Yes, of course, and I know where you are coming from. I felt that way when we left the plot.' She stopped conscious of his anger. She put down her glass and went over to him.

'What if we come to a compromise? Mr Morgan said himself that it's possible that it wouldn't fetch very much. Shall we agree on a certain amount and if it goes over that, we walk away?' She put her arms around his neck, waiting for an answer.

***

The consensus was for the four of them to leave Bristol at eleven o'clock, but by early Friday morning, all previous plans had changed.

'It can't be helped, Sab,' Roger said, irritated. 'I know you've tried to take the day off, but this happens to be a very important new client.' He waved the letter in front of her, biting into his toast. 'Besides, the meeting is only preliminary, mainly a bonding exercise. It will leave us plenty of time to get to the auction before it starts.'

'It's always the same, Rog, whenever we make plans, you can guarantee something crops up. It's most disappointing. And what about Cass? We promised her, she's counting on our support.'

'I'm sure she'll understand.' He leaned over and kissed her forehead.

'Mark might, but I wouldn't count on Cass!' She called after him. 'And you can tell her, Roger, because I'm not.'

***

Darkness had already descended on Chippenham when they arrived. Mark looked over at her. 'Nervous?'

She nodded. The day had not started well and Mark, against all his promises to take the day, had gone into the office after speaking to Roger.

'I can't believe they wanted a meeting with us out of the blue. Roger is more than capable of handling it – his people skills are much better than mine. I know he hopes to finish up in time to come over. It's got to be a good omen.'

'Let's hope it extends to the auction,' Cassie whispered anxiously.

Chapter Ten

On finding the hotel, they drove through a pretty arch into a cobbled courtyard. The rain glistened on the uneven stones as they walked towards reception. The hotel thronged with perspective buyers and interested parties. Passing the chaos at the desk, Mark guided her into one of the bars.

It was one of those old-fashioned hotels with heavy embossed curtains, complemented by a patterned carpet in the same navy blue, giving the room a regal feel.

'It's certainly humming. I bet there are a few speculative buyers here hoping to make a quick profit,' Mark commented, looking around at the business suits.

'We don't stand a chance!'

'Of course we do! Remember, most of these are after the big properties. You'll find they will dwindle away after they have been sold.'

'Is Ross coming?'

'It's unlikely, but he will have someone representing him.'

The voices grew louder as the excitement mounted. Avoiding a drunk with a full pint, Cassie ducked as he threatened to spill it.

'This is impossible, let's find somewhere else – I think there's a wine bar farther down the high street.'

***

Sabrina had a message from Roger, asking her to pick up his laptop from the office. This so-called 'getting to know you' meeting seemed to be dragging on. Sabrina tucked the computer under her arm and was about to leave when the phone rang on Mark's desk. Reluctant to answer it in case it meant more distractions, she ignored it. Then, thinking it might be Roger, she changed her mind.

'Is Mr Campbell there?'

'No, he's out of the office today. Who's calling?'

'My name is Joseph Morgan; I'm the solicitor on the auction. Forgive me but I must speak to him, I'm rather anxious.' Sabrina listened to his laboured breathing.

He had her attention. She put down the laptop, gripped the receiver with one hand and pulled out a chair with the other.

'Go on, Mr Morgan. My name is Sabrina Henderson, and my husband is Mr Campbell's business partner. Mrs Campbell and I grew up together and I do know about the auction, but I'm afraid they have already left.'

'Are you able to get in touch with them? It's very important that they are aware of the full facts. I have only learned of them this morning.'

'I'm afraid not, they left their mobiles behind – they wanted to concentrate on the auction. But my husband and I will be joining them later. Could I give them a message?'

'No – that will be too late.'

'I don't understand. You're making me nervous!'

'I'm sorry, let me explain. You are probably aware that Mrs Campbell came to see me a week ago. She asked me if I had any information on the property off Sandy Way. I believe Ross Meridian filled her husband in on all the details, including the family and daughter losing their lives in the fire.'

Sabrina gave a sharp intake of breath.

'I'm not telling you anything that you don't already know am I, Mrs Henderson?'

'Please carry on, Mr Morgan.'

'I thought about it after Mrs Campbell left and I did some research of my own. The more I delved into it, the worse it became. The property is bad news – I would almost go so far to say it's cursed.' Sabrina gasped. 'What Ross didn't know,' he hesitated, 'is that it had happened before to another family and their daughter, and she was exactly the same age as the girl in this latest tragedy.'

'My God, I had no idea. This is the first time I've heard about this. I see now why you want to warn them.'

'There is more.' Sabrina could hear him rasping. 'The fire started in the same way – with an electrical storm. The parents' charred bodies were huddled together, but their daughter's body was never found. More significantly, when they came to rebuild the house several years later, the excavator unearthed the human remains of a small child buried in a rockery farther down the garden. At the time, the human bones were passed off as those of animals.'

'I can't take this in.' Sabrina heard him coughing, trying to catch his breath. 'Mr Morgan, are you okay? Where are you calling from?'

'My office. I will be all right. I get these twinges now and again, brought on by stress I'm told.'

'Is your secretary with you?'

'It's her afternoon off.'

'So, you're alone?'

'Yes. Please ring the hotel, Mrs Henderson … you must let them know … tell her … Mr Morgan ... a remarkable woman, hair the colour of autumn …' He became incoherent.

'Mr Morgan, listen to me carefully. I'm going to ring for an ambulance. I want you to keep perfectly still until it arrives. Have you anything to wrap around yourself? A blanket, perhaps?' She heard him gasping for breath.

'I'm going to ring off now, but please don't worry. I'll

get that message to them somehow and thank you for your concern.'

It suddenly occurred to her that she had no idea where the solicitor's practice was based. Her mind in turmoil, she began flicking through the directory, remembering Cass saying something about south of Bristol on the coast road. Finding it, she rang for an ambulance. Picking up her handbag, she made straight for the hotel to collect Roger.

Pulling off the slip road, Sabrina joined the motorway, just as she got through to the auction venue.

'Yes, that's right, a message for Mr and Mrs Campbell. Could you please tell them …?' Background noise of laughter and the tinkling of glasses jarred in her ear. Checking her mobile, she noticed how low her battery was.

'Message for Mr and Mrs Bell to ring – what name was it, madam?'

'Henderson. And it's not Bell, it's Campbell!' she shouted irritably.

'Sorry, there's no one here answering to that name. Yes, all right, sir, I will be with you in a minute …'

The phone went dead.

'Blast!' She threw the mobile on the back seat in disgust and took the next motorway exit.

***

Sabrina parked in the waiting bay, watching the hotel entrance, her head all over the place. What in hell's name was she going to tell Cass? And why had she not told her about the history on the plot? Feeling disappointed, she began to think about Mr Morgan's rapid deterioration. She had made a few bad decisions in her life, mainly to do with her career, but answering the phone on Mark's desk this afternoon had been the biggest one of all.

***

Roger had finished the meeting and was pleased with the outcome. All he needed to do now was to get the costing on to his computer as soon as possible. He had discussed a few possible scenarios with Mark before he left for the auction, and everything he had put forward had been acceptable to the client. He snapped his briefcase shut and walked away from the conference room with a smile on his face. He waved to Sabrina, walked across the car park, and got into her car. She leaned sideways and he kissed her cheek, glancing over her shoulder for his computer

'Sab, don't tell me you've forgotten my laptop!'

She rounded on him. 'Roger! Have you any idea what I have had to deal with this afternoon? Your bloody computer was the last thing on my mind!'

***

Bidding had started by the time Mark and Cassie entered the room. There was a stage at one end where the auctioneer sat at a long table. Next to him sat a clerk, writing everything down.

Immediately behind sat a bespectacled man who, after taking off his glasses, whipped out a handkerchief and dabbed at his forehead; he was speaking on the telephone.

Occasionally, he would lean forward and cup his hand over the mouthpiece when the auctioneer turned to speak to him.

'Are you certain you want to bid on it?' Mark whispered, indicating a row of seats.

'It's okay, I prefer to stand,' she answered nervously, edging her way through a group of people.

They pushed between two affluent looking executives to

get a better view. A mobile went off beside them and the man turned and left the room, one finger in his ear.

Mark unbuttoned his overcoat. 'God, it's hot!'

'There are so many people here, what if …?'

'Look. What did we say at dinner? We both agreed that ten thousand pounds is a fair price to pay for it. Besides, Ross seems to think it won't even fetch the reserve of six.' He smiled at her. 'We could go farther back if you like?'

The businessman returned and began marking his catalogue with a gold ballpoint pen. Tense, Cassie found her confidence deserting her with each fall of the hammer.

'And now, ladies and gentlemen, we have an interesting lot in this evening's autumn property auction. Lot number ninety-eight, situated off Sandy Way, overlooking the Bristol Channel.' The auctioneer glanced around the room. 'Who's going to open the bidding? Come on now, somebody start me off, an opportunity like this rarely comes on the market. Stunning views and a lovely, elevated position. I would have it myself if I could get the wife to move.' A small group in the corner of the room forced a laugh at his attempt at a joke. 'And I daresay it's only a matter of time before planning will be allowed on this plot again.' He stopped to take a sip of water. The audience started to talk amongst themselves, adding to Cassie's apprehension.

'Quiet please!' He banged his gavel. 'Okay, then, I'll open the bidding at five thousand. Come on people; let's have a bit of interest. Do I hear five thousand, five hundred? Thank you, sir. Five thousand, five hundred it is.'

Cassie felt that her heart had jumped into her throat; she glanced over at Mark for support. Someone in front of her entered the bidding, and she had a sinking feeling it would all happen around her before she could get a bid in.

'Do I hear six?' Mark nudged her but it was too late; another bidder came in, taking the place of the person in front. 'Six? Six.' The auctioneer looked at his first bidder and the man nodded. 'Seven,' he said to the man in front who also nodded. He looked at his first bidder again and pointed a finger at him. 'Seven thousand, five hundred, sir. It is against you at the moment.' The man shook his head and, pushing through the crowds, left the room.

'Nine.' Cassie found her voice at last, thankful at the chance to put in her bid. The businessman standing next to her looked at her, surprised.

'It's with the lady in the middle.' The auctioneer glanced down at the bidder in front.

'Nine, five.' The bidder lifted his catalogue in response. The auctioneer pointed at Cassie. 'Ten thousand pounds madam?'

'Yes.' She could hear her heartbeat echoing in her ears. Mark felt for her hand, but found it clenched into a fist.

'Ten thousand, five hundred?' the auctioneer asked and the bidder in front nodded, waving his catalogue in triumph.

She shook her head, the disappointment unbearable. Her eyes filled with tears, and she brushed them away, determined not to let her emotions get the better of her.

'Have we all done on this one, ladies and gentlemen?'

He raised his gavel 'Ten thousand five hundred we have then. For the first time, for the second time, for the third and final time …' Mark slipped his arm around her shoulders.

'Eleven thousand!' The voice, clear and concise, intensified around the room.

'Just in time.' The auctioneer looked directly at Cassie, and then behind her. 'Eleven we have then.' He turned to the man in the front.

'Twelve,' he said tersely, looking behind him and fixing Cassie with a malevolent stare. Where had she seen him before?

'Thirteen.' The same clear voice cut into the crowd,

commanding attention. The man in the front row shook his head, his face like thunder as he pushed his way through the thinning crowd. Of course, how could she forget the ill-mannered estate agent in Bedminster?

'Thirteen we have then.' The gavel came down hard. The clerk looked up from his invoices, and exchanged a look of relief with the auctioneer.

She had never felt so disheartened in her life. She turned to look at the new owner, two rows behind her. Their eyes locked, almost as if he had been waiting for her to face him. All the activity in the room fell away in an instant, and she was back on the bridge, feeling the same mixture of emotions. Then he smiled – a big generous smile that lit his face, his teeth gleamed. It was the man on the suspension bridge.

'God, Cass, whatever got into you? I thought we agreed on ten thousand. I can't believe you bid thirteen. We will never get our money back on it, even if we sold it tomorrow.'

She stared at him. 'I didn't. It was the man behind us – look.' She pointed, but the man had disappeared. Cassie looked around frantically. 'He's gone.'

Mark gripped her arm. 'What are you talking about?' She looked up at him, her eyes bright. 'Don't you see, Mark? He wants us to have the plot, its part of his plan.'

Mark guided her out of the room for some fresh air, a nagging doubt in the back of his mind. As for Cass, he had never seen her so happy.

***

Roger decided not to aggravate the problem by prolonging the discussion of the laptop. Sensing her tiredness, he had suggested driving to Chippenham, and she had welcomed it, spending most of the time staring out of the window, deep in thought.

'Want to share it?'

Sabrina smiled over at him, nodding. She told him about the phone call from Mr Morgan but she left out the sinister details. He caught hold of her hand, and squeezed it gently. His instincts had been correct, but this was even worse than even he thought.

'I knew it! Ever since Mark talked about buying it, I've had this feeling … In one way, I hope they're not successful tonight, Sab. It feels like bad luck. What's more, I don't want it rubbing off on us.'

'Concentrate, Rog,' Sabrina indicated the car in front. He pulled up sharply, changing gear. 'I agree with you, like you, I don't intend to get involved with any of it. Cass or no Cass.'

***

The auction had wound down by the time Roger and Sabrina got there – they found Mark and Cassie at the bar.

'We bought it, Sab, it's ours!' Cass said, getting off the bar stool to hug her.

Sabrina saw the animation on her face. 'Cass, I'm pleased for you, I know much you wanted this,' she said, returning her kiss. 'There is a reason why we are late. Mr Morgan rang the office. I took the call when I picked up Roger's laptop. He wanted you to know he had more information on the property. I tried to ring the hotel but …'

'We ate somewhere less crowded. Anyway, Mark already knew the history from Ross.'

'But that's not all. The stress has made him ill … he had a heart attack as we spoke.'

'Oh, my God, no!' She gripped her friend's shoulders. 'Is he all right?'

'I organised an ambulance, but we won't know until this

evening.' She glanced at her watch. 'Tomorrow, now.'

Cassie sat down on one of the leather chairs, her earlier excitement forgotten. She had a faraway look in her eyes. 'You know, he went out of his way to see me last week. I'll never forget that. He is such a gentleman.'

Sabrina sat down beside her and held her hands. 'I'll ring the hospital tomorrow. He was concern for you, Cass.'

'I know. I felt a connection when I met him.' Her eyes welled up.

'I'm so sorry to put a dampener on your day.'

Cassie hugged her again. 'My dearest, Sab, what would I do without you?'

'Now tell me, what happened at the auction?'

'We got lucky today. Everything went our way.'

Sabrina looked at her, surprised. 'Is that all? I thought you were going to tell me something profound! Sabrina added

'What more information did Mr Morgan have?'

'Oh, nothing that you didn't know already, Cass. Come on, let's round up our husbands. It's been a long day.'

Encased in a luxurious Egyptian towel, Cassie stepped out of the shower. She had hoped the hot water would clear her head and help her creative process. Mrs Lethbridge had left a message yesterday suggesting a particular William Morris design she had in mind. Shaking her head at her choice and knowing that particular pattern would look hideous for the room she had in mind, she set about going into the study to come up with an alternative.

She found it therapeutic browsing through her swatches. It was a world away from the auction, and the events that had led up to it. To get back to some normality was just what she needed. Visualising the colours she had in mind, she pinned the different materials against the cushions. She knew she would have to come up with something spectacular if she wanted to keep this commission. The phone rang.

'Cass, Mr Morgan died last night.'

'Oh, Sab! I hoped he would make it.'

'I can't help feeling I could have done more. After all, it now seems that I was one of the last one to speak with him.'

'You know the answer to that. At least you had the presence of mind to ring for an ambulance, giving him the best chance. Personally, I think this auction stressed him out, Sab, and with Ross Meridian on his back – poor man. He only wanted to retire and play golf.'

'Do you think I should ring his wife?'

'Leave it, Sabrina. Why don't you send a condolence card with a note inside, explaining what happened? Oh, and include your telephone number.'

'Excellent idea, Cass. I'll do that.'

Mark drew alongside Don's expensive white Mercedes and reversed into the space behind. It was one of those gorgeous clear days, and even the sight of the industrial chimneys on the distant Welsh coastline couldn't deter his enthusiasm. It had been almost a week since the auction, and he wanted to tie up a few loose ends with Don before they went on holiday.

He had another reason to feel optimistic; after Cassie's low spirits from Mr Morgan's death, they had both found their appetite for the plot again. Roger had come up with some innovating and exciting designs, mainly in glass, to maximise the sunny aspect. Mark was working closely with the planning department and had suggested some interesting angles on how to overcome the current objections. The only obstacles had been the access and the boundaries. He needed to think about that while he was away. Kicking a stone, he watched it bounce down the track before resting against the fence.

Seagulls screamed overhead, owning the sky. There is something gratifying living this far up he thought, watching them circle.

'Got your work cut out here, Mark. Don't know where to start, to be honest.'

Mark swung round and saw Don at the entrance of the property. 'Hoping to fit it in around my main work, but that's not going to happen.'

Mark squeezed through the gap. Don's negative attitude was already irritating him. He had to use him of course, too many people had heard him accept Don's offer to clear the site.

They walked towards the building. Don indicated the blackened shell and the mangled steel rising up in front of them. Looking at it, his earlier enthusiasm disappeared in an instant. Reality stared back at him. The same despair greeted him – a reminder that the fire had claimed a family. A cloud passed over the sun, leaving the plot in the shade.

They hurried around the building and disappeared to the back, only to emerge minutes later from an underground storeroom.

'What an awful place! Must have been hidden there for years.' Don bent to retrieve a card. 'Do you know a Mr Morgan?' He handed Mark a hospital card.

'Yes, he was the solicitor on this place. Where did you find this?'

'Over there, by that door.'

'How strange.'

'Everything is strange if you ask me,' Don nodded towards the building. 'What the bloody hell went on in there? It's enough to give anyone the creeps, and it doesn't like me that's for sure. Almost fell on my face as soon as I set foot inside.'

'I know what you mean,' Mark said, remembering the fight with the washing line.

'With your permission, Mark, I'll dismantle as much as

I can by hand, and then get my digger in to level it. Although I'm at a loss to know how we will get it up here.'

'We could always airlift it.' Mark laughed, slapping him on the back. Don didn't see the funny side and instead, looked at his watch, anxious to go to his yacht club.

'By the way, the estate agent was here when I arrived, he seemed quite familiar with the place. Came looking for the sale board, or so he said, but he left without one. Rude bugger, nearly knocked me over, he was in such a hurry.'

'I didn't give anyone permission to come up here, maybe Ross did. Okay, Don, concentrate on doing as much as you can, and I'll see you on my return.' They shook hands and he left.

Mark lingered, although he had no desire to stay. He listened to the sound of silence, devoid of any birdsong. His spine tingled as his eyes were drawn to the stairwell and the shadows of children jumping from side to side. Seriously spooked, Mark stumbled down the path, followed by the chilling sound of children's laughter.

Chapter Eleven

The plane touched down at eight-thirty local time. Cassie breathed a sigh of relief as they taxied into the airport perimeter. The oppressive heat was stifling inside the terminal building. Thankfully, the overhead fan gave some relief when they passed underneath it on their way to the baggage carousel. They had decided at the outset to travel as light as possible.

The busy airport was smaller than she had imagined. Nearby, a small group of boys were arguing amongst themselves, and she noticed their unkempt appearance as they ran around each other. Catching her eye, one of them sprinted towards her, dodging through the crowds.

'Missy wants help with baggage?'

Cassie looked down at his bare feet and guessed his age to be eight or nine. He grinned, showing a row of small, even teeth. She burst out laughing, finding his grin infectious. Before she could reply, a man carrying a nameplate approached the boy from behind. He spoke tersely in dialect and the boy ran away.

'Are you Mrs Campbell?' he asked, referring to his sign.

'Yes,' she replied.

'Mr Campbell?' She pointed to Mark walking towards them. 'Ah, then please come with me. I have a car waiting outside. By the way, Mrs Campbell, a word of warning, be careful to whom you talk. The boys just now – not everyone in Jamaica are what they seem.'

'You must be from the Hotel Blue Mountain.' Mark shook his hand, noticing the hotel name on the breast pocket of his blazer.

'Yes, Sir, allow me,' he said, taking their bags. 'I'm sure you are eager to reach your destination after such a long flight.'

'It's stifling,' Cassie remarked, fanning herself with a magazine.

'Always the same here at the airport. Thankfully we have air-conditioning. Soon you will have the breeze from the mountains then you will feel the real Jamaica.' He chuckled and slammed the boot shut. 'The Hotel Blue Mountain is the new hotel of Port Antonio – the jewel in the crown, as we say.'

Mark gave an exhausted smile as he listened.

The air-conditioning in the car kicked in as they left the airport, enabling them to continue the rest of the journey in comparative comfort.

***

The hotel leapt out of the night like a magic lantern, with impressive white lights hanging from every wall that illuminated the way through to the main reception area. Coloured lights studded the vast grounds, creating a kaleidoscope of reflections, highlighting the many features surrounding them.

'It's magnificent!' Cassie exclaimed, listening to the tinkling of water next to her.

'You've made an excellent choice, Cass,' Mark said, as they made their way up the marble steps. All was quiet save for the distant sound of crickets.

The octagonal foyer had an enormous crystal chandelier from which light reflected in the gilt frame mirrors that adorned the walls. Cassie caught sight of herself, at the unflattering angles the mirrors threw up.

'You look beautiful,' Mark whispered, reading her

thoughts, following a commissionaire to the reception to sign the register. A light breeze disturbed the plant next to her.

'The weather can be very changeable this time of year,' the clerk said matter-of-factly, motioning a porter to take their bags. They followed him through one of the arches into an identical room. Central to the room stood a brass statue depicting a servant alongside his employer. A large palm behind, lent a realistic touch to the scene.

'What a splendid statue!' Mark said, getting in the lift.

'Here, in the foothills of the Blue Mountains, many are descendants of the slaves.' He nodded boisterously. 'Held in very high esteem

The room was beyond impressive; luxury oozed from every corner. Two bedside lights threw pools of soft light on to the gold-threaded bedspread and, turning back the sheets, Cassie ran her hands over the bed sheet, revelling in the silk. She left the bedroom and went into the bathroom.

'Mark, come and see this. I'm sure these taps are gold. I can't wait to get in!'

'Oh yeah,' he laughed, throwing her towels. 'You have a bath, and I'll unpack our bags,' he said, kissing her head.

After he had finished, he lit a cigar and went out on to the balcony. There seemed to be more breezes here, possibly because the wharf was nearby. Mark blew the smoke into the night, relaxing for the first time since the auction. Stars studded the sky and the lights from Port Antonio twinkled below. Savouring the moment, he listened to the distant sounds of Jamaica. Stubbing out his cigar and yawning, he went inside to join Cass.

They slept until late morning. Cassie had already showered and was putting the rest of her clothes away. She looked over at Mark who had begun to stir. He stretched and rolled over towards the balcony window, wondering if the view would hold the promise of last night.

'Room service, I think,' she said, shutting a drawer.

When it came, they took it out on the balcony. The breakfast consisted of home-baked bread, muffins and scones with honey and Blue Mountain coffee.

Port Antonio lay lazy in the midday sun; a heat haze hung like a gossamer web.

'It's breathtakingly beautiful.' Cassie shielded her eyes from the mountain's shadow. 'I hadn't realised we were actually up in the mountains.'

Mark stood beside her, leaning over the balcony rail. 'I'll say it again, Cass – you made an excellent choice of hotel.'

'I wish I could take all the credit. I think someone is watching over us,' she mused. 'What do you say we stay around here for the rest of the day, Mark?'

'That suits me fine. I must admit, I still feel a bit jet lagged. Let's go and see what this excellent hotel has to offer us, Mrs Campbell. You've already showered, haven't you, Cass?' he asked, going through into the bathroom.

'Yeah!' she shouted absently, watching a cruise ship coming into the port.

***

After a good night's sleep, and an early start, they decided to explore Port Antonio. After asking for directions at reception, they set off for the main square and the local market.

Musgrave market bustled with hagglers preparing for the day. Cassie had slipped on a cerise voile blouse over her camisole, giving her some protection from the already fierce heat. They wandered among the local craft stalls, hand in hand. Cassie caught sight of a tall building. 'What's that red building over there?' she asked, pointing.

'It's the courthouse,' replied a voice from behind. They turned to see a tall, good-looking Jamaican. Cassie judged him to be in his early thirties; he was standing so close that she could feel his breath on her neck. 'Forgive me, I did not mean to interrupt. It's because I'm very proud of my town. Please let me introduce myself. My name is Cudjoe. It's an old name that belonged to a Maroon leader many years ago.' He gave them a friendly smile. 'It means Monday. If you would like a tour of my town, I would be very glad to show you around.'

They looked at each other, not sure what to say. Mark replied for both of them, introducing Cassie he shook Cudjoe's hand.

'Thanks, Cudjoe. We'd appreciate that very much.'

'By the way, please call me Joe; most people do.'

The farther they went into the market, the hotter it became. At least we are shielded from the sun, Cassie thought, stopping to fan herself with a torn-off piece of cardboard she had found. The smell of charcoaled meat mingled with the sweet smells of coffee and vegetables.

'Allow me,' Cudjoe said, disappearing into a crowd of women who were bargaining over Rastafarian berets. He reappeared, carrying slices of meat.

'What is it?' Mark asked, the aroma wafting up to him.

'Only the most famous dish in Jamaica – jerk pork. Their recipe originated from my ancestors,' Joe said, proudly.

'It's delicious, Joe, but very hot!' Mark added.

Joe laughed. 'That's the sauce. The truly authentic recipe requires the meat to be grilled over a pimento wood fire. In a perfect world, that is.' He grinned.

Having toured the flea market, Cassie decided to buy a beret she had seen earlier – many of the local women wore them.

'I can't see Sab wearing it.' Mark picked it up and inspected it.

'You'll be surprised – she likes everything to do with her

Jamaican roots,' Cassie said, paying for it.

They wanted somewhere original to eat and Cudjoe suggested a restaurant off East Harbour. When they arrived, it was little more than a rickety bamboo shack. They followed Cudjoe inside. Finding difficulty in adjusting to the dark interior, Cudjoe led them to a table in the middle of the small room, where a small crowd of locals were enjoying an array of dishes. A colourful Jamaican woman produced a fan and placed it abruptly in front of her, thankful to be sitting down, Cassie removed her hat; tendrils of damp hair escaped, fluttering against the fan.

'I can recommend the curried goat,' Cudjoe proposed, turning towards the woman, speaking to her in dialect. Mark caught Cassie's eye and squeezed her hand reassuringly.

It was mid-afternoon when they eventually left the restaurant. Mark wanted to find a beach and Cudjoe recommended one at Norwich, a mile west of the town. The rest of the afternoon passed in an idyllic haze. There was only one other couple and they were so far away, it hardly mattered.

Cassie felt the white sand sieve through her fingers. She had discarded her shorts in anticipation of a swim in her cerise bikini. She sighed, contentedly, stroking Mark's face with her finger.

'I've been thinking. You realise we don't know anything about Joe? I mean, did he talk to you, about himself?'

Mark looked at her. 'You're right. He did suddenly appear, but he was kind enough to take us to lunch and we would have never found this wonderful beach without him.' He lay back in the sand, completely relaxed. 'Anyway, he told us we could always find him in the square.'

'Yes, I know, but it seems strange somehow.' Cassie propped herself up on one elbow and lifted a long leg in front of her, applying sun lotion. 'This really is like the brochures,' she said, gazing at the aquamarine sea and the palm trees swaying in the breeze, their roots resembling shoehorns. Cassie flicked at the sand with her toes.

'I suppose Don knows what he's doing, Mark? We haven't seen any of his work.'

'Where did that come from? Remember we are on holiday. Anyway, he is only dismantling at this stage. I know he thinks he has a chance for the new build contract, but for what we have in mind, my darling, he will not be in the same league.'

'So many things are strange though, Mark. Finding Mr Morgan's appointment card at the plot. I wasn't aware that he had been up there. At least, that is what he told me.'

'Come on, lazy,' he said, poking her in the ribs. 'Forget all that, let's go for a swim.'

They ran towards the waves, the hot sand burning their feet. After several minutes of swimming together, Cassie decided she wanted to sunbathe. Mark watched her stroll back, her long legs tantalisingly brown against the white sand. She bent down to pick up a towel. How happy she looks, he thought, as she wiped her shoulders before spreading the towel in the shade.

Turning towards the sea, he decided to swim out to a group of rocks he had spotted in the distance. It made the challenge more enjoyable. With a warm breeze in his face, he struck out. It felt good to stretch his body and feel the water rippling around him.

Exhausted by the swim, Mark sat on a rock, having decided the island was not as interesting as he first thought. He lingered, overwhelmed by the view, before diving off and swimming vigorously back to shore.

Chapter Twelve

It was on Navy Island where they first met the Americans.

They walked down to West Harbour to catch the early morning ferry, hoping on the off chance they might see Cudjoe again. Apart from a few traders in the process of setting up their stalls, the square was empty.

Sitting on a seat, waiting for the ferry to arrive, they watched the hurly-burly of the wharf. Even this early, the heat was becoming unbearable. Cassie adjusted her wide-brimmed hat and Mark pointed out a freight ship in the distance heading towards Boundbrook Wharf and the banana plant.

The trip on the ferry was interesting. With so much to see, they were almost sorry when they reached Navy Island. They stood and marvelled at both the contrast and tranquillity of the place. Although such a short distance from Port Antonio, it could have been in another country.

The gentle landscape gave way to tall palm trees and well-tended gardens full of vibrantly coloured plants.

They ate on the other side of the island in the shade of a bougainvillea, enjoying a local dish of ackee and salt-fish. Taking time to photograph and explore the island, they were treated to a display of egrets swooping down in front of them – they soared to great heights where they were joined by other water birds.

'Say, you guys,' a male voice said, addressing no one in particular.

By chance, they found themselves in the private marina resort. It was mid-afternoon and they were both thirsty. Mark went to the bar and ordered two orange and sodas, while Cassie found a seat amongst walls full of Errol Flynn memorabilia.

'Say, are you English?' Mark, who was about to re-join Cassie, looked surprised.

'Yes, I am.'

'I'm sure glad to meet you. My name is Vernon Holder, but my friends call me Vern.' He shook Mark's hand robustly and indicated a table nearby. 'My wife, Mrs Holder, and our dear friends, Bob and Mrs Forbes.'

'Mark and Cassie Campbell,' Mark responded.

'Come and join us. Can I get you some more drinks?'

'No thanks, Vern.' He indicated the full glasses.' Cassie, following Mark, went over to them. The group were older than they were, somewhere in their mid-fifties, she guessed. Both men were well over six feet tall and well built. The women, in comparison, were slightly on the heavy side. Cassie thought it most odd that the men did not refer to their wives by their first names. Vern offered Mark a Macanundo cigar, and the three men went outside to smoke.

'Do you live anywhere near London?' Mrs Forbes asked. Cassie laughed.

'No, not really. We live in Bristol – it's about a hundred and thirty miles away from London.' She could never understand why some Americans thought everyone lived in or around London. She waited for the next obvious question, but it never came.

'We have been to Scotland,' Mrs Holder informed her. 'But that was years ago when Vern had more time. We travelled a lot then, you see.'

They turned as Vern, followed by Mark and Bob, came back into the bar.

'What do you know? Mark here is in the same line of business as us – real estate.' His cigar bobbed at the side of his mouth.

Vern pulled up a chair, his large frame filling it. The two ladies sat side by side, with Bob and Mark at the end, and Cassie completing the circle.

'Well, what a coincidence,' Mrs Holder said, slightly miffed at being interrupted by her husband.

'Hell, we've been trying for years to get a contact over there, eh Vern?' Bob added.

'Just a minute, you two. Don't get carried away – I *design* houses, I don't sell them.'

'Nonsense, course it's the same,' Bob said, having none of it.

Mark and Cassie spent the rest of the day with them, and they later decided to have a meal together in the restaurant off the main area, where there were more reminders of Errol Flynn. The room was tiny by comparison but intimate and yet, there were no other diners. Shown to a table that overlooked the ferry route, Marge Holder took the window seat, from where she had a view of the lush vegetation in the grounds of the Marina.

'Look you here, Betty; you can just see that ferry leaving. Oh my, look at the view of Port Antonio from here.'

They dined on grilled lobster steeped in butter and garlic, followed by 'matrimony' – a dessert of orange segments and crushed apples in cream. Darkness fell while they ate, and the lights of Port Antonio twinkled on the black water.

'What time is the next ferry?' Marge asked, sitting back in the chair.

'Don't worry about that, darling,' Vern said, blowing out smoke from one of his fat cigars. 'I've already arranged for a water taxi when we want one.'

He turned to Mark. 'Say, Mark, I've got an idea. Bob and I have arranged a fishing trip tomorrow. A client of mine has a property out here and he has arranged to take us out on his boat. Reckons we can fish for marlin. How about coming along?'

'I can't, Vern. I mean, if it is you two, he's invited…'

'Don't worry about that. Besides, he owes me. It's settled then.' He looked at the ladies.

'You both have something arranged, anyway, haven't you?'

'Sure have,' Marge said on cue. 'Betty and I are going to Moore Town. It is an ancient Maroon town in the Blue Mountains, and then we are taking a hike up to the falls. You'll just love it, Cassandra.' She saw the expression on her face. 'We won't take no for an answer, will we, Betty? And we have the best guide on this side of the island. He told us there is a mountain village up there – the site of Nanny Town. The villagers make crafts for the market in Port Antonio.'

'It'll be an early start, Cassandra, before the heat sets in.'

'But I haven't any suitable footwear.'

'Don't worry about that, honey. We're about the same size, I guess.' Marge put her foot alongside Cassie's. 'I have a spare pair back at the hotel; I'll bring them with me tomorrow.'

Usually, they had a few drinks before turning in but tonight they were so exhausted.

The resident pianist played a painful tune on the grand piano and the barman nodded to them as they walked by. They paused, looking over the balcony, watching a party in evening dress come in from the restaurant. On cue, the pianist upped the tempo.

'I think we were frogmarched by the Americans tonight, Mrs Campbell.'

'I agree,' Cassie said, laughing.

She decided on a khaki cotton shirt with a pair of old shorts and dug out a pair of Mark's heavy-duty socks.

'And don't forget your hat.' He tossed it at her, and she put it on.

'God, I look like I'm going on safari.' She looked at

herself in the mirror.

'You soon will be when you get Marge Holder's hiking boots on.'

Her hat missed him by inches as he ducked into the bathroom.

'Seriously though, Mark. Can you imagine anyone bringing an extra pair of boots with them on holiday?'

'By all accounts, they go on long distance walks, I expect it's one of those foibles people have. Always making sure they have over and above what they really need,' he said from the bathroom. Cassie had stopped listening; concentrating instead on checking what would be needed.

'Did they say their hotel would be providing a packed lunch?'

'Yes, don't you remember? They said they would take care of all that.'

Mark was also looking forward to the day. The fishing trip promised to be interesting, and he wanted to learn all he could. Don had already offered him first refusal on his old boat, and they had arranged to go out on it when he returned. The plan was to meet Vern and Bob at their friends' mooring in the Marina, and Mark intended to go there by taxi.

Cassie, meanwhile, went in the opposite direction towards Bonnie View Hotel, where the Americans were staying.

The sun hit them as soon as they left the shade of the hotel. Cassie hung on to her hat, glad of the shelter as they walked towards her taxi.

'Take care, darling, I'll see you back here about four-thirty.'

'You too, Mark, enjoy your day.' She said returning his kiss.

***

'Cassandra!' She turned to see Mrs Holder waving frantically from her hotel entrance – a pair of boots in her hand. 'I see you have a hat, most wise, we need as much shade as possible today.'

She handed Cassie the boots. 'Marlon our guide has a picnic for us and plenty of bottled water.' She glanced at her wristwatch. 'Oh, where's Betty? The men went over an hour ago.' Exasperated she sat down on a wall and fanned herself.

Cassie sat next to her and adjusted her socks before pulling on the boots.

'I thought our hotel was impressive', she said altering the laces. 'But this is even more superior. What's over there?' Cassie shielded her eyes pointing in the direction of a group of factories on one of the wharfs.

'I think Vern mentioned it was a banana plant. Ah, Marlon, we're just waiting for Mrs Forbes.'

Marlon, a small wiry Jamaican had an engaging smile and an easy manner.

He took off his backpack and checked it diligently. Taking out a compass, he shook it, looked up at the sun, and put it back.

'We seem to be quite high up here?' Marge said pulling out a handkerchief as she mopped her forehead looking at Marlon for confirmation.

'Oh yes, Mrs, six hundred feet here? And that there,' he swept his arm towards the back of the hotel, 'is twenty-five acres of plantation and the Blue Mountains behind them'? He drew out a machete. Marge Holder screamed. 'You don't worry, missus, some of them paths like jungle.' He cut through the air, demonstrating.

'Thank you, Marlon, I understand.' She mopped her face again. 'Thank goodness, Betty, whatever kept you?

They never did find out what kept her. All they knew was that it had made them late and the car Marlon had hired was old and uncomfortable. He started shouting above the noise of the engine to make himself heard. They passed through plantations, villages and women surrounded by stockpiles of green bananas.

'Them for the market!' he shouted over his shoulder. They began to ascend into mountainous country. 'John Crow Mountains.' Marlon pointed through the window and leaned forward to enable the women to get a better view. The driver slowed, struggling with the gears. Marlon said something to him in dialect and the driver replied by thrusting the car forward, crashing the gears in the process.

'It's okay, ladies, car no like mountains,' Marlon laughed nervously. They sat back in the rear seat. Cassie began to feel sick as the car jolted over yet another pothole, and wished she had not hurried her breakfast.

With a sense of disappointment, Cassie noted that Moore Town wasn't any different to the other villages they had seen on route. It consisted of one street that wove uphill.

'You all right, Cassandra?' Marge asked, waving her map to create a breeze. Cassie nodded, helping Betty out of the car. Marlon said something to the driver before he drove down a side street to wait.

'We will rest first, and then I will show you the town before we go to Nanny Falls.'

They found a small bar and Marlon ordered water. Cassie sat with the ladies, looked out at the street, and thought about Cudjoe. This was his town.

'Okay ladies, you feel better now.' Marlin reappeared with a tray of ice-cold water and placed it on the table. Placing his backpack on the seat, he shook out a full-scale map in front of them, briefing them on the path they would be taking. Packing it back into the bag, the women noticed the machete jammed in one of the side sections of the guide's bag and glanced at each other.

Feeling refreshed, they followed Marlon. Five minutes into the journey, Betty cried in agony, stumbling. She caught hold of Cassie's arm.

'I'm not usually this clumsy, it's not like me at all,' Betty said apologetically. They looked ahead at Marlon, who began chattering excitedly.

'Ladies, this is a monument to Nanny, most famous leader of the Maroons.' He grinned proudly and pointed to a plaque, waving his arms around and then looking with reverence at the grave. 'It's been said she had the supernatural powers … It was she who fought the British all them years ago.'

They all stood looking down at the grave as a mark of respect to Marlon, and Marge took a photograph with him standing beside it.

Passing a derelict church, they followed the route up a steep mountain path to Nanny Falls. They walked in single file, with Marlon setting the pace at the front and Betty languishing at the rear.

'Cassandra!' Cassie turned and held out her hand as Betty tripped on a root and almost lost her footing. Gripping Cassie's hand, she thanked her.

The higher they climbed, the denser the forest became. Every now and again, the path opened up into a clearing bathed in bright sunshine. Lush green plants surrounded them, oozing sap when they trod a path through the thick undergrowth.

Marge let out a high-pitched scream. Everyone stopped. A lizard had darted in front of her.

'Okay, ladies, we rest here.' Marlon slipped off his backpack and began searching for their packed lunches. The women collapsed, exhausted, against a clump of cotton trees, much to Marlon's disgust. 'Them not good,' he said, shaking his head. 'Duppies.'

'What are you talking about, Marlon?' Marge lay against

the tree and closed her eyes. The drone of a hummingbird somewhere nearby created a sense of peace.

'All around us, in trees.' He looked into the bushes as if he expected something to burst through them.

'What are duppies?' Betty sounded scared.

'They have two souls, one in heaven and one in tree. They follow us.' He got up and the others followed quickly. Marlon announced they would go straight to the village where they make the crafts because there wouldn't be time to go to Nanny Falls.

The route was overgrown with tree ferns and the cool air created an eerie jungle ambience. The screech of a white owl in full flight threw an echo around the party.

'Patoos.' Marlin quickened his pace, his machete slicing through the vegetation. 'This means bad luck to follow.'

'Marlon, have you any idea where we are?' Betty Forbes's question voiced the concern they all felt.

Relieved at eventually reaching the top, Cassie stood still, getting her breath back. The forest had ended at a wide track that further opened into a space with habitable dwellings in the distance. They were so high up, that even the heat of the day could not prevent a chilly mist swirling around them. Marlon helped Marge with a wrap she had brought with her, while Betty sat on a boulder, massaging her feet.

'My God, Marlon, you sure had us all worried back there in the mountain,' Betty said. 'Is it the part of the tour guide to scare us? because if it is, it sure worked.'

Cassie went over to a ledge and looked out into the distance. Marge joined her, linking arms.

'My, this is so beautiful. I feel as if we are on the top of the world.'

'Follow me, ladies.'

If Marlon had lost his composure earlier, he had certainly regained it now. 'We now are going into the mountain village.'

He set off at a pace. The path had turned into a dust track, making it easier on their feet. Marlon proceeded to inform them of the various trees and plants on route.

'Look ladies, a lack-billed parrot.' They followed his finger, only to see the bird fly away. As they approached the village, it was obvious how simply the people lived. A dog lazed in the shade, only to be disturbed by a toddler who goaded it into action with a stick. Cassie watched the child wander off. Shaking her head, she followed the others.

Chapter Thirteen

The village consisted of no more than a dozen rundown shacks in various stages of disrepair. Marlon told them the crafts the villagers made were for the market at Port Antonio.

An old man whittling away at a carving fascinated the women.

'Look how he's chipping away at that lump of wood, Betty,' Marge said.

Cassie took off her hat, and mopped her forehead. It was far too hot. Leaving the ladies discussing the woodcarving, she strolled under the welcome shade of a corrugated roof. The dog she had seen earlier waddled towards her, wagging its tail, and then changed direction and flopped next to a large woman who was breastfeeding – her eyes dull with boredom.

Marlon called them together. 'Ladies, this village is typical of the Blue Mountains, but with a difference. Here we have a direct descendant of Nanny.' Marlon placed a finger to his lips; his eyes wide open with conspiracy. 'You must respect, ladies. Beneba is of great age, her daughters protect her. I will go first, you wait here please.'

Marlon was gone for quite some time. Betty Forbes sat on a wall watching the shack. Marge gazed around with trepidation at the village people coming towards them.

'Okay, ladies, we go now. Follow me.' He led them to a tiny room where they stooped to enter.

Cassie suppressed a shudder at the dark room. She could just make out an old woman in the corner, sitting on a rush mat, wearing some kind of cloth that completely covered her.

Her body seemed awkward, as if she had been dumped

on the floor and abandoned. She began swaying from side to side, reminding Cassie of a lion she had once seen at Bristol Zoo.

She stepped towards the old woman, looking into her sightless eyes, the colour of cloudy marbles. Marlon began talking to the other women, presumably her daughters. They seemed to be striking some kind of bargain for goods to sell at the market. Suddenly, the old woman let out a screech followed by a wail. Marge and Betty jumped and turned to look at her.

'Bad, Beneba!' one of her daughters scolded, and then continued to talk to Marlon as if nothing had happened. Beneba screeched again. This time the wail continued, and the Americans turned to leave.

'No, no, ladies please.' Marlon went over to them. 'Don't be alarmed, it's okay. Her daughter Jessie says she has something to say, which is a rare privilege indeed, as Beneba speaks very little these days. I have never heard her speak in all the times I been here with other tourists.'

They all stood still, as if the slightest movement would break the spell. Her daughter Jessie said something to Marlon in dialect.

Cassie stared at Beneba and the old woman's rheumy eyes stared back, as if she were now sighted. All the time, she was rocking.

'She senses your nearness. She wants to touch you.' Jessie caught hold of Cassie's hand, drawing her to the old woman. A claw-like hand came out from under her garment and touched her.

'Your face, she wants to touch your face,' her other daughter said.

Cassie sat on a makeshift stool in front of the old woman – a stale odour permeated from her. As she leant forward, her bird-like fingers gently traced Cassie's features. The stench in the shack became overwhelming and Cassie felt sick. She glanced around at the others, but they had already gone.

'There is no need to be afraid.' Beneba's voice was no more than a whisper. 'I know you have de power.' The old woman's lips parted, showing anaemic gums. Quickly, she withdrew her hands as if she had been burnt. 'Bears of the devil, it be coming, it be the Loa,' she started whimpering. 'But you have the strength. He must be destroyed. You have first to look inside yourself.' Beneba shook her head. 'That not your fault what happened as a child.'

Cassie stared into her sightless eyes in amazement, the nausea returning with a vengeance. 'How do you know about me?'

Beneba pointed to her eyes. 'Beneba need no eyes, I see the whole.' She leant forward, gripping Cassie's arm. 'Listen to Beneba, he needs your help now, all the years in the wilderness must be put to rest, before the next rise ...' She broke off, looking into her lap, and began to whimper.

Cassie stood up, desperate to leave.

'Wait!' It was a command. 'Danger happening now.'

Cassie swung round, surprised at the forceful eerie voice of the old woman.

'There is water; there is a boat, Baka!' As she spoke, the old woman's white-marble eyes changed into dark pools.

'What is it, Beneba? Tell me.' Cassie dropped to her knees in front of her. 'Is it Mark?'

'Marassa, Marassa,' she chanted, rocking from side to side. 'Beware Marassa.' She clutched Cassie's hands as though to make her understand.

'Do you mean Mark? Is Mark in trouble?'

Beneba's head lolled, her energy spent. Her daughters gathered around, trying to calm her.

'Please leave, our mother is tired.'

Once outside Cassie rushed behind a stack of wood and threw up.

'My, Cassandra dear, whatever is the matter?' Marge put an arm around her shoulder. 'Here have this.' She thrust a napkin at Cassie who took it and disappeared behind the woodpile again. 'I think it's been too much for her, Betty. Where the hell has Marlon disappeared to?' She looked around 'We got to get out of this God-forsaken place. I only hope the taxi's waiting for us when we get to Moore Town.'

'It sure gave me the creeps in there,' said Betty. 'Did you see the way she sat propped up with cushions on the floor, as if she was some sort of queen? And the noise she made? I tell you, Marge couldn't wait to get out.'

Marlon blinked in the dazzling sunlight. 'Ah ladies, there you are.' He swung around. 'Where is Mrs Campbell?' Betty nodded in the direction of the woodpile, just as Cassie reappeared.

My God, child, you're so pale.' Betty led her to a makeshift seat under a mango tree.

Marlon followed, looking concerned. 'Sometimes, difference from dark to light makes for giddy.'

Cassie went up to him. 'I have to get back to the hotel as quickly as possible, Marlon.'

'Is better to eat more food before we go down …'

'You don't understand! I have to get back there now! Please, it's Mark. I know it is.' The tears flowed and she angrily wiped them aside. 'Please, Marlon!'

'He's in safe hands, honey. Why, Vern and Bob wouldn't let anything happen to him, being their guest and all.' Marge took her hand.

Cassie listened with a sense of hopelessness as Marlon insisted on finishing the rest of the pack lunch. The nausea stayed with her as she chewed on a salt-beef sandwich.

'Is there a shorter route back, Marlon?' she asked.

'If we cut through the steepest part of the mountain, we will arrive sooner.' He drank deeply from a water bottle and offered it to Marge Holder who turned her head to decline. He extended the bottle to Cassie. 'Should drink, Mrs Campbell, must settle stomach.'

But Cassie reflected on Beneba's words and in particular the truth about her parents. She knew she would have to face the truth one day. She had managed to shut the memory of the car accident out of her mind, but perhaps Beneba had been right. She had blamed herself too much.

'Okay, ladies, follow me.' Marlon went ahead and they all followed. Cassie stopped to take a last look at the village and, particularly, Beneba's shack. It crossed her mind that she had come all this way, not only to be faced with the truth, but also to find a kindred spirit that understood her. She wondered if she would ever find anyone like that again.

'Not long now, Mrs Campbell!' Marlon shouted over his shoulder. Clutching at an overhead vine to stop herself from slipping, she thought about that day all those years ago.

Her parents had lived for each other. They saw the arrival of their only child as an intrusion into their lives. It had been a difficult birth for her mother, a fact she would never let Cassie forget.

On the day of the accident, she had been arguing with her mother. Normally, she would let her jealous remarks go over her head, but that day she responded.

'I hate you both! I wish you were both dead! You never wanted me anyway.' Cassie remembered storming off to her bedroom, crying. An hour later, both her parents were killed in a head-on collision on the outskirts of Bristol.

'Of course you didn't make it happen,' Mark had told her when they first met. 'It was a terrible, tragic accident.'

They never spoke of it again and she had almost succeeded in burying it at the back of her mind. Until today.

Chapter Fourteen

Mark sank into the plush cream upholstery. Some boat, he thought, surveying the fifty-foot cabin cruiser.

'The Wahoo' came with impressive decks and a sumptuous lounge area. The owner, introduced as Al, handed him an ice-cold Red Stripe from the fridge and joined him on the sofa. Mark drank deeply, watching Vern wrestle with a fish.

'That Marlin is as slippery as you,' Al laughed, pulling his baseball cap down over his eyes.

The mid-afternoon sun bore down on them. Al had already dropped anchor half a mile out at sea and with it came a welcome breeze. Leaving Al to doze, Mark strolled over to the starboard side, and gazed down at the ripples lapping against the bobbing cruiser. He picked up a pair of binoculars and looked towards shore. The bright orange of Folly Point lighthouse came into view. Adjusting his sight, he surveyed the Blue Mountains, steeped in greenery and pockets of heat haze.

'Impressive, isn't it?' Al said, joining him. 'Why would I want to live anywhere else, with all this on my doorstep?' He swept his arm, taking in the vista.

'Al, you must know just about everyone in this area?'

'Sure do, why?'

'Cass and I met someone on our first day, in the market square, and we haven't been able to locate him since. His name is Cudjoe do you know him.

'Yeah, I know him, Cudjoe has been here for years, and I think his family originally came down from the mountains to find work at the ports as many did. I suspect the reason you can't find him is that he has probably gone back to Kingston University. He is well educated and lectures on Jamaica folklore. Although I think there is more to it than he lets on.'

'He made a good impression on us, and even took the trouble to show us this town. Now it seems unlikely we will meet him before we go back.' Mark pulled out a business card. 'If you do come across him, Al, give him this. We would love to return the favour if he ever came to Bristol.'

'Sure thing Mark, leave it with me.'

***

It wasn't long before Bob caught his first serious fish, a snapper. He danced around the deck proudly parading it in front of everyone. Mark and Al laughed at the challenge Bob threw at Vern to match him, but it was short lived. A commotion came from the cabin.

The native Al had hired for the day came up on deck gasping for breath, smoke billowing behind him. Vern and Bob dropped everything and rushed to his aid. Mark and Al went down into the galley.

'Where's the extinguisher, Al? Mark shouted through the smoke. Al held a handkerchief over his face and pointed to a glass cabinet. Mark smashed the glass with the heel of his hand, cutting himself in the process.

'Dyok! Dyok!' The native screeched.

'What's he saying?' Vern asked.

'He's saying it's the evil eye,' Al replied, coming up for air.

'Where's Mark?' Bob looked down the galley.

A sudden explosion and the caustic smell of melting plastic made them step back.

'Mark! God dammit where are you?' No answer came from the galley.

***

When they arrived at Moore Town, the car was exactly where they left it. Startled by their voices, the driver dozing at the wheel roused himself. Catching sight of the half-chewed sugar cane melting in the passenger seat, he reached over and threw the fly-infested object out of the window.

Soon they were heading down the mountain road to Port Antonio. At the hotel, Cassie said a hasty goodbye to Marge and Betty, with a promise to call them later.

'Mrs Campbell, before you go!' Marlon ran after her as she was about to get into one of the taxis parked under a pergola of sun-drenched palms.

'Marlon, I'm sorry, I'm so anxious about my husband that I forgot to thank you.' She pushed a fifty-dollar bill into his hand.

'Thank you, Mrs Campbell, but Beneba say, give to you.' He held out his hand.

Cassie looked at the object, inspecting it. 'What is it?'

'Garde. She says it will safeguard you. Beneba say to keep it always near you.' He looked at her earnestly as the taxi pulled away. 'Don't forget, Mrs Campbell!' he shouted after her.

'I won't, Marlon. I will see you before we leave.' She waved as the taxi turned the corner and drove out of sight.

At the hotel Blue Mountain, Cassie went straight to the reception.

'Was he supposed to report here, madam?' the receptionist enquired, looking startled at the state of her appearance. The suit she wore had been immaculate at the start of the day, and even Mark had complimented her. Well aware of how she now looked, Cassie went to the bathroom and dabbed at her scratches. She washed her face and generally tried to straighten her creased suit, aware it was beyond repair.

The air-conditioning disturbed the tendrils of her damp hair when she removed her safari hat on the way out of the hotel.

'What time did you arrange to meet him, madam?'

'I didn't. We're staying here. My husband went on a fishing trip with friends, and I wondered if you had seen him?'

'No, I haven't seen any one prepared for a fishing trip, and I have been on duty all day. I'm sorry.'

She glanced up at the clock, it was four-thirty, and the time they had arranged to meet. Cassie forced herself to think logically. He wasn't late and, as Marge had pointed out, the men were with Al. Yet this still didn't allay her fears.

Sudden laughter interrupted into her thoughts; a group of residents sat around one of the fountains, enjoying happy hour cocktails before retiring to dress for dinner.

She walked past them, going into the hotel grounds. Darkness had already fallen. Cassie saw a figure in the distance near the perimeter. Convinced it was Mark, she ran towards it, only to find whoever it was had disappeared. Disappointed and realising she had gone farther than she intended, she walked back to the hotel.

A waiter ran towards her. 'Mrs Campbell! Mrs Campbell! A telephone call for you.'

She stood motionless, bracing herself for bad news.

'Mark, is that you?' The line was bad and voice on the other end began cracking up. Her hand trembled as she gave the receiver back to the receptionist. 'I'm sorry, I can't hear.'

'I will get you a better line. It should be okay now.'

'Mark.'

'Cassie? It's me, Sabrina. Thank goodness I managed to get hold of you!'

'Sab, what's happened? We're coming home the day after tomorrow.' The pause alerted her. The headache that started when she came down from the mountain became a series of thumping hammers inside her head.

'Sabrina!'

'It's bad news, Cass. Don has had an accident at the plot.' She hesitated. 'He's in the intensive care unit at the Bristol Royal Infirmary.'

'Oh my God! How bad is he?'

She stopped before continuing. 'He is on a life-support machine, Cass.'

'What?' Completely drained, with the hammers threatening to split open her head, she stared at her dishevelled appearance in one of the mirrors.

'Cass … are you there?'

'How did it happen?'

'He fell off the roof over the bathroom, hit his head on one of the girders, and crashed into a glass shelf over the bath. He has severed an artery in his arm. The doctor said he would have been killed if the bath had been empty, but the rain we've had since you left thankfully broke his fall.'

'If only we had left the work up there until we got back. I feel responsible.'

'How's Anne taking it?'

'As you would expect, badly. She is completely distraught – she keeps blaming the move to Bristol. I offered to stay with her, but she is at the hospital most of the time.'

'What are his chances, Sab?' 'Fifty-fifty at the moment. It depends if they find anything else, internally I mean. It's so sad. He isn't the most endearing person but he has a big heart. Anne said everything was beginning to go so well for them. Only last week he took delivery of a brand-new boat. In fact, he sailed in it that very morning. Apparently, he had found a disused mooring near the plot.'

'Beneba!' Cassie gasped.

'What are you talking about, Cass?'

'It's okay. I'll explain when I see you. Surely he had workers with him?'

'Only one, and he didn't see it happen because a freak wind had sprung up, from nowhere, and Don had asked him to go down and check the mooring. He heard Don's piercing screams as he walked back up. When he got there, he said the whole plot was a war zone, with a willow tree whipping up at the end of the garden – at least that was his take on it. Anyway, he found Don Semi-conscious and literally lying in a bath full of blood.'

'Oh, my God.' She felt sick again, perspiration sliding down her hands as she clutched the phone. For a split-second she was there once more – the frogs, the indescribable sense of evil. She felt her body shake uncontrollably. 'Sab, we'll get the next flight back.'

'No point, Cass. You can't do anything, none of us can. I was against ringing you, but Roger persuaded me. He said if anything happened to Don, I wouldn't be able to live with myself, and he was right.'

'You did the right thing, Sab, and please tell Anne we are thinking of her.'

'One other thing, Cass. Lorna has disappeared. Felix rang to ask if I had seen her. Apparently, she hadn't been to work for over a week and there is no answer on her landline or mobile.'

'Perhaps she's gone away for a few days?' Cassie had no interest. 'Anyway, keep me informed.' She replaced the receiver, deep in thought.

'Is your husband all right, Mrs Campbell?'

'What? Oh, I still don't know. I'm going up to my room. Please let me know if there is any news. Also, could you tell room service to send up a bottle of Chardonnay and a glass,' she said, exhausted.

'Better make that two.'

She swung round at the sound of his voice. 'Mark!'

Chapter Fifteen

Thick grime covered his face and she hardly recognised him. Her tears began falling, smearing his face as he took her in his arms.

'I've been out of my mind with worry,' she said, holding him close. 'What happened to you?' She stood back and surveyed him. 'How did you get so dirty?'

'A fire started in the galley of the cruiser, and I helped to put it out,' he said, picking at the bandage around his wrist.

'Mark!' She gasped in horror at the sight of his wound.

'Don't fuss, Cass, it's not as bad as it looks.'

'How did the fire start?' She inspected the blood-encrusted bandage.

'No one knows. One minute we were relaxing on deck and the next, Al's native came rushing up from the galley shouting incoherently. Al and I extinguished the fire but unfortunately, I cut my hand when I broke the glass to get the extinguisher. I personally think Al's man got a bit careless, but who knows? The heat was enough to melt the plastic worktop, though. Anyway, that's enough of that, how was your day?' He looked her up and down. 'It looks as if you've had a full day as well,' he said, guiding her to the lift.

When they got back to their room, Mark immediately went into the bathroom, ran a bath, and then poured them both a glass of wine.

'I know why don't we ring for room service and have dinner up here? Neither of us feels like making much of an effort tonight.'

When it came, the meal included locally caught lobster

with pureed vegetables and sweet potatoes. But Cassie had little appetite. She was trying to find the right moment to tell Mark about Don. Guessing that he had not eaten for some time, she decided to wait.

'It seems you're not hungry after all,' he said, pulling apart the grilled lobster. 'What happened then? Did Marge and Betty put you through it?' he teased.

She did not reply, helping herself to salad instead. Mark offered her the lobster, but she shook her head.

'My day began well. The Americans have a fabulous hotel, set in its own plantation in the hills.' She described what happened and when she mentioned Marlon, Mark burst out laughing. Then she told him about Beneba. 'You would never believe how old and wise she is, Mark. She is descended from the Maroons and although she is blind, she singled me out. It's as though she was waiting for me to come here.' She lowered her voice. 'Beneba also knew about the black man at the bridge.'

Mark flinched. 'We have been through all that, Cass.' He looked directly at her and took her hands. 'Cass, my darling, you're forgetting one thing – you are the only person that has seen this man, whoever he is.'

'I know! That's why it's so significant that Beneba knew as well.'

Mark had thought Cassie had got over this fixation and, that meeting new friends, they were back to some sort of normality.

'Did Marge or Betty hear any of this?'

'Well, no, they were doing other things. Beneba knows so much, even about my parents' accident. She told me not to blame myself.'

'Cass, you said you never wanted to discuss that ever again.'

'Yes, I know I did. You see, she has made me face up to

it. She told me I had the strength. Beneba even knew about the boat and the danger on the water. At first, I thought she meant you, but I know now she meant Don.'

'Don? What's happened to Don?'

Cassie bit her lip – it was not supposed to come out like this. She told him about her phone call with from Sabrina.

'Christ, Cass, why didn't you tell me sooner?'

'You weren't in the right frame of mind; I wanted you to eat first.'

'Well, I am now! I'll ring home straight away,' he said, looking for his wallet.

'There's no point. Sabrina says there is nothing we can do.' She looked at him. 'He's in intensive care'

'My God, it gets worse.' Mark opened the door. 'Come on; let's go down to the bar. You can tell me everything that Sabrina told you. I have a feeling I'm going to need something stronger than wine.'

***

Don's accident had put a dampener on the last two days of their holiday. As far as Mark was concerned, the sooner they got back to England, the better.

He looked up and saw Cassie make a perfect dive. He absent-mindedly followed her silhouette gliding under the turquoise water, only to emerge a few seconds later at the other end of the pool. Pushing back her hair, she searched for a comb in her bag and leant over and kissed him on the lips.

'I'm going up to get changed; it's already two-thirty.' Her tone was subdued.

Mark smiled up at her. 'I'll be up in a minute.' He watched her walk towards the hotel.

Lying back on the lounger, his thoughts were all over the place. If only he had not been so eager to get things moving.

If only he had waited until they got back, the chances were that he would have supervised the work up there himself.

Pulling the peak of his baseball cap over his eyes, he tried to find some peace.

***

The bustle of Port Antonio continued well into late afternoon. Their sole purpose was to find Cudjoe, to say a final goodbye before leaving Jamaica.

They left the square disappointed, and instead, they walked to the medical centre to get Mark's wound dressed.

Back at the hotel, there was a message for Mark to ring Vern. Cassie left him and went upstairs to pack.

'He's asked us to dinner tonight at their hotel,' Mark said, closing the door. 'It seems its Al's treat – a thank you, and a farewell all in one go. What do you think?'

'Sounds like a good idea. I want to say my goodbyes to Marge and Betty, anyway.'

'I'll tell Vern we'll be over there at eight.'

'Mark, give Sab a quick ring, she's expecting us to call about the arrangements at the airport.'

Deciding to wear a black linen suit, Cassie found the cream silk camisole she usually wore with it. Piling her hair into a French knot, she secured it with a tortoiseshell comb.

'There's no change,' Mark said, looking at her reflection. 'I spoke to Roger. Don is stable but the doctors won't commit themselves. They still aren't sure of the extent of his injuries and are running more tests.' He shook his head. 'I can't help blaming myself, Cass.'

She turned and faced him, putting her arms around him. 'You told me once; we are not responsible for other people's actions. It was when I felt guilty about my parents' death.'

'Yes, and you're right. It's only that we seem to be

surrounded by catastrophes, even here in Jamaica.'

'Talking of which, did he say if anything is happening at the plot?'

'Roger thinks that one of Don's men is working up there, but he's not sure. We spoke about the business mainly – more work has come in, and he's champing at the bit waiting for me to get back.' Mark took a black polo shirt off the hanger and laid it on the bed.

'Cass?' He called from the bathroom. 'You didn't tell me Lorna was missing?'

She stopped mid-track. She had forgotten to tell him. 'Mark, I'm sorry,' she said, joining him in the bathroom. 'What with Don's accident and worrying about you, it went completely out of my mind. Has she turned up yet?'

'No, apparently not.'

'I told Sabrina she may have taken a few days off.'

'That's what I told Roger, but the university says she wasn't due any leave, and she hasn't rung in sick. Felix has been to her flat, but there is no sign of her, and the police will not be interested as yet.' He threw a towel at her. 'Now, get out of here and let me shower.'

She turned to leave. 'Cass?' She turned. 'You look beautiful.' She blew him a kiss and closed the door.

The hotel Vista Port, Antonio, took on a different atmosphere at night. The plantations directly behind were lit from the lights of the hotel, highlighting the dense green trees that swayed gently in the breeze, merging with the dark shadows of the Blue Mountains farther up that formed a sinister backdrop.

'Look down there, Mark.' Cassie was eager to show him the view towards the harbour and the lights from the wharf that twinkled into the night. Arranging for the taxi to collect them later, Mark came up behind her, placing his foot on the low-level wall where Cassie had earlier put on Marge's walking boots. He took in the view, impressed with what he saw.

'It's stunning, darling,' he said, looking at Boundbrook Wharf, where a cargo ship was waiting to be loaded.

'The bananas are taken all over the world. Europe mainly, Marlon told me.'

'Good old Marlon,' Mark said, laughing.

They walked towards the hotel; it was more high-profile then their own. And with a declining charm and a unique position, it made it a very desirable place to stay.

Al greeted them, shaking Mark's hand robustly.

'And this, I presume, is Cassie.' Al kissed her hand. 'You sure are a lucky man, Mark,' he said, slapping him on the back. 'Come and meet my partner in life and crime.' Al beckoned to a tall, elegant woman dressed in full-length jade silk, embroidered with cerise hummingbirds and white gardenias. Walking towards them, Cassie noticed her long hair crazily out of control, the curls framing her exquisite features. She was beautiful and Cassie warmed to her immediately.

'Please call me Della, all my friends do.' She held out a long arm in greeting. Cassie smiled, mesmerised by her hazel eyes.

They both looked towards the bar, where Al was holding court and treating them all to farewell drinks. Cassie recognised Mark's laugh as Marge scolded Vern.

'I reckon you two have made friends for life.' Della observed.

'I hope so, you are all good people.' Cassie watched Betty coming towards her.

'Are you feeling better now, dear?' Betty asked, kissing her on the cheek. Marge joined her.

'We were worried about you, Cassandra, especially when Mark told Vern that you had bad news from England.'

'I'm sure Cassandra doesn't want to be reminded, Marge.'

'Unfortunately, a friend of ours had a serious accident and he's on life-support.'

'Oh, my child, I'm so sorry. It must have been a terrible shock,' Betty said kindly.

'Didn't that old woman, Beneba, warn you about danger? Marlon told us she spoke to you …'

'The great Beneba spoke?' Della stared at Cassie incredulously.

A waiter showed them to a nearby table lit by candles of varying sizes, the flames unwavering in the stillness. They all settled down to a warm ambience of al fresco dining consisting of chicken wrapped in bacon, stuffed with onions and deep-fried cheese, side dishes of vegetable curry, mushrooms and rice, followed by candy apple walnut cheesecake and sorbet.

As they walked on to the terrace Al recollected the boat incident. Vern, tapping his glass, stood up and made an emotional speech to Mark and Cassie, describing how he would love to visit them in England.

Della refused coffee and asked the waiter to bring a bottle of rum. She pushed back her chair and stood up.

'Yeah, bootleg liquor. The stronger the better, eh honey?' Al said at the other end of the table.

'You know me, babe,' she answered, walking towards the balustrade.

The party moved back to the bar, and Cassie saw an opportunity to speak to Della.

'It's a reminder of my humble beginnings,' she said, raising the bottle and drinking deeply. Cassie stood beside her, leaning on the railings, and looking at the lights twinkling down below. Della continued 'I can't help thinking … Beneba speaks to no one.' She turned to look at Cassie. 'What did she say?'

Cassie told her of the meeting in the mountain village.

'Della, there is no way she could have foreseen events

halfway across the world. It's impossible.'

'You must understand, there is a lot of superstition on this side of the island, especially here on the John Crow and Blue Mountain area. Mountain people have powers that you and I cannot even guess.' Della paused and filled two glasses. 'Here, try this, you can't leave the island without tasting it,' she said, handing Cassie a glass. 'Bon voyage.' The spirit had a bitter-sweet taste, causing a slow intense burn as she swallowed. Coughing, she handed the glass back, much to Della's amusement.

'When Beneba warned me of danger, she mentioned 'Baka.'

'It's an evil spirit with supernatural powers; these things can take the form of anything they choose – or anyone. There are many stories of these spirits, they can instil such terror that it's been said some people die at the sight of them.' She put her hand on Cassie's arm. 'I'm sorry; I didn't mean to frighten you.'

'Can they take on the appearance of a child or children?'

'Yes, without a doubt. Spirits like these can be very coquettish and mischievous, almost irresistible. Although, I can't see why Beneba should warn you about Baka. I am at a loss to see the connection with Jamaican and African folklore and the link with your country.' Della had a puzzled expression, and stared into the distance.

Sudden laughter filtered through the French windows, and they turned absently. Cassie leant against the balustrade, remembering the beautiful face of the little girl in the bonfire.

'Beneba also mentioned Marassa several times.' She swung round and faced Della, feeling the light breeze against her face coming from the mountains behind the hotel.

Della looked even more puzzled. 'Marassa means twins. In the Voodoo religion, they are said to be more powerful than a Loa God.'

'Isn't Loa part of Voodoo worship?'

'That's what I don't understand. I know it's still popular in Haiti, and although our countries are not that far apart, Obeah is the preferred alternative religion here. But then, Voodoo originated in Africa, and since they were brought over as slaves, it's logical to think that older generations of Maroons such as Beneba would be aware of the cult and its superstitions. If she's thinking along those lines, then you'll have to watch your back, Cassie. Voodoo can have far-reaching consequences. You never know who practises it, and the network goes so far underground you will never …' Della paused to light a cheroot. 'No wonder she told you not to trust anyone.' She drew thoughtfully on the cheroot. 'What else did she say?' Della expelled the smoke into the night air, looking directly at Cassie.

'Nothing more. She laid a few ghosts for me. Oh, she did give me this, she told me to wear it at all times.' Cassie opened her evening bag. 'Although, it isn't possible to wear it all the time.' She showed Della the charm.

'But you must! It's a Garde – a protective charm.' She caught hold of Cassie's arm again. 'You must take these warnings seriously, especially in light of what you told happened before you came here …' Della took a chain from around her neck. 'Now, put this on.' She threaded the charm on to the chain. 'I strongly advise you not to take it off but if you do, don't forget to put it back on. Remember, while you're wearing it, you are protected by Beneba.'

Cassie stared at her, unsure if it was the drink talking. She looked sober enough, but it was a strange thing to say.

'In the meantime,' Della added, 'I will find out as much as I can about the religion. Have you a fax, or email address?'

'Sabrina has a fax you can use for anything urgent. It will get lost if you use the one at the office.' They exchanged addresses and telephone numbers.

'Cassie, I'm surprised you didn't mention any of this to Cudjoe. After all, he is much more knowledgeable than I am.'

She stared at Della in astonishment. 'I had no idea you knew him.'

'I don't, Al said you were looking for him. He has a reputation for being a recluse – it's part of his enigma. You must have caught him on a good day.' She laughed.

'He went out of his way to show us around Port Antonio, and we had a memorable lunch with him.' Cassie hesitated. 'Funny, Mark never said he spoke to Al about him but what with the fire and the hysteria surrounding it ...' She shrugged her shoulders.

'Hey, honey, I know you're both bonding out there, but I haven't had a chance to get to know Cassie.' Startled, they looked over at the French window and Al's frame filling it.

'We're coming, babe.' The two women walked across the terrace towards the pleasant music now filling the room.

'Della thanks for listening. It's such a relief to talk about this sensibly. Only please don't mention this conversation to Mark, especially the subject about Voodoo. He already thinks I'm on the edge. Tell him that and he will think I've gone over it!'

Della laughed, linking her arm in Cassie's. 'One other thing, Della. Why did you say Cudjoe knew more about Voodoo than you did? I don't understand.'

'Ah, there you are, Cassandra. I'm afraid Bob and Mark are a little worse for wear – and Vern is up there with them.' Marge sniffed, knocking back another gin and tonic.

***

They said an emotional farewell to the Holders and the Forbes, vowing to write often.

'And don't forget that little business deal we discussed,

Mark. So long, buddy,' Vern said, clapping him on the shoulders.

'What was that all about?' Cassie asked, waving to the Americans.

'A business plan Bob is putting together. I'll tell you if I get anywhere with it.' Mark smiled at her. 'You were in deep conversation with the beautiful Della. What was that all about?'

She faced him, a wicked glint in her eye. 'I'll tell you if anything comes of it.'

'Touché.'

'So, you think Della is beautiful, do you?'

'I'm not falling into that trap, Mrs Campbell. Come here.'

The taxi continued its downward journey to their hotel. When they got back, Cassie headed straight for the shower. She felt the water flow over her face and hoped it would settle not only her doubts but also, more importantly, her mind.

She wrapped herself in a towelling robe, put her charm back on and went to join Mark on the balcony. She stood next to him, and toyed gently with the rough edges of the charm.

'This place is so beautiful, Cass.' She felt his arm around her shoulders. 'Whatever we face when we get home, we must always remember it here.'

***

She sat bolt upright, soaked with perspiration. The room was in complete darkness – she knew immediately what had woken her. Mark, breathing heavily next to her should have reassured her, but she was drawn to the open window and the gauze curtain wafting in the breeze. Futile sound of drums beating louder and louder outside in the darkness had stolen her dream.

She went out on to the balcony. The drums were getting closer, and she could hear crude laughter underneath the window. Shuddering, she bolted the window and went back to bed.

Cassie began thinking about the conversation with Della. Could it have been possible that Cudjoe had targeted them on their first day? She dismissed the idea even faster than she thought it. Why would he? He didn't know them. Her muddled mind drifted into a disturbing dream of witch doctors chanting 'Marassa, Marassa.' Drums began beating louder and faceless people wearing Voodoo masks dragged her into a circle of fire. She looked up into Cudjoe's laughing face. He turned to his left and her eyes followed him. She screamed at the sight of Don's head on a stake, a tortured expression on his face.

Chapter Sixteen

The dull grey buildings of Heathrow airport only increased the feeling of despondency they both felt. Cassie sighed, and looked up at the sky; rain began to fall. She had been privileged to see the real Jamaica in a totally different way from most tourists. It had given her an understanding and fascination that she didn't think she would ever perceive.

'Are you ready to come back to earth with a bump?' Mark grinned, raising an umbrella.

'I wish we had met Della earlier in the holiday, Mark.'

'Yeah, they're a great couple,' he agreed, catching her melancholy mood. 'Cheer up; I'm sure we'll get a letter from the Americans before too long. Anyway, who says the holiday is over?'

Mark had arranged a surprise for her. It had been Sabrina's idea to book a hotel and arrange for them to take in a show. 'It'll have to be a budget one, Sab,' he had told her.

'Look, Mark, just because you're spent out, it doesn't mean that Roger and I have to slum it.'

Mark smiled at the recollection. Taking hold of her elbow, he steered Cassie out of the airport building.

'Sab!' Cassie flung her arms around her. 'I'm so pleased to see you! I have so much I want to tell you.' She looked over at Roger. 'What are you both doing here?' she laughed, hugging Roger. 'Mark, did you know anything about this?'

'It was my idea, Cass,' Sabrina said, producing tickets for the opera 'Nabucco.'

'How thoughtful, Sab – our favourite opera!' They hugged again.

A dark chill met them as they crossed the terminal road. Puddles of rainwater reflected the orange glow of industrial London. Oblivious of the cold, they walked towards the car park. Sabrina had booked them into a hotel near the airport and after they had eaten and had a drink at the bar, they decided to call it a night.

***

Cassie had half-expected to see blue skies and a view of Port Antonia when she pulled back the curtains. Instead, she saw a bank of umbrellas below her on the pavement.

She had overslept. Clicking open her suitcase, she soon found something to wear. After a hot shower, she went down to find the others.

Mark and Roger had already finished breakfast and were discussing business.

'Coffee, darling?' Mark asked, getting up.

'And some croissants!' she called after him. 'Where's Sab, Rog?' She sat next to him.

'She had to go into central London on business.' Shuffling papers, he smiled at her before placing them in his briefcase.

'Strange, she didn't mention it last night.'

'She's under quite a bit of pressure at work, rearranging structure plans or something. We're linking up later this afternoon. She has already made reservations for dinner and all we have to do is to turn up. Ah, here comes more coffee.'

Cassie bit into her croissant, studying Roger. If only he was not so weak, she thought. It irritated her when he let Sabrina make all the decisions. She loved Sab dearly, but Cassie knew from first-hand experience how forceful she could be.

'Roger's been telling me the latest on Don.'

'Yes, he's much the same. Anne told Sab she is worried

about the business. She thinks she may have to lay off some of the men. Without Don they're kicking their heels.' Roger sighed and shook his head.

'Don't forget the site still needs levelling, Rog. It's obvious they will need some direction. I'll see if I can get up there to jolly them along.'

'I think they are afraid they won't get paid, Mark, and Anne's no businesswomen. Thankfully it appears she's financially secure, but I really can't say the same for his business.'

'I'll go and see her when I get back to Bristol. At least it will take the pressure off Sab.'

'She can't wait until you get back, Cass; it's pitiful to see her. Sabrina has encouraged her to come over after she has visited Don, for company more than anything else. None of us know her very well, but it's almost as if we are all she has now.'

'Surely she has some family?' Cassie prompted.

'Apparently not.'

They fell silent, until Cassie rattled her coffee cup as she replaced it on the saucer.

'What about his guy that worked with him that day?' Mark asked. 'How is he?'

'He's still in shock, and according to the doctors won't be working for some time. I think mental health issues are involved, it seems he struggles with terrible nightmares and can't be left on his own. They told Anne he's full of remorse and blames himself because he was checking out the moorings when it happened and didn't hear Don's screams.'

'He wouldn't have been able to, Rog. Not that far down,' Cassie added. 'What happened to the boat? Wasn't it brand new?'

'Yeah, the company came and collected it. Anne wants to sell his original boat. You could probably name your own price, Mark.'

'That's callous, Roger. How could you say such a thing?' Cassie scolded.

'Do you think she will stay in Bristol?' Mark added.

'Your guess is as good as mine. She hasn't mentioned selling up, but I wouldn't be surprised if she sold and moved back to Somerset – if anything happens to Don, that is.'

They sat back with their own private thoughts, watching the rain lash against the window. Some executives came down the stairs with suitcases and arranged for a taxi to take them to the airport.

'And Lorna, Rog?' Mark asked, watching one of the men pick up a menu.

Roger shook his head. 'It's a complete mystery. She is officially missing now. Felix reported it after he came back from Newport. He thought she might have visited her sister, but she hasn't seen her for almost a year. That man is a saint,' Roger added. 'I can't think why he bothers. It was obvious there was no love lost between them at the dinner party.'

'I think he's just a decent person. There are still a few of us around,' Mark said, trying to lighten the mood.

'Anyway, it's in police hands now. By the way, they held Constable Palmer's memorial service while you were away. A double spread in the second edition. It seems he had a long and distinguished career that could have taken him to the top of his profession. But it appeared he wanted to remain a constable and a good copper, his wife said.

He glanced at Cassie. 'It seems the tree falling on him was a freak accident, Cass.' 'I kept the article, in case you both wanted to see it.

'Thanks, Rog, but I don't think I'll need it. I'm going to get our things together … Mark?'

'I'm right behind you,' he responded, also getting up.

Roger crossed the car park and opened the car boot.

Putting his bags to one side, he took the luggage that Mark handed him.

'We should make central London before the traffic starts building,' he said, looking at his wristwatch and getting behind the wheel. Before they left the hotel, Roger took a call from Sabrina.

'Four o'clock at the Glass Menagerie,' he said, smiling at Cass in the driving mirror. He manoeuvred his way out of the car park on to the busy A4.

Cassie closed her eyes and felt for her charm, holding it tightly. She appreciated the trouble Sab had taken to organise the surprise, but she really wanted to return to Bristol, there was so much she needed to settle in her mind. One of them was Anne.

'What made her choose a central restaurant? Covent Garden is not exactly car friendly,' Mark said, frustrated at the traffic queues.

They found the restaurant down a side street, near one of the theatres. It was dark and dreary inside, not the sort of restaurant she would associate with Sab.

Sabrina sat, writing, at a corner table with a small table lamp. The dark red of the shade threw a shadow over the scattered papers. Hastily packing them away, she got up to greet them.

'I hope this is all right,' she said, snapping her briefcase shut. 'It was recommended.'

'Bit claustrophobic,' Mark said, taking in the surroundings and hanging up his coat on an old-fashioned coat stand. Roger gave her a swift kiss, and sat next to her.

'Where did you park, Rog?' Sabrina asked, responding to his kiss.

'Don't ask,' he answered, ordering wine.

'What time is the performance?' Cassie asked, unfolding her napkin.

'Seven-thirty. Actually, I had better check now you've mentioned it, Cass.' She began looking in her bag.

'I suppose we will hear about this holiday one day,' Roger said, filling everyone's glass.

Mark told them about Port Antonio, Cudjoe and their hotel. He went into detail about the Americans and Cassie explained about the trip to the Blue Mountains and about Beneba. Cassie showed Sabrina the charm Beneba had given her, and Sabrina studied it closely.

'It's rather a clumsy piece, Cass, not the sort of thing you would normally wear.'

'That's why I like it, and it reminds me of Jamaica,' Cassie said defensively.

Sabrina reached over and touched her arm. 'Sorry, Cass, that was unkind. I didn't mean it. You took me by surprise.'

Mark caught hold of his wife's hand and squeezed it.

'My work programme is quite intense at the moment,' Sabrina said for no reason, as though to wipe out the earlier remark. 'The higher up the ladder one goes, the more the pressure builds.' She laughed nervously. 'And I suppose Roger has told you about the complication with Mr Morgan?'

'What about him?' Mark looked at her.

'As I was the last person to talk to him, they've asked me to make a statement.'

'That's normal, isn't it?' Mark asked.

'He fell into a coma after our conversation and died without gaining consciousness.'

'We didn't know that. We assumed he died at the hospital,' Mark added.

Sabrina sighed. 'His widow has requested a private autopsy. The results should be known within a couple of weeks.'

'Why, though, Sab? It was common knowledge he had a weak heart. Don even found his appointment card for the cardiology clinic.'

'Anyway, Elizabeth, his widow, is not altogether satisfied with the verdict of the first autopsy. She said he became very agitated after he had been to the plot.' Sabrina looked at Cassie. 'It seems your influence spurred him to go up there to see for himself. Anyway, he became convinced that someone was stalking him. She said he was literally frightened for his life.'

'Surely a second autopsy isn't going to make any difference?' Cassie said.

They ate in silence, and left Mark and Roger to settle the bill. Sabrina linked arms with Cassie as they walked towards the central arcade. Cassie looked up at the decorations that graced the roof, relieved to leave the dismal atmosphere of the restaurant behind, but she had little appetite for Christmas.

'I'm looking forward to this, Cass. This is everything we are, you and me.' Sabrina blew into her gloveless hands. They headed toward Shaftsbury Avenue, dodging evening shoppers and commuters alike.

'Nabucco' embraced all that Cassie remembered and stirred so many memories of when she first saw the opera in Victoria Rooms Clifton, with Sabrina's parents.

Cassie looked across at Sabrina. As the story unfolded.

Nabucco led his people from exile and adversity to eventual triumph. The opera led into the Chorus of the Hebrew Slaves. The emotive laments of a people plucked from their native land were embodied in the chorus. The opera, as always, stirred her, only this time she felt she had a purpose. Caught up in its overwhelming emotion, she silently vowed to be the salvation of the one that needed her.

Chapter Seventeen

Anne looked through the window at the close-cropped lawn, thankful that it would not need any attention until the spring. The hard frost covering the lawn glistened on the well-tended beds and the neat edges. She was disappointed that only three out of the eight conifers she planted had taken root. She remembered it had been one of those sunny weekends and Don had helped her in the garden. Anne pinpointed the one he had planted; it was growing strongly.

'There, my bird, I'm going to watch this one grow every day,' he'd said, treading the earth around the root. Her eyes misted over, and she had an overwhelming urge to cut it down, just as her Don had been cruelly cut down. Anne turned her back on the window, feeling isolated and lonely. Smoothing the back of his chair, she sat in it, sobbing.

It was much later when she woke. She went into the kitchen to make a cup of tea, forcing herself to think positively. After all, the doctors had told her he had a fifty-fifty chance, but somehow she had already resigned herself to a life without him. Sabrina had explained to her that it had been a tragic accident. What a friend she had turned out to be she thought, sipping her tea. Sabrina's kindness had surprised her; she was always ready to listen. She had invited her into her home and kept asking about Don's progress. It was a great comfort to know that she could be relied upon.

Anne looked up at the cuckoo clock Don had bought her. Better get a move on, she thought, going upstairs to change into her tweed skirt and a blouse. Yes, she had been lucky to have people who supported her. Even Felix, whom she hardly knew, had sat with her one evening. They had discussed Lorna's disappearance – mainly to occupy her mind, she supposed. When they were introduced at Sabrina's dinner party, Anne had taken to Felix immediately; he had a way of putting people at ease. Anne had another reason to feel optimistic, Cassie and Mark were due back in Bristol today, and she couldn't wait.

***

Don's room was empty when Anne arrived at the hospital.

'Don't worry, Mrs Berry,' the staff nurse said from behind. 'The doctor has decided to move him to another room.' They walked down the corridor to another part of the building. The doctor looked up as they entered the room.

'You'll be glad to hear he is breathing on his own, Mrs Berry. It is early days yet, but I think we may have turned a corner. It will be a gradual process, of course, and I am still waiting for the results of the second CT scan, but all things considered …' He peered over the top of his spectacles and smiled. 'Fingers crossed, Mrs Berry.'

'Thank God, doctor. I can't thank you enough.' She looked over at Don. 'Is he conscious?'

'Not really. You have to remember that with coma patients, it is very slow progress but having said that, he did respond to Sister this morning. Please be patient, Mrs Berry.'

'That is one thing I have always been with Don, believe me, doctor. I have had no choice.' The doctor turned to speak with the ward sister. Careful to avoid Don's heavily bandaged arm, Anne leant over and held his hand. His eyelids flickered at her touch but didn't open.

'Doctor, do you think it would help him if I brought some of his friends to visit? I mean, it might stimulate or trigger something …'

'I don't think it would do any harm, Mrs Berry, as long as you realise it has to be low-key. By that, I mean he must not be taxed in any way.' Anne nodded and kissed Don on his forehead before she left.

She left the hospital with a feeling of euphoria – her earlier self-indulgent outpouring forgotten. She walked up Park Street, vowing to be stronger. A sweater caught her eye in one of the shop windows. Don would like that she thought, and went in.

***

Cassie was just finishing unpacking and had begun loading the washing machine when Anne rang.

'That's wonderful news! I'm so pleased. Mark and I have been so worried. We almost decided to come home early. Needless to say, we feel somewhat responsible.' She hesitated as Mark came in. 'Yes, of course, Anne, if you think it will help. I'll pick you both up at eleven-thirty unless I hear differently.' Cassie hung up and turned to Mark.

'Don's making some progress. He's responding to drugs and his doctors are quietly confident.

'That's the best news I've heard all day,' Mark said, going into the kitchen. He came back with two glasses of wine and raised them. 'To Don and a speedy recovery.'

Mark sat down next to her. 'Have you heard from Sabrina?'

'Not since we got back, but I will see her tomorrow. Anne wants us go and see Don, she thinks our presence may help with his recovery.' She shrugged her shoulders. 'It's worth a try, Mark.' He nodded in agreement.

'What about the Lethbridge job? I thought you were planning to start as soon we returned?'

'Mrs Lethbridge was very understanding when I spoke

to her and explained. She's happy to leave it until I'm ready and besides, she hasn't made a decision on the colours yet.'

'That's because you're the best. Come on, we'll go out and eat.'

***

The first thing Mark did the next day was to find out if any of Don's staff were working at the plot, so he left the office and drove over.

Very little had changed, the building still held the same intimidation. He looked around, disappointed. Choosing not to go into the bathroom, he glanced down to the end of the garden at the outline of the willow. He called out but no one answered.

***

Don opened his eyes for the first time on Friday morning. Cassie and Sabrina waited in the corridor while Anne went into his room. Eventually, the sister came out and proceeded to tell them what to expect.

'Whatever you do, don't ask him any questions. His memory is limited, and he mustn't be stressed.'

They found him semi-conscious with a monitor attached to his bed, surrounded by an alarming amount of surgical equipment.

Anne walked tentatively towards the bottom of the bed followed closely by Sabrina. Seating herself beside Don, Anne held his hand and stroked it. She whispered to Sabrina who responded by pulling up a chair next to her.

Almost as if he knew they were there, Don opened his eyes, and focussed on Sabrina. He uttered a strangled sound; his whole body was shaking. Horrified, Anne pushed back her chair to get help. Don caught hold of her sleeve without turning his head. They watched him, terrified.

'Do something,' Sabrina said, backing off. Cassie, nearest to the door, ran from the room, followed by Anne.

The doctor looked at Don's heart monitor. 'I think you'd better leave. Sometimes after a huge trauma of this kind, the brain reacts in unusual ways. I think perhaps with the benefit of hindsight he wasn't ready for visitors.' He bent over and gave him a sedative. 'That should steady him and give him some peace.'

The three women left the room and went over to get coffee from the machine.

'I don't understand, that wasn't my Don in that bed, he was so frightened,' Anne sobbed.

'I agree, he certainly seemed a different Don to the affable man I met at your party, Sab,' Cassie said, handing Anne a tissue.

'Whatever was in his mind had terrorised him beyond belief. I only hope it wasn't me – he seemed to react to the colour of my skin.'

'But why should he, Sabrina? I've never known him to be racist. Besides, being neighbours, he practically saw you every day.'

'Mrs Berry, may I have a word?'

Anne got up. 'What's wrong, doctor?'

He took hold of her elbow and led her down the corridor out of earshot. 'I think we had better leave any visiting for a few days.' He saw her look of alarm. 'We want what is best for Don, Mrs Berry. It will be for a couple of days, and don't forget you can ring Sister anytime. She will keep you up to speed.' He watched her eyes fill with tears. 'There is one piece of good news – the scan we took is clear.'

'That is good news, doctor,' she said, wiping her eyes.

Cassie dropped Sabrina off at the centre and went back to Anne's to catch up.

***

'Everything's gone to pot!' Mark tossed a set of plans on the desk.

Roger swung round in the swivel chair, pen in hand. 'What has?'

'Don's whole workforce.'

'What do you expect, Mark? The poor bastard is fighting for his life, and you're worried about …'

'I accept that, Rog, but surely someone could have gone up there, or at least lifted the damn telephone, for God's sake. I mean, what kind of bloody outfit is this? Christ, I should have known better trusting someone I didn't even know. What the hell was I thinking?'

'Calm down, Mark,' Roger said, offering him coffee. 'Don't forget his foreman's laid up as well.'

'That's why no one is up there. We must have other contacts, Rog.' Mark started shuffling papers.

'Is this what you want?' Roger asked, holding up a well-worn book.

Mark got home later than expected, and the fish pie Cassie had cooked was almost ruined.

'If I had known, Mark, I wouldn't have put it in so early,' she said, getting it out of the oven.

'Yes, you're right, I should have rung. It's not been a good day, Cass,' he said, helping himself to some claret.

'You and me both.'

'Sorry, darling. Of course, you arranged to see Don. How did it go?'

'Nothing like I thought it would. I'll tell you later.' Mark looked at her, surprised. 'Anyway, what happened to spoil your day?' Cassie asked, playing with the dry cod.

'What do you think, Cass? The only topic that does these days – our plot. Nothing is happening up there. Anyway, I've sorted it now.' He helped himself to some pie.

'Keith is starting after Christmas.'

'What? Keith Poole? I thought you were never going to use him again.'

'I know, Cass, I know, but we need to clear the site as soon as possible.'

She nodded in agreement, and began stacking the dishwasher. 'Mark, I thought we might invite Anne over one evening – it will take the pressure of Sab. Besides, she's very low since the doctor has put a ban on any visits at the moment, including Anne.'

'What! But why?'

They went into the lounge and Mark made himself comfortable in the corner of the sofa. He listened with increasing horror when Cassie related her visit to Don, and when she mentioned his extraordinary outburst, he got up, and drew the curtains. He turned to face her. 'Cass, my darling, we have to face facts, don't you think we've had enough of this plot? Think about it. Our entire conversation tonight has been about it. This place is not making us happy. I found myself ranting and raving at Roger earlier. That's not me, Cass, you know that. I'm frightened what this is doing to us. I think we should sell it.'

Cassie went over to him, but the phone interrupted them. It was Sabrina. The coroner's office had rung her at work with the results of Mr Morgan's second post-mortem. It had been a straightforward case of heart failure.

'At least it is confirmed, Sab. I know it was on your mind.'

'You have no idea. It would have been so undignified if his last moments were clouded with suspicion. I am worried about Anne, though. I thought you and I could take her shopping; choose a few Christmas gifts for Don?'

'Oh, I don't know, Sab. I haven't even thought about it

and to be honest, I really have no appetite for Christmas.'

'You okay, Cass? You sound upset.'

'It's the shock of seeing Don, and everything that went with it.'

'I know, it affected me as well. I can't get it out of my mind. I wasn't going to mention it, but since you brought it up I ...'

'Sab, I don't want to discuss it now. I'll think about your suggestion and ring you tomorrow. Say hello to Rog.'

'That was a bit abrupt,' Mark said, as she sat down beside him.

'I didn't feel like getting involved in a long conversation tonight.'

'Listen, Cass. Let's run with it for a while, we will get our money back if need be. I know it means a lot to you. Is it a deal?'

'It's a deal. And Mark? Nothing is more important than you.'

Chapter Eighteen

The strains of 'Silent Night' echoed through the halls of residence. Finishing his mid-morning lecture, Felix began preparing for his next one later that day. Collecting his tweed coat, he went out into the corridor. A giant Christmas tree confronted him as he entered the great hall, the imitation candles twinkled impressively as they balanced on the branches. He had a heavy schedule in front of him and was also due to meet the sergeant at Redland Police Station. He would now be late. It was all because he had taken a call from an old university friend.

David had taken up a pathology post at the Bristol Royal Infirmary and now that he had settled into the job, he was eager to renew their friendship. Felix, happy to accommodate, had arranged to meet for a liquid lunch.

Turning a corner into the square, he looked up at the lights strung in loops across the street between old lampposts. With Christmas drawing ever closer, the only thing on his mind was complete rest. It had been particularly hectic this term and then with the added pressure of dealing with Laura's disappearance … Sighing, he wrapped his scarf further around his neck and rubbed his hands together. He had decided to stay in Bristol over the holiday, and Anne had invited him over for Christmas day. He had agreed only on the condition he provided the turkey. He crossed the road and went into the police station.

'Did you hear what I said, sir?' The sergeant looked at him. Felix was miles way.

'The file will still be open, won't it? I mean, she is still a missing person.'

'I know that, sir, but until we have more to go on – for example a body,' he said sarcastically, 'we can't do a lot more. All the usual leads have drawn a blank. Place of work, hospital … nothing. My guess is she has probably left the area and is keeping a low profile for some reason. A racy woman from what I hear. Could be an affair with a married man?'

The sergeant shuffled the papers on his desk and walked over to the filing cabinet. 'Anyway, Mr Moss. If I find out more, I will have to notify her sister first,' he said, offering his hand.

Felix slumped in the back seat of the taxi, reflecting on his conversation with the sergeant. He had told him precisely nothing. Why did he bother? No one else seemed to care; even her own sister had made it clear there wasn't any love lost between them. Sabrina, bless her, had spent hours phoning mutual friends, without success. What he found even more astonishing was that the police had already drawn their own conclusions. Even Lorna, for all her faults, did not deserve such a character assassination. He took a deep breath. It was about time he stepped back from this investigation and left it to the police; he leaned forward to look out of the window.

'Here will be fine, thank you, driver,' he said, fumbling for change. He walked towards the wine bar and went down the steps. A small group of session musicians were practising in the corner, using a wooden palette as a makeshift stage. Adjusting to the dim surroundings, he recognised David sitting in the corner, nursing a pint.

'Good to see you, my old friend.' Felix shook his hand robustly. 'That's new.' he laughed, pointing to his moustache.

'You certainly don't look any different, Felix. God, it must be all of fifteen years.'

'So why Bristol?'

'After my marriage broke up, I needed a clean break.

Plus, I wanted to be nearer to my elderly mother in Swindon, so this is a step in the right direction. I applied for a pathologist post at the Bristol Royal Infirmary, not thinking I would get it, of course.'

'Of course,' Felix laughed, taking off his coat. 'You'll find it much quieter here in Bristol, though.'

'You're joking, Felix. I've already had more unusual post-mortem cases than I ever had in London.'

'You were always gory, Dave,' Felix said, taking their drinks from the barman's tray.

'Remember that cat you dissected outside one of the don's rooms?' They laughed at the recollection.

'But seriously, Felix. There is another reason why I wanted to see you. I wanted to pick your brains on your knowledge of the transatlantic slave trade.'

Felix nearly choked on his pint. 'What has that got to do with anything?'

'Call it a hunch. Have you heard of a 'hex'?'

'Well, yes,' Felix added, puzzled. 'It's part of the black arts, isn't it?' He looked at David, wondering where the conversation was heading. 'I know it's said people have died from Voodoo spells but surely you don't really believe that?'

David leant towards him. 'I wouldn't have believed it either, but I have first-hand experience, Felix.'

'I first came across a case of 'vagal inhibition' ten years ago. I was working in a hospital in West Africa on a short-term exchange contract. One night, a young man was admitted with the classic symptoms. Total panic swept over the patient, the heart accelerating to the point where adrenalin was pumping into every cavity. Then the reverse happens, the heart begins to slow, the blood pressure drops. Death is instantaneous. The young man had literally been scared to death.' Felix looked at him. 'Look, the guy I did the autopsy on already had a heart condition. It was exactly the same as I had seen in Africa. All his large blood vessels were dilated which flooded his major organs, including his distended heart.' He looked at Felix. 'In the circumstances, it seemed easier and kinder to determine the death as heart failure. Anyway, I believe the old man's cremation took place not long after. Best thing, given the situation.'

Felix sat back in the chair, staring at him for several seconds. 'Let me get this straight,' he said, incredulous. 'Are you telling me there is Voodoo activity in Bristol? And if so, why?'

'That's where I hoped you could help. I remembered you specialised in that area.'

'But it's insane, Dave! Okay, I do know a about the subject of slavery, but not Voodoo! I get what you're telling me, but can you honestly expect me to believe it? You know what happened here, it was no more sinister than ships bringing goods from the West Indies into this city, even though I admit the whole triangle was ruthlessly exploited at the time. But anyway,' Felix got up and put on his coat, 'I'll go through my library and see if I can come up with anything remotely similar. It will be easier now that the end of term is approaching. I'll ring you next week, old friend,' Felix said.

Felix decided to walk back to his flat in the hope of clearing his head. Turning up his collar against the bitter east wind, he walked quickly across the Downs. The uneasy feeling of David's revelation had taken the edge off their reunion. The very idea of a West African religion infiltrating its way into life here was inconceivable.

It was one thing to teach his subject to the students, but quite another when he thought it could become a reality. He needed to talk to Cassie and Mark as soon as possible, especially now. Unbeknown to David, Felix was left in no doubt that the autopsy David referred to was that of Mr Morgan.

***

Mark, weary of all the corporate events that surfaced at this time of year, welcomed the opportunity to be able to leave his office at a sensible time. He looked forward to his evening. Cass had invited Felix for supper to catch up and, not having met since Sabrina's party, there would be plenty to talk about.

Cassie had spent most of the afternoon putting the final touches to the flat, placing gold baubles next to candles decked with red and green tartan ribbons. She was pleased with the effect, and she went into the kitchen to prepare supper. Taking a tray of sausages rolls out of the oven, she left them to rest. She thought about her shopping trip with Sab, it had been a lot of fun, just like old times. Unfortunately, Anne had declined to go with them. The doctor had reinstated her visiting again. The sound of Mark's key in the door made her jump.

'Wow! This sets the scene, Cass, it looks fantastic,' Mark said, looking around the flat. 'I'm sure Felix will appreciate your efforts,' he said, following her out to the kitchen. 'What time is he expected?'

'Oh, not for another hour yet.'

'Good, it gives me time to get a shower,' he said helping himself to a sausage roll. 'Any news?'

'Sab and I went shopping this morning. Anne is visiting Don again, but Sab says the house is always in darkness. She's worried about her, Mark.' She put the sausages rolls to one side and began to prepare lasagne.

Felix, despite his earlier conversation with David, was in sparkling form.

'You both look well; you obviously had a nice time.'

'We did,' Cassie said, filling his plate with lasagne. 'I'm afraid you're going to have to look at the dreaded holiday snaps later.'

'No problem. I enjoy observing other people's lives.'

After they had finished eating, they settled in the lounge. Felix sat back, contented, and Cassie handed him the photos, describing the views of Port Antonio and Musgrave market.

'Just a minute, Cass. Let me see that photograph again?' Felix studied it closely.

'Good Lord! You didn't tell me you met Cudjoe Jefferson?' He took off his spectacles, looking across at Mark for an answer.

'Why would we? He befriended us when we arrived in Port Antonio.' Mark flicked the photograph with his nail. 'In fact, that was the only time we were with him. Cudjoe took us to a charming little restaurant in East Harbour and he got a local to take this snap of us together. It was a special day, wasn't it, Cass? We tried to find him before we left Jamaica, but we were told he had probably gone back to Kingston. Anyway, I left a business card at the same restaurant we ate in. You never know, he might get in touch one day. You sound like you know him, Felix?'

'Not personally.' He handed the snaps back to Cassie. 'He's a leading authority on Afro-Caribbean history and folklore. I've come across his papers many times.'

Mark gave a low whistle, looking at Cass. 'Thinking about it, Al more or less hinted that he was involved with the subject the day we all went fishing. No wonder he knew so much history of the area. But what an amazing coincidence, Felix?'

'That's what Della must have meant, when she asked me why I had not spoken to Cudjoe about meeting Beneba,' Cassie said, feeling for her charm.

Felix looked puzzled. Mark poured himself some more wine. He offered some to Cassie, but she covered the glass with her hand.

'Felix, you remember the evening of Sab's party when

we first met, and we briefly discussed a plot of land we had seen the previous day?' He paused. 'Well, my friend, that's when it began' Ignoring Felix's bewildered expression; Mark told him everything that had happened at the plot and the bridge on the night of the storm.

'And then we went on holiday as you know. And with Mr Morgan's untimely death, we were more than ready, believe me.'

Felix flinched at the mention of Mr Morgan's name.

'Even then, events seemed to follow us,' Cassie interrupted. She told Felix about Beneba and her premonition that turned out to be Don's accident at the plot.

'In fact, the only normality on the holiday was our American friends, Bob and Vern and their wives,' Mark said, smiling at the memory. 'To be honest, Felix, I'm relieved to get this out in the open.'

'It's beyond belief; you must have thought you were in some kind of on-going nightmare.' Felix said glancing over at Cassie.

'I'll go and make coffee,' she said, heading to the kitchen.

'So, what's happening at the plot now?' Felix looked over at Mark.

'Roger says Anne has lain off the whole workforce. I personally question whether she's in a fit state to make that kind of decision but ...'

Cassie came back with a tray of sausage rolls, mince pies and coffee. Felix bit into a mince pie, trying to find the words ... 'I also have something to tell you and, ironically, it is connected to what you've been telling me. I met up with an old friend of mine – he's taken up a position in the B.R.I. as a pathologist.' He paused. 'And he had some worrying news. It seems that he did the second autopsy on Mr Morgan and is convinced it is exactly the same as a case he witnessed in Africa where the patient died of a Voodoo spell.'

'Mr Morgan wanted to get in touch with us on the day of the auction. He told Sabrina he had more information about the plot. What if he knew something we didn't? My God, Felix, do you think there was a connection?'

'We found his hospital appointment card when I met Don up at the site.' Mark watched Felix, deep in thought. 'Anyway, Sab said it was a straightforward case of heart failure!' he added.

'From what David told me, he felt it was appropriate to leave it at that, but I know it has shaken him. He asked me to find out more about the slave trade, and particularly the Voodoo religion. But to be honest, I can't see where it will lead.'

'Felix? If, hypothetically, there are dark forces at work, why do I feel an empathy with the man on the bridge? Why do I long to understand it fully? It's almost as if there are two different energies.'

Felix sat up in his chair. 'That never occurred to me, Cass. What was the word Della used when describing the Loa?'

'Marassa. It means twins. They are granted unique supernatural powers and are said to be more powerful than Loa. She also warned that when they take possessions, they very often take the form of little children – capricious, and ruthlessly cruel.'

Felix ate a mince pie in silence. Flicking crumbs from his trousers, he said, 'I think it might be helpful if we called on Mrs Morgan. She might be able to tell us what was so urgent that Roger needed to speak to you both about on the day of the auction.'

'I won't be able to go but it's a good idea. Cass could take you up to the plot at the same time,' Mark said, walking into the hall.

'One thing, Felix,' Cassie said, receiving his kiss. 'I

think it would be better if you didn't mention any of this to Sabrina, she already feels she could have done more to hurry the paramedics. She would be distraught if she knew his real condition.'

'I appreciate your interest, Felix,' Mark said when they were out of earshot. 'Although I don't understand why you should be so interested.'

'For one thing, I promised David. I also have a lot to gain, Mark. Can you imagine what it would mean to have my name on a paper that discovered unknown facts, not only about Jamaica, but part of Bristol's history in the eighteenth century?' He laughed. 'It would be almost the equivalent of the Nobel Prize! It's not only very exciting to be in the middle of this adventure of unearthing facts; the bonus is to be able to do this with people I have a lot of time for.' He hugged Mark.

'Well, I appreciate your involvement, for Cassie's sake. She needs an ally. I know her, Felix. She won't rest until she gets all this out of her system.'

Chapter Nineteen

A strange stillness met staff nurse Pearce as she prepared for night duty. With only days to go before Christmas, she had at last completed her shopping and welcomed the solitude of the ward. Flicking through her daily report, she noted there were no new messages. Good she thought, perhaps it will be an uneventful night. Arranging patient medications, she pushed the trolley through the swing doors.

At midnight, she went to check on Mr Berry. She had done this earlier, but he had been asleep. She walked down the corridor to the private ward he occupied, her uniform shoes squeaking as the rubber soles made contact with the highly polished floor.

It was dark in his room, so she was not able to see if he was still asleep. For some reason, the light over his bed had been turned off, leaving only the glow of his heart monitor pulsating in the pitch black of the room. Nurse Pearce leaned over his pillow to switch on the overhead light. Nothing! Realising it was not plugged in; she pushed the connector back into its socket.

She felt isolated as a malevolent presence threatened her. Sweat beaded her forehead and even in the grip of terror, she knew she had to get some light into the room. Turmoil made her disorientated as she scrambled to get to the main light inside the door. She accidently knocked over a steel tray, which spooked her even more.

With the room, at last, flooded with light, she leant against the wall to calm herself. Barely glancing at Don, she picked up his chart on the end of the bed – acutely aware of the silence in the room. She thought it strange that Don was lying on his side – how could he have possibly turned himself over? She moved towards him, feeling the fear returning with every step. Reluctantly, she put out her hand to take his pulse but recoiled in horror. His flesh was cold.

Alarmed, she rolled him on to his back, conscious of an appalling stench that came from him. Her blood-curdling scream filled the room.

Don Berry's eyes were empty black holes. As she stared down at him, blood began filling his sockets, the dark crimson staining his face. She screamed again, rushing out into the corridor, waking not only the other patients but also attracting the ears of the duty doctor.

***

Cassie threw back the duvet – sleep eluded her. Filling a glass of water, she tried to make sense of everything. The staggering coincidence of Felix recognising Cudjoe and then the disclosure of Mr Morgan's post-mortem. She switched off the kitchen light, wondering where it was all heading.

When she got back to the bedroom, she was surprised to find Mark on her mobile.

'It's for you, Cass. I've no idea who it is.'

'But it's the middle of the night?' she queried, taking the mobile.

'Hello, Mrs Campbell? It's the sister at the B.R.I. I'm sorry to ring you at this hour but Mrs Berry has asked me to call you. I am afraid she is very distraught.'

'Why? What's happened?'

'It's her husband. He's dead.' Cassie put the mobile on her chest and looked at Mark.

'Mrs Campbell?'

'Yes, I'm here.'

'Could you come to the hospital?'

'We'll be there as soon as we can,' she said, putting down the phone and looking for her clothes.

'What is it, Cass?'

She looked him in the eyes. 'It's Don, Mark. He's dead!'

***

The wards were in a state of chaos by the time they reached the hospital. Doctors passed each other with a look of panic. They found Anne huddled in a corner, staring into space. A young nurse sat next to her, holding her hand. Cassie ran towards her.

'I never had a chance to say goodbye, Cass. They won't even let me see him and now he's gone.' She began sobbing. 'They've already taken him away; I'll never see him again.'

'It's okay, Anne, we're here now.' Cassie held her tightly. As Mark went to find the reception area.

'Is it possible to have a word with a doctor – concerning Mr Berry?'

The nurse put down her pen. 'Are you next of kin?'

'No, but his wife ... I mean his widow is over there with my wife, and as far as we know she has no relatives. Look at her! She is so very distraught, and no one has told her anything about the circumstances of her husband's death. It's inhumane!' Mark banged his fist.

'I'll make sure a doctor will see you as soon as possible.'

Half an hour later, Mark was able to see the doctor.

'I have to tell you, doctor. I'm not his next of kin.'

'Yes, I know,' the doctor said, offering a chair opposite him.

Anne was taking a sip of water, when Mark came back into the room he glanced over at Cassie indicating the doctor wanted to see Anne.

'Should I go with her? She asked, noticing his pallor as he slumped in the chair next to her.

'The doctor wants to see her on her own; he wants to assess her reactions.'

'Mark,' she reached out to comfort him. 'What did the doctor say?'

He stared in front of him, his hands in his pockets. 'Cass, Don suffered terribly in his last moments! The doctor wouldn't go into too much detail; in fact, I felt he was finding it difficult to find the right words. He did emphasise the need to support Anne.'

'Why do you think he wanted to talk to you?'

'I think to prepare us for the ordeal ahead. There's something strange going on and I can't put my finger on. It's as if he's hiding something.'

'You're not serious?'

'No, I suppose not, but even so ...'

'I feel so sorry for her, Mark. I don't think she's strong enough to cope.'

'That's what the doctor said. Coming here to the hospital to sit with him kept her occupied. One thing, though – he's adamant that she does not see Don.'

'What?' Surely, he can't expect that. It's unrealistic.'

'I know, but it's what he wants,' Mark said, yawning.

'That will be difficult. Did he say how he died? We all thought he had turned a corner.'

'He led me to believe it was an accumulation of his injuries. He was very cagey. That's why I feel he's holding something back.'

'I was just about to ring Sab. I left the mobile in the bedroom!'

'Calm down, getting stressed is not going to help. Anne did ask them to ring Sabrina but there was no answer.'

'How did Anne get down here? She's only wearing a

lightweight jacket.'

'Taxi, I guess. Cass, save your energy, all you're doing is winding yourself up.' She took his advice and waited, but not for long.

Anne came out of the room, supported by the doctor; she held out her hands to Cassie. Her small frame was wracked with sobs. Cassie held her.

'Is she able to stay with you?' The doctor glanced wearily at Mark.

'Yes, of course.'

Mark placed his overcoat around Anne's shoulders and she caved into him, grateful for male comfort. The three of them went out into the December morning, Christmas far from their minds. Doctor Harris leant his back against the closed door, thankful that the arduous task of dealing with Mrs Berry was over. He hadn't expected her to be so vulnerable. She was completely bereft, insisting on seeing her husband's body. The only way to appease her was the promise to see what he could do later.

It had been a long and tiring shift. He and the duty doctor had even tried to shock Don back to life – knowing it was useless. He sat at his desk, running his hands through his hair, looking down at the blank sheet of paper that would be his report. What the hell was he going to say? That he had found Don with empty eye sockets, blood oozing relentlessly, even in death.

They had hurriedly moved Don's rapidly decomposing body out of the ward and down to the basement. The angst was evident as they shook hands on an unspoken promise.

He called staff nurse Pearce into his office and told her gently but firmly that Mr Berry had suffered a severe haemorrhage. To his relief, she either believed him or wanted to, because it was never mentioned again.

Taking a deep breath, he put away his file – he needed

time to word it correctly. Pushing the cabinet shut, he flicked off the lights and took the lift up to the next floor to collect his personal belongings. Something made him stop as he walked past the room that Don had occupied for so long. He stared into the darkness and felt the hairs on the back of his neck bristling. Confronting his fear, he went into the room.

The stench of death invaded his nostrils, even though the bed had been remade with fresh linen, as if nothing had happened. One never gets used to it, he thought.

But it was a different odour that hung in the air tonight.

'Excuse me, could you point me in the direction of the pathology unit?'

Doctor Harris swung around and faced a tall black man silhouetted in the doorway.

'Yes, it's on the …'

But the man had already disappeared. Incredulous, the doctor went out of the room and looked up and down the empty corridor. Hastily collecting his things, he left the building. It occurred to him to alert security, but it was cold, it had been a bastard of a day and he wanted out. Besides, it probably wasn't anything to worry about. Even so, he found the fact that the man appeared from nowhere and vanished just as quickly very unsettling.

His ex-wife had accused him of burying his head in the sand, suspecting at the time it was to gain a better divorce settlement. Yet as the dawn began breaking, he was sure as hell going to do exactly that and if the pathology boys had any sense, they would do the same.

The familiar bleep of his keypad deactivated his car. He drove off in the half-light, the cold morning swallowing him up.

***

Anne slept in the green room – the only room that had been given a makeover. The overall effect had been one of serenity and calm, except for now.

'Is she okay?' Mark asked as Cassie got in beside him.

'Did she mention Don's ring to you?' Cassie asked.

'Not that I remember. I thought she said he didn't wear jewellery?'

'I don't think we can depend on anything she says at the moment. Are you going to the office tomorrow?'

'No, I've left a message for Rog.'

'Good, that means Sab will ring. I'll be glad of her support. It's going to be a difficult time.' She yawned, almost asleep.

Chapter Twenty

David peeled off his gloves and looked over at Don Berry's body. If the evidence weren't in front of his eyes, he would have said he had imagined the last four hours. It was with apprehension that he reached for his tape recorder. All the preliminaries had been carried out, including the photographs. That only left his report. He was alone, his colleague having left as soon as he could. With a shaking hand, he spoke into the tape recorder.

'Penetrating wounds were found on the major internal organs causing massive haemorrhages to the liver, pancreas, spleen and kidneys. The deceased also suffered peritonitis, caused by perforation of the bowel.' He broke off and replayed the tape.

Walking towards Don's body, he continued...

'Therefore, loss of blood and subsequent shock were the major contributory factors to the cause of death.' He turned off the machine and paused. Then he rewound the tape. 'Hello, is anyone there?' He turned towards the door, listening intently. A surgical tray clattered to the floor behind him. 'Hello?' he shouted in the direction of the noise.

The appalling smell from Don's body made it imperative that he concluded his report quickly. He needed to refrigerate the body as soon as possible. He spoke into the tape again.

'I conclude that the cause of death was heart failure.' Switching off the tape, he prepared to put Don's body into storage, well aware that he had compromised the situation. Reaching for his mobile, he rang Felix. He spoke rapidly, as Felix's voicemail kicked in.

'Felix, it's important that I see you as soon as possible.' He spoke in hushed tones, as if he were afraid of being overheard. 'It's happened again. Only this time it's much more serious. I just closed the autopsy on a man, and it bears all the hallmarks of a Voodoo death. All his internal organs are in a severe state of decomposition and his eyes have been gouged out.' David paused. 'Christ!' He felt the cold of the steel pillar against his forehead as he leaned against it in an effort to pull himself together. 'Listen, mate, I'm tired, and it isn't the best place to be on your own. Meet me at the usual place, say one-thirty, but I can't stay long I have to catch the four o'clock from Temple Meads. I'm going to my mother's for Christmas. Any different, let me know.' He slipped the mobile into his trouser pocket.

In the cloakroom, he noticed his overcoat in a heap on the floor. That's strange, he thought, looking at the hanger swaying where it had been disturbed.

In his haste to get away, he realised he had forgotten to refrigerate Don's body. He walked over to where he had left him. In that short time, Don's body had decomposed beyond recognition.

Recoiling in horror, he quickly refrigerated the body, snapped off the light and headed for the lift, shaking as never before. Ignoring the 'no smoking' sign, he jabbed a cigarette between his lips, and fumbled in the pockets of his coat. 'Where the fuck is my lighter?' Throwing the cigarette away in frustration, he stumbled into the lift.

***

Sabrina turned her back on the window overlooking the square. Screwing up her paper cup, she aimed it at the wastepaper bin, but missed. She sat down behind the desk, her head in her hands. So, Don had died. Cassie had rung her as she was leaving for the office.

If only she didn't have this meeting. Unfortunately, it had been arranged months ago. She assured Cass she would leave the office as soon as she could. Things would have to be rearranged, of course. God, what a Christmas this was turning out to be! Chiding herself for being so selfish, she thought of Anne, and how she must be feeling. She decided to ring Roger.

'Have you heard?'

'Yes, Mark rang.'

'Oh Rog, what are we going to do? We all thought he was coming through it.'

'Take one thing at a time, that's what we're going to do.'

'It's such a shock …'

'Do you want me to come over?'

'No need, darling, I'm meeting Cass, but if you can pick up the turkey it would be a big help. Otherwise, it will be beans on toast on Christmas Day. Oh, and Rog? Check on next door? Heaven knows if Anne locked her door when she left for the hospital.'

'No worries, sweetheart, see you when I see you.'

What a rock he is, Sabrina thought, replacing the receiver. She smiled as her secretary entered.

'Sorry to disturb you, Mrs Henderson, but the meeting you're chairing is in five minutes.'

'Thanks, I'm on my way.' Sabrina picked up her agenda. 'Good morning,' she said, entering the boardroom with a fixed smile.

After much soul-searching, Sabrina and Cassie felt it would be best if Anne stayed with Cassie, until she felt able to face going back to her own house.

Cassie picked up the Christmas mail and glanced at the postmarks. Placing the mail on the work surface, she made herself a slice of toast. It was ten-fifteen and Anne was still asleep. Glancing at the mail, she sat down with a coffee, intrigued by a large blue envelope.

She smiled to find it was from the Americans. Apart from seasonal greetings, it also contained a letter. Cassie laughed at Betty's reference to the day they went up to the Blue Mountains in the clapped-out old taxi. It also described how they had sent a card to Marlon. Still laughing at Marge and Betty's endearing chat, she held up a brown envelope that bore the Jamaican postmark. Curious, she slit it open. It was a card and letter from Della, asking if she had received the fax and if there was anything else she could do.

Puzzled, Cassie read it again. Sab hadn't mentioned a fax from Della. Then again, was it any wonder, with everything that had happened?

***

Felix picked up his voice mail messages at two o'clock. He rang David immediately but there was no answer. He left the building and walked across the grass. Most of his students had gone home for Christmas.

'Have a happy Christmas, Mr Moss.'

'And you,' he said absently. There was no point in going to their usual watering hole now. Instead, he headed in the direction of Cotham, deep in thought at the revelation of David's latest voicemail.

Felix accepted the cup of tea Cassie offered him.

'What happened at the hospital, Cass? Sabrina left a message on my voicemail. Here, let me help.' He saw her hand shaking.

She felt for the chair behind. Sitting, she told him everything.

'Where is Anne now?'

'Upstairs. I managed to persuade her to eat breakfast.

Her grief is tangible, Felix. Sab is already wondering how to cope, and there is no one more confident than her. To take the pressure off, we've organised that she stays with me until Anne's ready to go back.'

'It was David that did the autopsy on Don, Cass. His message left me in no doubt that what we have in Bristol is no coincidence. It seems it was the same as Mr Watson's autopsy but a lot more serious. Apparently, his body was in an advanced state of decomposition which is probably why the three of you were not able to see him.' Cassie looked at him in horror.

'But it's impossible, Felix. He's been dead less than twenty-four hours!'

Felix told her about the other injuries to Don's body, including his face.

She stood up and walked over to the window, the low sun making a pale impression on the windowpanes.

'Oh, my dear God. All I know is that we have to keep this to ourselves.' She swung round and faced him. 'Now I understand. Mark said he thought Dr Harris knew more than he let on. Felix, what are your thoughts, you're the expert?'

'This is way out of my depth, but if you pushed me, I would say it could be a ritual death. David said his organs were targeted one by one.' Images of Voodoo dolls flashed through her mind, making her shudder.

'I know I am asking a lot, Felix but please hold back on the extent of Don's injuries. I hate holding information from the others but coming so soon after Mr Morgan's death, I don't know how they would react, especially Mark, he's constantly worried for my safety these days.'

'And I agree with him, Cass, you must watch your back. Things are becoming more intense, and we need to keep one step ahead. It might be a good idea to postpone Elizabeth Morgan until after the New Year.'

She nodded. 'That's a good idea. I can go up to the plot at the same time. I need to go when things have settled down anyway. Anne is convinced Don's gold signet ring is still up at the site. Apparently, he has never taken it off since the day they married. Anne thinks it was wrenched off his finger when he fell.'

'I'm surprised you still want the place, Cass.'

'I know it's the key, Felix.'

Mark had been right, she had to deal with it in her own way and nothing would stop her.

'What about his funeral?' he asked, putting on his jacket.

'In the New Year. Mark and Roger are organising it. Felix, do you think Lorna's disappearance is connected with any of this?'

'The police think she wanted to start a new life somewhere else. And as there isn't any information to the contrary ...' He shrugged his shoulders. Kissing her swiftly on the cheek. She opened the door for him.

'Have you any plans for Christmas?'

'Only that I'll have the library to myself – there are plenty of dusty manuscripts on Bristol to keep me occupied.' He laughed.

Closing the door behind him, she listened to Anne crying. Depressed, her own tears flowed as she thought about a man she hardly knew, but who deserved more from life.

Leaving the flat, Felix pulled his scarf even tighter, bracing himself for the drop in temperature. It was late afternoon and cold. Finding his gloves stuffed in his jacket pocket, he pulled them on and noticed something that fell to the ground. He picked up the crumpled white envelope he had put in his pocket earlier. Tearing it open, he smiled at the humorous snowman on the front of the card. Inside, he read the greeting. Glad we met up again mate, regards, David.

Realising he hadn't sent his friend a card, he made

straight for Broadmead. I'll give it to him when he gets back, he thought to himself, as he descending Christmas Steps walking towards the centre.

Chapter Twenty-One

Temple Mead station hummed with excited people returning home for Christmas. David paid for the taxi, collected his belongings, and jostled his way through the crowds. Sensibly, he had booked his seat the previous week. Just as well, he thought, escaping the queue for tickets.

Squeezing through more people, he checked the overhead screen. Good, it was still on time. He went over to buy a newspaper before going through the turnstiles and on to the platform, and through the throng that lined the edge, waiting for trains. A girl in her early twenties barged in front of him, her black nylon backpack winding him in the chest. Catching his breath, he sat down on one of the benches, looking up at the intricate metal roof – designed by Brunel. It reminded him of a huge umbrella with broken spokes. Calmer now, he wished he had been able to meet up with Felix. He needed to get every detail of last night off his chest, and Felix would be the only one that would understand. Even now, sitting amongst the crowds, the entire episode was unbelievable, and he couldn't get it out of his mind. He stood up, impatient for his train.

It was only when a girl in a Santa Claus suit detached herself from a group of boisterous students and linked arms with him that David decided to move farther up the platform. He watched, bemused, as a little girl dressed as an elf skipped in front of him. Looking up, she gave him a dazzling smile, her golden curls held in place by a pair of Rudolph antlers.

He passed under the sound system, informing of a five-minute delay. A cold blast of air ruffled his hair. David put down his holdall and blew into his hands.

'Manic, isn't it? It only needs one delay. I'm catching a flight to Jamaica; I hope my onward connections are on time. What's so annoying is that I left my office in good time. Even Bedminster can get grid-locked.' David glanced at him, nodding in agreement.

Frustrated and cold, David left the man and walked towards the curve of the platform – it was a bad move. A group of children in school uniform chatted to their teacher excitedly; all were laden with presents and end-of-term items.

He hoped his mother had not gone to the trouble to meet him at the station. She was still recovering from a major illness. He knew she was looking forward to spending Christmas with him. From where he stood, he could see the ice-cream coloured terrace houses at Totterdown. For the first time since he came to Bristol, he actually felt like celebrating the holiday.

David caught a glimpse of the train. It coursed snake-like towards the curve in the track. Irritated by a drunk behind him, he smelt the alcohol on his breath as he blew a paper whistle in his face. The fool stumbled farther along the platform, mumbling, with his paper hat askew.

It was what David saw behind the drunk, which made him shiver. The black man who had spoken to him earlier lit a cigarette and immediately David recognised his own lighter. The man drew on the cigarette, smiling, with pure hatred in his eyes. The small girl dressed as an elf stood beside him, holding his hand, and snarling. Confused, David watched, fascinated, as the school girls formed an arch with their arms, inviting other children to play. The small girl let go of the estate agents hand and joined in, her golden curls bouncing. With a malevolent expression fixed on him she raised her voice to a deafening pitch

'Here comes the chopper to chop off your head!'

David turned his back on them and looked along the platform at the train thundering towards him.

'Chip chop, chip chop!' Disorientated he put his hands over his ears, the sound of the nursery rhyme ear-splitting.

'The last man's dead!'

David's foot became tangled in the strap of his holdall, pitching him forward. The train powered into the station. The screech of brakes pierced the air as he fell. The train had decapitated him.

Chapter Twenty-Two

Christmas was a sombre affair and, as expected, they all spent the day at Sabrina and Roger's. Despite the heroic effort Sabrina had made with lunch, a gloom had settled on the day. It was not helped by the heavy rain.

Shortly after four, Anne announced her decision to return home.

'Are you sure, Anne? You really don't have to. Why don't you spend the rest of the holiday with us, and then decide?'

'Thanks, Cassie, you and Mark have been so kind,' she sighed wistfully. 'I'll have to go back eventually. I feel that I'm ready to face it now. Besides,' she caught hold of Sabrina's hand, 'these two will be watching my every move,' she said, smiling up at Sabrina.

'Anne, I really don't think …'

'Leave it, Sab. I'm sure Anne has thought it through.' Roger laid a hand on her arm.

'I'll go and check the heating, Anne,' he said, looking for his coat.

'And I should be going as well.' Felix roused himself out of the armchair. 'I'm expecting a call from my sister in the States. Thanks, Sab, for making the best of today. I'm sure I speak for everyone, it was a lovely meal.' She responded by hugging him. Two days later Mark packed away the last of the Christmas decorations. Never a fan of the frivolous side of the holiday, it was an attempt to get back to normal.

'Thank God you were able to arrange Don's funeral so soon after Christmas.'

'I think you will find it was Dr Harris who took responsibly for that, Cass, although I have to say that Roger organised a lot of it,' Mark said as he took down the stepladder.

'It was David, Felix's friend that performed the autopsy, Mark. Apparently another straightforward case of heart failure,' she lied. 'Felix said he sounded tired on the voicemail, they arranged to meet for a quiet drink, but they missed each other. I am worried about Anne though,' she said, changing the subject, 'She is not answering her phone. Apparently, Roger went around checking on her and the doors were locked.'

'Give her time, Cass, things will be better when we get the funeral over with.'

Don's funeral was arranged for the 30th of December. Trying to find something suitable to wear, Cassie settled for her favourite black cape. Her mobile rang as she flicked through the rest of her wardrobe. Sabrina began voicing her concerns about Anne's mental decline.

'Okay, Sab, I'll go round as soon as I can. But remember, it was her own choice to go back on Christmas Day,' she said, sifting through her blouses. 'We all told her we didn't think it was a good idea.'

'I know. I'm ringing from work, only it's taking a bit longer than I thought …'

'And you're worried she won't be ready. I can read you so well, Sabrina Henderson. Don't worry I'll sort it. Just make sure you're back in time,' she added, ending the call.

Cassie found the black cape she was looking for and went into the kitchen to charge her mobile. She was still smarting from the spat she had with Mark last night.

'I'll be going into the office early tomorrow, Cass, Roger wants to discuss our plans for the coming year,' he told her.

'Oh, that's great! Surely, it can wait. What will happen if she's difficult, Mark?'

'It will only be for an hour.' He said as she left the room.

With a heavy heart, Cassie looked up at Anne's three-storey house. The rain that had threatened since early morning now came down with a vengeance, with no wind to temper it. With only three hours to go to Don's funeral, she was beginning to panic. Angry at being left with no support she grabbed an umbrella from the back seat of the car and ran up the path. She knocked on the door, impatiently looking through a chink in the drawn curtains bunched on a wire rail. Finding the doorbell hidden under an ivy branch, she pressed it and stood back. Cassie looked up at the windows for a response.

Suddenly aware of a dull thud coming from the back of the house, she went in search, noticing that all the curtains were drawn as she passed by. The noise came from the bottom of the garden. She quickened her pace across the lawn, her stiletto heels sinking into the grass.

Horrified at the scene in the garden, Cassie shouted, but Anne took no notice.

Anne wore a sleeveless dress, the thin pink cotton clinging to her tiny frame and a pair of green wellingtons that were several sizes too big covering her knees. Wielding an axe, she glanced at Cassie before continuing to hack at a three-foot high fir tree.

'For God's sake, what are you doing, Anne?'

Anne's eyes were blank, staring at Cassie as if she was seeing her for the first time. The rain bore down on her, blending with the tears running down her face unchecked.

'We planted this tree. Now Don is dead. This has to die as well.' She continued to hack at the stump with a venom Cassie didn't think she possessed. Her normally soft grey hair hung thin and lank, plastered to her face, her fringe falling forward with every blow of the axe.

Cassie knew it would be difficult to stop her. Glancing

across to Sabrina's house next door, she wondered if she was back yet. Turning back to Anne, she knew she was on her own.

Uttering a cry, Cassie went forward to break Anne's fall, but unable to stop her, she watched, helpless, at Anne lying spread-eagle in the mud. A terrified scream racked Anne's body as she buried her face in the mud. Cassie could only stare, shocked at Anne's outpouring of grief.

With a struggle, Anne raised her head towards the grey sky, the rain bouncing off her upturned face she gave a high-pitched scream. Her thin arms were clawing at the earth beneath her, as if she wanted to disappear into it.

Cassie dropped to her knees and pulled Anne's shaking body towards her. The compassion she felt for this tormented woman threatened to overwhelm her.

'Come on, Anne.' She gently helped her up. 'You'll catch pneumonia.' She clung to Cassie, and looked up into her face.

'Don liked me in this dress. He always said I looked pretty in pink. He liked the shells; he said it reminded him of the times we went to the seaside. Look, Cassie.' Anne sobbed, wiping the earth from her dress, showing Cassie the pattern.

This is bizarre, Cassie thought, staring at the mud-streaked dress. 'Listen, darling, why don't we go back to the house?'

They made a forlorn couple as they crossed the lawn towards the house, arms around each other. Cassie's mind raced. How was she going to get Anne in the frame of mind for her husband's funeral?

Time was not on her side. Glancing at her mud-splattered watch and with the funeral less than three hours away, she had to get help quickly.

As they approached the kitchen, Cassie became aware of an acrid smell coming from the kitchen. 'Something's burning! Quick, Anne.' Anne had a blank expression. Frustrated and forcing herself to stay calm, she moved to open the kitchen door.

'Anne, the door is locked, have you got the key? 'Anne handed over the key from the pocket of her dress like a naughty child. Smoke filled the kitchen; Cassie began coughing, and ordered Anne to stay where she was. She opened the oven door and took out the burnt offering. Dashing over to the sink the water gushed over the wet towel she held under the tap.

'It's Don's favourite – steak and kidney pie.' Anne's small voice sounded rather pathetic. Cassie turned and hugged the broken woman. The muted sound of Anne's phone focused Cassie's mind, frantically looking for it, she found it under a tray of dirty dinner plates. Cassie picked up.

'Cass, I only rang to see how Anne is getting on I didn't expect you to be still there, what has happened?'

'I very much doubt she will make the funeral, Sab'. Cassie described what had happened.

'You need help, Cass. I'm about to leave the office, I will get hold of Mark. Stay with Anne. If anyone can calm her it's you.' Cassie took Anne upstairs and ran her a bath. Searching for a clean towel, she eventually found one at the back of the airing cupboard – the bathroom was in the same state as the rest of the house.

Cassie smiled, as she carefully massaged the shampoo into Anne's scalp, letting the soap cleanse her skin. She couldn't help thinking all Anne needed was a little tenderness. Wrapping her in the towel, she heard Mark.

'I'm up here, Mark; we'll be down in a minute.' She went through Anne's wardrobe for something suitable, as his widow and went downstairs.

She found Mark in the kitchen, looking around at the chaos. He held her as she clung to him in relief.

'What on earth happened in here?'

She shook her head, watching Anne inspecting her fingernails, oblivious of two of them.

'How are we going to deal with her, Mark?' He wiped away her tears and kissed her face as they went over to comfort Anne.

***

Despite the horrendous problems, Don's funeral took place on time. Sabrina arrived not long after Mark and had immediately taken charge, allowing Mark and Cassie to go home and change. Roger and Sabrina accompanied Anne in the funeral car and then met everyone at the crematorium.

The rain continued throughout the service, adding to the depression of the day. Roger had supported Anne throughout the ordeal, easing Cassie's fears that she wouldn't be up to it. Dr Harris had made a surprise appearance, nodding in acknowledgement as he made his way to the back.

The heavy perfume of lily petals filled the room scattered on the coffin. Anne had requested the only hymn, 'All Things Bright and Beautiful,' with a posy of forget me knots Anne placed herself. For a brief moment, she smiled when they all sang and she looked from Don's coffin up to a crucifix on the wall.

After the service, Sabrina took the opportunity to invite several people back to her house, where she had hastily prepared food.

'God, this headache is driving me insane,' Cassie said, joining Sabrina in the kitchen.

'There are some tablets in the first drawer,' she said, pointing with a sharp knife. 'It's probably everything that you had to deal with this morning,' Sabrina reasoned, cutting more sandwiches.

'Thank goodness you were able to accommodate

everyone. Anne wouldn't have been able to cope, that's for sure.'

Felix chose that minute to come through with a tray of coffee cups. He glanced at the women.

'Have I interrupted something?'

'No, of course not. Sab will tell you, Felix.'

Cassie offered him a sandwich and he went back into the living room. Dutifully passing a tray of food around, she talked briefly to Don's business acquaintances and his staff. She gazed at Anne, who sat meekly on Sabrina's leather sofa, responding to people who came over to offer their condolences.

Felix followed her into the lounge, and she saw him introduce himself to Dr Harris. They seemed to be in intense conversation, as they walked to the back of the room. Shrugging her shoulders and satisfied that everyone was now taken care of, she went back into the kitchen, where Roger and Mark were discussing Anne.

'He's coming tomorrow after surgery.' Roger handed Mark a lager.

'Who is?' Cassie asked, scraping plates, with one foot on the pedal bin.

They turned to face her. 'The doctor, Cass. Roger rang him after this morning's episode. Anne obviously needs professional help now.' Mark held up his hands as if warding her off. 'I know, Cass …'

She took his empty plate. 'Did you think I wouldn't agree with you, Christ? I looked after her this morning, remember, Mark? Anne wasn't the only one traumatised. Roger went over and put his arm around her shoulders. 'Don't get upset, Cass. We know how well you coped with Anne. I think we're all a bit edgy and is it any wonder?' Roger kissed her cheek.

Cassie turned her back and watched the rain against the windows. Her eyes followed the hedge that separated Anne's garden from Sab's. It still rankled that she had been left with Anne when everyone else had made their own plans.

'Anyway, I don't think we should be talking about her,' Cassie cut in. 'We have just cremated her husband. Surely it can wait.' She busied herself stacking the dishwasher.

'Sabrina, whatever is it?'

'Can you get a glass of water, Cass? It's Felix. He's had a terrible shock.'

Cassie filled a glass. Pulling out a kitchen chair, Felix sat down, his hand shaking as he took the water.

'What is it Felix, what's happened?' Roger asked, looking at his ashen face.

'I think he needs something a lot stronger, Sab,' Roger said, watching his reactions.

'Is Doctor Harris still here?' he asked, handing him a double brandy.

'No, he left after he told me.'

'Told you what, Felix?' Roger probed.

Felix looked at Cassie and Mark 'It's my friend David' His voice shook. I was due to meet with him on Christmas Eve.' Felix paused 'He is dead! Dr Harris told me he died a terrible and horrific death at Temple Meads Station.' He held his head in his hands. 'David tripped on his holdall and fell into the path of a train'. He sobbed, his eyes filled with tears. 'I will never see him again.'

'Oh Felix, I am so sorry. I know how much you valued his friendship.' Cassie went over to him.

'Let me get you another,' Roger said topping up his glass 'how did he trip?'

'Nobody seems to know, Rog. Apparently, it was a freak accident.' Felix shook his head. 'I really can't believe it. I posted his card on Christmas Eve. It must have been around the same time that they found his body.' He stifled a cry, and excused himself.

Sabrina left the kitchen to check on Anne. Most of the mourners were preparing to leave. She saw Felix come out of the downstairs closet and followed him back into the kitchen.

Felix heard Mark say, 'there was nothing in the local paper.'

'There were a couple of paragraphs,' Felix responded. 'But it's like everything else, because he wasn't local; it doesn't get the same coverage. And with it being Christmas …'

'What does Doctor Harris think?' Sabrina asked, standing next to Cassie.

'He didn't voice an opinion. Only to say he was one of the best pathologists they've had at the hospital. He inferred the transport police were still heavily involved and would get in touch if they need me.' Felix got up. 'If you don't mind, folks, I will get back to the flat. This means yet another funeral.' he said wearily, giving Sabrina a hug. 'Give my apologies to Anne'

'I'll walk you to the door, Felix. My God what a day, I think we would be wise to keep everything we have discussed to ourselves,' said Sabrina. They all agreed.

Sabrina's persona changed once she was in the company of Don's sailing friends. After making pleasant small talk, she went to get their coats. They walked over to Anne, who got up to receive their condolences once more, and Sabrina saw them out.

'That's it, thank goodness. You were marvellous, Anne.' Cassie sat down beside her.

'Has anyone found Don's ring yet?' Anne was completely unconcerned with the effort Sabrina and Cassie had put in to make Don's funeral as dignified as possible.

'No, not yet, Anne, but I'm sure we will,' Sabrina said, holding her hand. Later that evening, Cass confronted Mark with her concerns. 'Other people are involved now, and we are caught up in it. Even if we sold the plot, it wouldn't make any difference. It's never going to end, Mark.'

'It's because of David, isn't it? It has been a long and terrible day, but you were there for Anne. You're bound to feel insecure and to be fair, Cass, there is a chance it has nothing to do with you – we can't put the genie back in the bottle.'

Chapter Twenty-Three

A January sun crept over the horizon. Cassie drove over the Downs to pick up Felix. It was three weeks to the day since Don's funeral and things were slowly getting back to normal. She also felt better. A few nights of peaceful sleep, along with Sab taking over responsibility for Anne, meant she was able to get things in perspective. She wanted to make a conscientious effort to find out more about the history of the plot, to see, once and for all, if the latest wave of horrific deaths was anything to do with it.

Felix had made it clear that he would also be finding out as much as possible. He felt it would be his legacy to continue what David had asked of him. And with that in mind, he arranged a suitable time to meet Mrs Morgan.

Parking alongside the water tower, Cassie opened the window and took advantage of the fresh air.

'Sorry I'm late, Cass,' Felix said, out of breath, almost knocking into a jogger as he got into the passenger seat.

'Careful,' she joked, indicating her intention to pull out. 'Have you seen Anne?' she asked.

'No not lately, what with David's funeral coming so quickly after Don's.'

'How did it go?' She glanced at him, filtering into the one-way system.

'How does anyone's funeral go?' he said dryly. Their mood was momentarily subdued.

Felix was the first to break the silence. 'There's no doubt, David was well respected within his field. It was tragic to see his elderly mother. She couldn't understand why he had to go before her.' He paused. 'I wanted to find out more about what happened that day. I even went down to Temple Mead station. The transport police showed me where they recovered his body.' Felix looked out of the window. 'I still can't comprehend it.' He shook his head.

'It's no good beating yourself up, Felix. It was Christmas Eve, and it must have been busy, but I do take your point.'

They left the city for Easton-in-Gordano. It was the first time she had travelled the road since that terrible night. Avoiding looking up at the suspension bridge, she drove on towards Ashton Court.

'It's a pity Sabrina couldn't make it. I thought she wanted to meet Mrs Morgan.'

'She did but she says she's not able to commit at the moment.'

Felix rolled his eyes and stared out of the window as they took the coast road.

***

Elizabeth Morgan walked down the path in front of her cottage, almost tripping on the large tabby cat that weaved its way through her ankles. She bent to pick it up, burying her face in its soft fur. The cat began to purr, pushing its head under her chin as she stroked it.

It was a beautiful spring-like day, unseasonal for late January. She put the cat down and it scuttled across the lawn amid clumps of snowdrops.

Elizabeth took a deep breath. At last, she felt she was coming out of a dark tunnel. She missed Joseph, of course, and she always would, but on a day like this, she could feel alive.

She shielded her eyes, looking up towards the golf course and the golfers in the distance. She smiled. Joseph had loved the tenth hole and she could always time him by that point of his round. She picked up the cat and went inside.

Finding her reading glasses, Elizabeth looked down at her own neat handwriting. 'Mrs Campbell and friend, 11am.' Her mantle clock chimed the hour, and she placed her glasses in their leather case. Am I so lonely, she thought, that I am waiting for two complete strangers to pay me a visit?

Hearing the crunch of gravel on the drive, she went outside to greet her guests.

'Thank you for agreeing to meet us, Mrs Morgan. I realise it's still early days for you.'

Cassie took in the tiny cottage, saw the cat stretching in front of a newly lit fire, and then took the chair Elizabeth indicated.

'I'm sorry, I should have introduced you, and this is a friend of mine, Felix Moss. Felix is researching the coastline.'

Felix smiled and extended his hand in greeting, then stretched both of them out towards the fire, feeling the warmth. 'How long have you lived here, Mrs Morgan?'

'All my married life.' She faltered. 'Unfortunately, you can't see the channel from here. We are too far inland.' Elizabeth placed the tray on the coffee table and offered Felix a cup. 'You remind me of him; my Joseph had an open, friendly face like yours, Mr Moss.'

'Please call me Felix, Mrs Morgan.'

'Elizabeth, Felix.'

'Touché. The question on my mind is why do you want a second autopsy?'

'My husband suffered from a heart condition for many years, and we both learned to live with it. As long as he had his daily medication and regular check-ups, there was never a problem. Because we'd lived with his condition for so long, I simply didn't feel his sudden death to be a satisfactory conclusion.' She began to weep. 'I suppose I needed to know once and for all.'

Cassie reached over and touched her arm. 'It might be better if we make it another day.'

'No, I need to talk about this.' She took her cup over to the window seat and looked out at the garden. 'I remember Joseph being very upset. Ross Meridian had told him that you and your husband would be bidding for the plot, and said it was a done deal.'

Cassie glanced over at Felix.

'Joseph was furious at his casual attitude and vowed to find out as much as possible. He even made a point of going up there. He remembered that you had asked him if he had viewed the property.' Elizabeth smiled at her. 'He liked you, Cassie. Ross had told him that he had spoken to your husband about the fire but when Joseph got the file out and studied it more closely, he found two older deeds wedged in between an old map of the immediate area. From one of the deeds, he was able to trace the names of the first occupants. He then came up with a further two families who lost their lives in similar circumstances to the latest family. They also had a little girl of exactly the same age.'

'Extraordinary!' Felix said.

'Sabrina said he had new information ...' Cassie said to Felix.

'I must meet that remarkable young lady,' Elizabeth interrupted. 'I haven't had the chance to thank her for her kindness to Joseph. It makes it easier to think that she made his last moments peaceful, knowing help was on the way.'

Cassie smiled at her. 'Yes, she would have done that.'

'Where are the deeds now, Elizabeth?' Felix questioned pulling out a notebook.

'That's the strange thing. Joseph told me he kept them in his safe at the office but after his death, I went to sort his papers and they had disappeared. His secretary had no idea what I was talking about, and I began to wonder if I had imagined it.'

'Did Joseph say when the deeds were dated?'

'Yes, he told me it was 1777. It was only the land and outside stables then, the house was built much later.'

'Elizabeth, first of all, thanks for being so frank with us. Is there anything else you can think of, however trivial it might seem?'

'Yes, there is and it's not trivial. I suspect it was the information that he really wanted you to know.' She left the window seat and sat opposite Cassie.

'The day he went up there, he got into a conversation with an old man who'd lived in the area his whole life, and his father and grandfather before him. He told Joseph the story that had been handed down through the family, particularly of the imaginary friend that appears to be dominant in all the fires at the building, befriending every small girl that lived there. To the girls she was real, so much so that the old man saw her chatting to the empty space beside her. Elizabeth paused, aware of their eyes on her.

'Joseph said it was unnerving, and everyone assumed it was just that, an imaginary friend. That was until several years later when they rebuilt the house again. The excavator unearthed remains of a girl in the garden. The interesting fact is that she hadn't perished along with her parents in the house, as in the other fires. This time, her bones were unearthed in a crude grave in the rockery, along with belongings reminiscent of African rituals. The old man said no one discusses it in the area – the locals who know of the curse shun the place. Joseph took the legend to heart and said he must get in touch with you before the auction but sadly, that was never to be,' she said wistfully. Elizabeth saw the shock on Cassie's face.

'Are you all right, dear? Let me get you a glass of water.'

Cassie was back there, the foul night, the bitter taste of

the earth in the rockery, the evil holding her down in its grip so that she couldn't breathe and most of all, the slime of the toads as they crawled over her!

'Excuse me, I need the bathroom,' Cassie said, suddenly getting up.

'Is she all right, Felix? She isn't pregnant, is she?'

Felix laughed her comment off by asking, 'so this is not the last fire we are talking about, or the second or third, but the first one, in the beginning?'

Elizabeth nodded. 'Joseph was never the same after that.'

They took their leave soon after one-thirty. Cassie hugged her and thanked her.

'What you've told us helps toward making sense of this nightmare.'

Elizabeth watched the car drive out of sight and walked around the side of the cottage. She picked up her cat and stroked the length of her spine. Looking up at the golf course, she could have sworn she saw Joseph swinging his clubs.

***

'Now at least we have established that not only has there been a dwelling for hundreds of years, but that the fires have been a regular occurrence for most of them.' He looked over at Cassie.

'Cass, what really threw me was the child's remains in the rockery, the African paraphernalia then you leaving the room suddenly. What was that all about?'

'Something happened the evening Mark and I went up there for the first time. I had a bad experience with that particular part of the garden. The conversation with Elizabeth brought it all back.' She smiled. 'I wasn't expecting it. I wonder what your friend David would have made of all this, Felix.'

'Well, he was convinced there was Voodoo in Bristol, especially after the post-mortems he carried out. Mr Morgan and Don had links to the plot – we learnt that today. Even now, I still think there is a cover up with David's death. There are too many questions and not enough answers. I wish I had more time to go into it, although I did promise him I would find out all I could about the slave trade. He felt there was a connection. Cass, remind me of the name of the ship you remembered at Sab's dinner party?'

'You mean the 'Silas Hunt?' Where is this going, Felix?'

'It's something Elizabeth said about the old deeds that Joseph found. She said they were dated 1777. I've been keeping busy and going through the archives at the university and I found a map, if you can call it that, of the whole coastline down as far as Weston-Super-Mare. It was nothing like it is today, just a few buildings scattered the coastline at that time – the odd farm, the tide mill at Portishead and Salty Hill wharf. But the point is, we've now dated your building on the plot and all we need is an ordnance survey map of the surrounding area off Sandy Way.'

'I'm sure Mark can lay his hands on one, Felix. Not sure where the 'Silas Hunt' comes in, though.'

'I'm not sure either but there could be a link. You said yourself, Cass, that you felt empathy for the slave on the bridge. Yes, today has been a very interesting day. Here will do,' he said, kissing her on the cheek as she pulled up at the kerb on the Bristol side of the suspension bridge.

Cassie drove to Cotham, her head buzzing. With a heavy heart, she felt for the charm she now always wore. If ever she longed for Beneba's wise counsel, it was now.

Chapter Twenty-Four

'Bloody joy riders!' The duty officer voiced his anger after reading the response from the national database. He tossed the printout in front of his colleague. 'Another burnt-out car! Senseless, bloody senseless. If they're not mugging old ladies, they're nicking cars and burning them.' His colleague scanned the report.

'At least we've something to work on. Most of the registration is intact. Find out what DVLC can come up with,' he said, looking over the duty officer's shoulder at the reply.

'I remember she was officially missing at the time. Hang on a minute.' He went over to a filing cabinet and pulled out a file. 'Ah, here it is, Felix Moss is the person I saw.' He compared the name to the one on the file. 'Lorna Curtis, missing since November twenty-third. Let's get cracking on this one. Get in touch with the sister; she's the next of kin. Oh, and I promised Mr Moss I'd ring him if there were any developments. In the meantime, I'll get on to forensics.' He put on his overcoat. 'I want all the stops pulled out on this one,' he added over his shoulder. 'I want this woman found.'

The news spread. Speculation on Lorna became more fantastic by the hour. The university had taken a completely new stance on the matter. It was one thing to have a missing person, but quite another when the name of the university had unwelcome media interest.

Lorna's sister had travelled from South Wales at the request of the police, who had set up an interview room next to the bursar's office at the university.

Felix came out of the office and walked into the main

hall. It buzzed with speculation. The conversation stopped abruptly as he cut a path through the middle and strode purposely into the February afternoon.

He had spent two hours with the police, going over a statement regarding Lorna. The police had tried to make more of his relationship with her. Christ, he hardly knew the woman! Furthermore, what he did know, he didn't like very much. He had only taken up her cause because no one else seemed to care.

He picked up the latest edition of the Bristol Post and wasn't surprised to see the story had made the front page for the second day. Tucking the paper under his arm, he made for Mark and Roger's office. Felix's intention had been to pick up the ordnance survey map that Mark had for him.

'It's gone quiet again,' he said in answer to Roger's question. 'If they know what happened to her, I don't think they're going to tell me.'

'I don't know where he's put it, Felix.' Roger began pushing aside papers on Mark's desk. 'I know he had it earlier.'

'Felix, this is a surprise.' Mark's voice came from the doorway. 'Sorry I'm late, Rog.' He opened his desk drawer and flung the map at Felix. 'I expect this is what you're looking for. Cass said you were collecting it – she said something about tying up the plot with another old map of the area.'

'Thanks – this will be very helpful.'

'We were discussing Lorna,' Roger said, looking at Felix's evening paper.

'It's certainly strange. Apparently, the car was found in a disused quarry, on the coast road, not that far from our plot.' Mark began unfolding a gold foil coffee bag. 'Cass is unsettled by it; I've tried to reassure her it's a coincidence. Unfortunately, she's feeling the strain now. That's one of the reasons I'm late, Rog.'

'Are you sure you won't stay?' Roger asked.

'Well, if there's coffee going, I could be persuaded,' Felix said, trying to lighten the mood. 'I think it's got to be one of two scenarios. She either parked her car in the area, maybe to go shopping, and when she returned it had been stolen and dumped.'

'It's possible but it still doesn't account for her disappearance.' Mark reached for the carton of milk, breaking the seal. 'And even if that happened, can you honestly see Lorna going to a small seaside town to shop? Come on Felix, Clifton Village, maybe.'

'And the other theory?' Roger asked.

'Is that she met someone and decided to make a new life, destroying everything from her past.'

Roger nearly choked on his coffee. 'You don't really believe that do you?'

'I don't know what to believe, Rog. I didn't know her that well. Although others think differently,' he added sarcastically. He finished his coffee and stood up. 'I have to make tracks. Thanks for the coffee, and this.' He waved the map in Mark's direction.

'Hang on a minute, I'll walk with you. I need a newspaper anyway.' Mark opened the door and let Felix through.

As they walked down Park Street, Mark said, 'I wanted to thank you personally for your interest, Felix. I know it means a lot to Cass. Everything that's happened over the last few months has had a profound effect on her.'

Felix watched him closely. 'And you, Mark?'

'Yeah, me as well. It is different for me. I have the business and now that we've secured a major new contract, we'll be busy for some time.'

'Roger seemed subdued' Felix said.

'I think he's finding it difficult with Sabrina working

away at the moment, and then with Don's funeral …'

'To be honest, Mark, I think it's affecting us all in different ways. I even found myself losing it with the students yesterday.'

They sat down on a bench near one of the fountains.

'I'm frightened it will destroy her, Felix.'

Felix saw the anguish in Mark's eyes. 'Those are powerful words, Mark.'

'She said recently that even if we sold the plot, it would still be the same. She likens it to Pandora's box – once we open it, we can't shut it again.'

'Listen, mate, it could destroy all of us if we let it but if it's Cass they want, we need to protect her. She told you about our meeting with Mrs Morgan?'

'That appeared to break her. She made light of what happened on the evening we first went to the plot but believe me, Felix, nothing could be further from the truth. Then when Elizabeth told her, what Joseph had found out … if only we knew what we're dealing with.'

'Well, it's not your usual haunting or poltergeist, this is far more sophisticated. The fact that it has two different energies makes it more confusing. We need to understand it more; my historical expertise doesn't include the Voodoo religion, unfortunately. What I do find unsettling is that it's prepared to wait, almost as if it's on its own terms. Why?'

'Actually, I hadn't thought of that,' Mark reflected.

'The conversation you had with Ross Meridian, do you recall the month the fire started?'

'Yes, April. I remember being impressed at the way it tripped off his tongue.'

Mark looked at him puzzled. 'Don't ask … I don't know where I'm going with it either. All I'm doing is gathering as much information as I can.'

'If I can help in any way, Felix,' Mark said, as they

walked back to his office.

'Actually, staying on that theme, I wonder if Ross has any useful information from the land registry. That would tell us the month the previous fires started.'

'I'll see what I can find out,' Mark said as they went their separate ways.

'And Mark? You know Cass better than anyone, but I get the feeling she is much stronger than even you realise.'

Mark went up the stairs. By talking to Felix, he now felt a great weight had been lifted from his shoulders.

***

By late afternoon, Felix found the time to study the ordinance map Mark had given him. By late evening, he had cracked it. Having traced the coastline, it enabled him to tie it up with the older map from the university. He rang Cassie excitedly but reached only her voicemail.

'Cass, I'm making progress. There's only one farm on that stretch of coast and some old barns farther along the coastline. What could be of significance is that I've combined the two maps and I've found that the barns would have been on your plot. It's a start – a bit tenuous but still a start. I've arranged to go to the Ventures' Hall on a quest to find the 'Silas Hunt.' Catch up with you tomorrow.'

Cassie did not catch up on her voice messages until much later that night. She had just returned from the Bristol Old Vic, and a performance of Falstaff. Sabrina had been given complementary tickets. It had been a long time since the two of them had had an evening together. An hour later, she discussed Felix's message with Mark.

'Felix will enlighten you more in the morning, I expect,' he said, yawning. 'You should go out more often; I haven't seen you so relaxed since Jamaica.'

There had been a change of plan; Felix had an extra class thrust on him at the last minute. It wasn't until later in the day that he was able to find time to go to the Merchant Ventures' Hall. It was with a sense of optimism that he fetched what was to be the first of many heavy ledgers, housed in the lower rooms.

An hour later, he found what he had been looking for. His fingers traced column after column of slave ships, their sailing dates and owners' names. Anne Snow 1730-31 Jamaica; Betty Galley 1730 Anglo-Jamaica, the names went on and on.

Nearing the bottom of the fifth ledger, he could hardly contain his excitement. Before him, in scrawny writing, were the details he had hoped to find. Silas Hunt, April 2nd, 1777, ship lost in severe storms off Rockpoint Bay. Goods went down with the ship.

Disappointed that the ledger had not referred to the Coromantee slaves, he mentioned it to a member of staff, who suggested he look up the news of the day at the library's reference department.

His mobile rang before he had time to leave the building. 'Hi Cass, did you get the message I left?'

'Yes. Sabrina and I went to the theatre. It was too late when I got back. I'm intrigued to know what you've discovered, though.'

'Quite a lot. I've found the 'Silas Hunt.''

'What? Where? How exciting, Felix. Does it mention the crew?'

'No. I'm outside the Ventures' Hall and they've advised me to go to the central library. The old newspapers are stored there.'

'Okay, I'll meet you down there.'

'I'm not sure what time.' He looked at his watch. 'It depends how long it'll take me to get on to the main drag. I'm on a limb out here.'

'Don't worry, Felix, just ring me when you're near.'

Cassie watched Felix stride across College Green towards her. They climbed the marble staircase, she bombarding him with questions.

'Rockpoint Bay. Where on earth is that?'

'Possibly on your plot but I'm not sure,' he said, approaching reception. 'It's obviously an old name but I should be able to compare it with the maps here.'

She took off her coat and settled herself in one of the chairs, dipping into her handbag for a supply of pens and highlighters.

Ten minutes later, a member of staff came over, weighed down with The Bristol Society's publication volumes 0-7.

'Concentrate on the end of March and beginning of April,' he instructed, before turning back to the volume in front of him. Mindful of the task, she turned each page, scanning the thin paper.

'On cruising voyage to Jamaica, the good ship Virginia all gentlemen seamen, able-bodied landsmen to try their fortunes in faid ship shall apply to the captain.' How quaint; they use the letter 'F' instead of 'S'. Cassie looking at Felix for confirmation.

'Well, I can better that. 'Letters of marque were declared in the twenty-seventh of November, 1776, where Richard Bellamy was named as master of the vessel.' His voice shook with excitement. 'According to the pass, the Silas Hunt was bound for Africa and the muster roll shows it left Bristol with fourteen crew.' Felix shook his head. 'But there are varying reports here; it reads the return crew included only five of the original crew, with three new, enlisted for the return journey on the twelfth of February, 1777. One man died on the home run.'

'That left only seven! What became of the first crew members when they reached Africa?'

'Sometimes they mutinied but more often, they deserted.

You have to remember, a lot of these men were recruited against their will, lulled by false promises, like the article you just read.'

'What else does it say?'

'It seems they left the Cape coast as normal on the twelfth of February, with a cargo of miscellaneous objects, possibly gold or ivory, and because it was a direct trader, maybe red shell. All of these things were nearly always for a person of rank. But listen, Cass, it seems we were right; they were caught up in a severe storm as they neared Bristol. The Hunt, followed by the crew, but not before the Coromantee slaves were released from their shackles in the hold to help above deck with the captain.

'Interestingly, there is no pass return to say either the crew had deserted, or the slaves were ever brought up from the hold. I know what you're thinking but read this.' He turned the ledger around so she could see it. 'A certain Henry Potts is named as the registered owner, and bounty hunters were sent out to find the missing slaves. This leads me to believe they had already sold the slaves before they reached Bristol, possibly to merchant Ventures' as servants.' He closed the book and looked over at Cassie. 'What have you come up with?'

'Well, you'll be surprised to know that I've picked up on what you've just said. I'm looking at April fifth. Listen to this, "'six runaway male slaves, the second of April last and the property of Henry Potts, ran afoul of the Silas Hunt at Rockpoint Bay. The males are remarkably well proportioned – six feet two inches in height. Including a pair of identical twins. There is a handsome reward of three guineas for the return of the slaves, and all charges.'" Records show that the three enlisted men also deserted the Silas.

'Yes!' she said, punching the air. 'We certainly got lucky today.'

'Let's grab a coffee somewhere, Cass, before you get too excited. We still have to find a definite link with the plot.' He saw her face, 'but I agree, we got a little bit lucky.'

They made their way to a café in the corner of the square. If Cassie had thought for a moment that Mark was not going to be in his office, she would have gone straight back to the flat. Instead, in her excitement, she collided with Roger at the top of the stairs.

'Steady on, Cass,' he said, noticing her flushed cheeks. 'Mark's out on site.' He glanced at his watch. 'He should be back soon. What brings you over anyway – couldn't wait to see him, eh?' He winked at her.

'You can make me a cup of tea for that, Roger Henderson,' she chided, taking off her coat. 'Felix and I have been to the central library on a voyage of discovery. We've found the 'Silas Hunt,' or at least Felix has. And not only that,' she added, ignoring his lack of response, 'we think we have some idea what happened to the ship.'

Roger levelled his gaze at her, the silence punctuated by rain hitting the window. 'Well, I'm glad you're getting somewhere, Cass. That means I can tell Sabrina and she can put it to rest. Thank God.'

'I didn't think she was interested, she certainly didn't give me that impression,' Cassie said, surprised.

'I think we're talking about two different Sabrina's. She's always talking about it.'

They drank their tea in awkward silence. Deciding she couldn't wait any longer for Mark, she got up to go.

'I must go, too, if I'm going to catch my bus.' He went over to get his coat, his arm getting caught up in the torn sleeve lining.

'Looks like a spot of mending is in order, Rog, that or ask Sab,' she teased.

A nerve in his face twitched. 'I doubt if she's even home.' He picked up papers on his desk, and put them into his briefcase.

Cassie placed a hand on his arm. 'Working late again? Do you want to talk about it?'

'No, not at the moment.' He snapped his briefcase shut and walked to the stairs.

'Rog, before you go, you don't remember receiving a fax just before Christmas, do you? I keep forgetting to ask you both. Only a friend of mine in Jamaica sent one to your home fax.

'I'm afraid I don't, Cass. Sab would have told me if we had. Give her a ring, though, if it's important.' Roger hurried down the stairs and encountered Mark coming up. Their voices drifted towards her and when Mark eventually came into the office, he found her deep in thought.

'You look puzzled, Cass.' He kissed her absently. I have some great news – that contract we've been angling for. We have landed it, it's signed and sealed.

'That's good news! I heard you talking to Rog just now.'

'We were discussing setting up a meeting at their head office in Swindon with the development consortium. Are you sure you're okay?'

'Yes, I was trying to track down that fax that Della sent on Sab's fax machine but he's not aware of it.'

'Surely Sabrina is the one to talk to? Have you brought the car?'

'No, I walked to the library to meet Felix …'

'I'm sorry, Cass, there's me prattling on about contracts when I haven't listened to what you have to tell me. How was your day?'

'Mark Campbell, you're teasing me. I'm not going to tell you now.'

***

Getting off the bus, Roger looked towards the tall Victorian houses that graced his street. The rain had eased into a damp and murky feel to the evening. Sighing, he turned up his coat collar. He knew even before he reached the house that Sabrina wouldn't be home. Walking up the path, he began to think what had kept her this time, and what excuse she would give.

Unlocking his front door, he glanced over at Anne's house in complete darkness. It was difficult to tell if she was in or out these days, he thought sadly.

Collecting the mail, he tossed it on the hall table and went into the lounge. Exasperated that on top of everything else, Sabrina had forgotten to get the heating engineers in – the house was freezing.

***

Anne jerked the net curtain in the upstairs window, watching the shadowy figure walking along the pavement. For a split second, she thought he was about to come on to her drive. She placed her hand on her chest to still her beating heart. Was it Don? He would come home about this time.

The figure went next door and she realised it was Roger. Her thin fingers smoothed the net curtain as she reluctantly came back to reality.

She left the darkened room and switched on an upstairs light – the dull glow hardly enough to light her way down the stairs. She turned it off again when she reached the bottom. Treading carefully, she went into her lounge and switched on a reading light beside Don's chair. This was where she spent most of her time these days. Don had always encouraged her to read and become more cultured. Resting her head against the wing of the leather chair, she closed her eyes. She could still smell him. He had had a habit of leaning his head in exactly the same place.

Picking up a biography of Winston Churchill, she read the heavy sentences, knowing Don would have approved. Her eyelids began to droop as she felt her body relax.

She must have nodded off because she woke with a start to the shrill ring of the telephone. Her sudden movement caused the book she was reading to slide to the floor with a thud.

'Anne? It's Sabrina. I was just about to ring off. How are you?'

'Sabrina! Oh, I'm sorry; I was dozing in the chair. What time is it?' she asked, trying to focus. She looked over at the clock on the mantle, trying to distinguish the time in the gloomy glow of the low wattage bulbs she used now she was on her own.

'Eight-thirty. Roger was concerned he couldn't see your lights on.'

'My goodness! I must have slept longer than I thought.'

'Listen, Anne. I have a meeting at the Weston-Super-Mare office tomorrow. If you like, I could drop you off at Cassie and Mark's plot. I know you're anxious to look for Don's ring up there and the coast road won't be out of my way, and I can pick you up on my way back. How does that sound?'

'Oh Sabrina, would you? I would be so grateful. It's the only place left to look. What time should I come over?'

'Ten-thirty suit? I've already cleared it with Cass, so she knows.'

'Thanks, Sabrina. It means a lot to me.'

'I know, Anne. Are you sure you don't want to come over for a couple of hours now?'

'No, but thanks anyway. Say hello to Roger for me.'

'I don't know what all the fuss is about. She's fine,' Sabrina said, replacing the receiver and turning her attention to Roger.

He peered at her over the rim of his glasses, rustling the newspaper as he took them off.

'We haven't seen her for a few days, that's all.' He sucked the arm of his glasses, his expression pensive. 'Why she keeps the house in darkness is beyond me.' Replacing his spectacles, he began reading again.

'I've arranged to drop her off at the plot tomorrow morning. At least she can see for herself that his ring won't be there.'

Roger shot her a disapproving look. 'You can be very unkind at times, Sab.'

'I'm sorry, I don't mean to be. She has the knack of wearing me down, Rog, going on and on about Don's ring. At least it will settle her mind once and for all.'

She crossed the room and picked up a glossy fashion magazine. Thumbing through it, she headed for the door. 'God, it's cold in here. I think I'll have a nice bath and then go to bed.'

'But you've only just got in! What about food?'

'I'm not hungry.'

'We haven't talked,' he said, irritated.

'We can do that in the morning, Rog. I'm bushed.'

'But I wanted to tell you about the new contract. Sab, please.'

'What, Rog?' she shouted from the hall.

'Never mind.' He went back to reading his paper. 'Oh, and good luck with the bath,' he mumbled as she climbed the stairs.

Chapter Twenty-Five

The early sun dappled unusual shapes on the bathroom floor. Standing in a pool of warmth filtering through the window she wrapped herself in a thick towel.

How unselfish of my husband she thought Not only had he had the immersion working before he went to work; he had sacrificed the warm water so she could shower. It was a temporary measure, but at least she felt clean.

Booking a table at their favourite restaurant was the least she could do, and she looked forward to surprising him.

She went into her walk-in wardrobe to find something suitable to wear. Her reflection stared back at her as she opened her eyes wide, applying mascara and adding a touch of lip-gloss to finish off her look.

The doorbell rang as Sabrina straightened her suit. Opening the door, her smile froze as she looked Anne up and down. She wore a floor-length coat made of fur covering her entire body.

'They forecast rain later, so I thought I would wear the coat Don bought me for my birthday. Can you believe it; I haven't even worn it yet? 'It suits you, Anne,' Sabrina lied, 'although it would be a shame to get it wet. I am running late – will instant coffee be all right?' She watched Anne stroke the fur lovingly, a smile on her face. God, Sabrina thought if it wasn't so sad, it would be comical.

'Are you still attending hospital?' Sabrina asked, handing her a mug of coffee.

'No, not any more. I've finished the course and they've given me a clean bill of health.'

'What about your visitors? You know the people that sat with you?'

'Oh, you mean the counsellor that has stopped as well. I tell you, Sabrina, I am well now. Coping with the grief of losing Don and not being able to see his body was such a shock.'

'It would be a shock to anyone, Anne,' Sabrina said tenderly. 'But you have us now.'

'Yes, and I'm grateful for so many caring friends.'

'Now, you're quite happy with the plan,' Sabrina said, rinsing the mugs. 'I will pick you up at four-thirty, give or take ten minutes either side. I'll wait for you at the bottom of the track that leads up to the plot – there are streetlights in that area.'

Anne looked at her, surprised. 'I didn't know you knew it?'

'I don't, I have heard Cassie talk about it.' Sabrina glanced at the clock. 'I'm definitely going to be late now.' Snatching her document case, she ushered Anne out of the kitchen. Eventually leaving the city, they headed for the coast road.

Dropping Anne at the entrance, Sabrina drove off without a backward glance.

Anne took the path Sabrina had described, stopping only to take off her fur coat to catch her breath, before putting it back on again. She wondered for the life of her why Cassie would buy a plot of land so far up with only a track for access.

Shocked at the scale of work involved, she stared in horror. Not even in her wildest dreams did she imagine it like this. Sidestepping bulldozer tracks gouged in the mud, she looked around.

Don's tools were scattered everywhere, she noticed his upturned cement mixer and the spilled contents that had created a river of crusted lava.

What was he thinking? He would never have been able to clear this! It was way out of his league – no wonder he never discussed it with her. Poor deluded Don wouldn't have thought about that – he wanted only to impress – he had always been like that. Anne sighed and took a deep breath, holding on to a steel pipe stuck in a bed of cement she caught hold of it to steady herself. Why did every thought lead back to him? She despaired at her on-going grief.

Dismissing her negativity, she began focusing on Don's ring.

Heaving from the musty odour of debris that trashed every room, the silence only broken by the sound of her pushing rubble with her feet. It would be easier to search by hand, but the thought made her retch again.

A breeze sprang up, lifting the pages of forgotten illustrations from a well-thumbed children's book. Anne systematically covered the area where Don had obviously worked. A rat darted over a pile of waste in front of her. She felt the flick of its tail against her ankles, making her scream. She found herself in the very room she wanted to avoid.

Don's congealed blood had stained every conceivable area of the bathroom. Anne's horrified cry vibrated inside the shell, followed by a chilling echo. She gave way to the nausea she felt earlier and vomited amongst the chaos.

Outside, the rain came from nowhere, driving into her. It was a mistake coming here she knew it now – she wasn't ready. Trying to retrace her steps, she became confused. Everywhere she turned, it appeared the elements were against her, an invisible wall of fear had closed in on the plot, taking on a different atmosphere, not wanting her to leave, and not giving her up. Thankfully, she saw a gap in the fence, but the mud made her progress slow.

'Mummy, Mummy, please don't go.'

Stunned, she turned in the direction of the tiny voice

hardly audible above the gathering storm.

Even in the rain, the little girl was lovely. Anne gazed at her, captivated, as she walked towards her. Her eyes were the colour of forget-me-nots on an early summers morning and she guessed her to be about six or seven years old. She looked down at her, noticing how the rain had encouraged her golden ringlets to frame her oval face. Her dress had a sense of a bygone age, blue like her eyes, with bright red embroidery.

The small girl watched Anne with a forlorn expression, clutching a ball.

Unexpectedly, the rain stopped, leaving showers and mist, under a darkening sky. Anne bent down to the girl's level.

'I'm not your Mummy, dear,' Anne said gently. 'Where have you come from?' The girl pointed in the direction of the building. 'But there are no more houses up here,' the child giggled, and Anne became infatuated She threw the ball to Anne, her blonde curls dancing.

'Hide and seek mummy?' She suggested throwing the ball back over her shoulder as if she expected someone to catch it. Anne followed, only too eager to play her game.

Here was the daughter she always wanted. It must be fate, she decided in her confused mind. Don had wanted her to come today. This was his parting gift to her. She named the girl 'Lily May' in memory of her beloved Don's Mother.

Anne's joyous laugh rang out, she had not been this happy for a long time. Struggling to keep up, she shouted, 'Coming, ready or not!' Listening to silence, she peeked through her fingers and shouted again, frightened now, that she had lost her. Anne began searching, frantically sliding in the mud. Exhausted and weary from playing the game, she noticed the wind had dropped. Then she heard a giggle.

'There you are you little devil. Just you wait until your

father comes home, he will be very cross.'

The child stood on the steps of the building and beckoned; her silhouette casted a sinister outline in the gloomy afternoon.

'No, Lily May. I am not going up there again.'

Picking up a stone, the girl threw it in defiance. 'Don't do that, Lily May, that's naughty.'

The charm that had so bewitched Anne earlier had disappeared and been replaced by a hardness that disturbed her. For a split second, the moon came out from behind a dark cloud, giving the plot a surreal atmosphere. She had no idea of the time, and she did not care.

'Come on, dear. We must go home. Daddy will be waiting for his supper.'

'Where is your precious Don now? He can't help you anymore. I know because I was there.' The words from the child's mouth were vile and unnatural, her laughter chilling, but she continued, desperate to hold on to her dream.

'Please, dear, daddy won't like you talking that way.'

The little girl jumped down from the steps and walked towards Anne, snarling and tugging at her fur coat, pulling her down towards the rockery, and the lower garden. Anne smiled and watched indulgently as the little girl urged her to go with her.

Anne's mood changed and she began shaking with fear as the girl dragged one of the boulders from the rockery. She listened to the willow's unrest – the branches began twisting and thrashing into frenzy. She stepped back in horror as she turned her attention back to the child's harrowing laugh. The girl looked up at Anne – a depraved expression on her face.

Underneath the boulder, a thin grey leg flopped out of a gaping hole. The girl, sensing her advantage, cruelly began unearthing more boulders from the rockery to reveal a body almost beyond recognition. The flesh had either been nibbled or had naturally decomposed, attracting maggots that moved greedily over the corpse. Anne began wailing, staring at the little girl she called Lily May. She held out her arms towards her, willing her to come to her. Anne was completely broken. The dream she had nurtured earlier had been snatched from her grasp.

Ignoring her, the girl picked up a length of sawn timber. Giggling, she began prodding the body, disturbing more toads deeper in the rockery. Anne's wail grew louder, piercing the relative quiet that prevailed. She distanced herself as the toads began springing towards her.

'Do something, Lily May!' she screeched as the toads regrouped around her ankles, trying to climb her legs she screamed again, pushing them away with her coat the girl snatched another toad and carefully stroked the creature's skin, kissing its head, all the time leering at Anne.

'What kind of child are you?' Anne screamed. 'You're a monster!'

The girl's eyes narrowed. Shaking with rage, and with an aim directed at Anne, she hurled the toad.

She began mumbling incoherently, tears staining her face. She didn't care about the corpse, or even how it got there. She had lost the only thing that for a brief moment had been hers and Don's.

'Lily May. I'm sorry. It's time to go home now.'

The girl grimaced, baring her teeth like a jackal, her small hands clenched into fists. 'I'll show you what daddy really wanted, shall I?' She began scrambling in the rockery with her hands, removing rocks, and boulders.

Anne stared at the head of the corpse, instantly recognising the spiky peroxide hair and the red-chipped nail-varnish that belonged to Lorna. Anne gave a gut-wrenching gurgle, her vacant eyes boring into those of the child's.

The girl tugged at a chain around the corpse's neck.

Anne recognised a bathplug chain and threaded through it she saw Don's gold signet ring.

She tugged at it. 'And it wasn't you, mummy. He gave it to her!'

Anne stumbled down the path, the words following her. She covered her ears, wanting to shut them out. Hampered by the bramble hedges snagging her coat, she fell, losing her shoes. She had no idea if she had reached the road or not, all she knew was that nothing mattered. She had lost Don and Lily May.

'How could you, Don?' she wailed, wiping her drooling mouth; she had without doubt lost her mind.

Chapter Twenty-Six

Cudjoe came back into their lives as suddenly as he had left it. Cassie's mobile rang as she went up Bridge Valley Road.

'Cass? You'll never guess who I have here in the office?' Mark's voice was full of excitement.

'Cudjoe?'

'How on earth did you know?'

'I have a sixth sense, remember. How is he Mark, and where is he staying?'

'That's already sorted. I insisted he stayed with us.'

'Brilliant. I know a butcher where I can get some goat meat for dinner – I have a Jamaican dish in mind.'

What a lovely surprise. She had hoped he would find them and come to Bristol one day, and now he was here. Although neither herself nor Mark knew him well, she trusted her instincts as far as Cudjoe was concerned, and she intended to make him as welcome as he had made them.

Putting an apple pie in the oven, the thought crossed her mind that it would be a perfect opportunity to introduce him to Roger and Sabrina. She rinsed her hands and went into the hall. Sab answered immediately.

'Cass, oh thank God!'

'Why, whatever is it, Sab?'

'It's Anne. Remember you suggested I should take her to the plot to look for Don's ring the next time I went to the Weston office? Unfortunately, I had to wait over an hour for her. By then I was out of my mind with worry. I began to think she had forgotten where we had arranged to meet, and it was almost dark … Then from nowhere she wrenched the door, nearly pulling it off its hinges. God knows what happened to her. She was an incoherent wreck, not making any sense at all. Then she just cowered in her oversized coat and stared ahead.'

'Is she okay now?'

'Not really – I had to get her out of her wet clothes. Cass, it was her monstrous fur coat that got me! She convinced me she was over her grief, and I believed her, Cass. I even asked her if she was still taking her medication, but she has stopped, she insisted that she doesn't need it. Roger gave her a cup of tea, but all she wanted to do was to go home.' Sabrina sighed. 'Anyway, I'll check on her later, before we go out.'

'Oh, I didn't realise you were going out?'

'Yes, I'm treating my long-suffering husband to an Italian meal. Why?'

'It's just that we have had a surprise guest. Sab, can you recall I talked about Cudjoe, the friend we met in Jamaica?'

'Yes, I do remember, Cass.'

'Well, he turned up at the office. Anyway, as he's staying with us, I was rather hoping you two would join us for dinner, but if you've made other arrangements …'

'The table is booked for nine, but we could come over for drinks, if it fits in with you?'

'Great! I'd love you to meet him, he's so interesting.'

'We'll try to get over at about eight.'

***

Cassie's mood was exuberant – not only about meeting Cudjoe again but also because of the news she had received that morning confirming her pregnancy. She could hardly contain herself as she stood watching Sabrina talking earnestly to Cudjoe.

Mark came over, helped himself to a canapé and nodded towards them.

'Sab seems to be a big hit with Joe.' he whispered in Cassie's ear.

She followed his gaze, desperate to tell him about the pregnancy. They had not been alone from the moment Cudjoe had arrived, but now was definitely not the right time.

'I must say, he cuts a fine figure in that pin-stripe suit. He's not as casually dressed as the last time we saw him, that's for sure,' Mark continued.

'I think 'professional' is the word you're looking for, Mark.'

He reached behind her, winking, and grabbed another salmon canapé. 'He was pleased to have found us, though. He couldn't stop talking all the way home. Apparently, he came to Bristol over the Christmas period but didn't have chance to look us up until now.'

'Really? How strange.'

Mark missed the pensive look on her face. 'It is a pity Felix wasn't able to join us.'

'I did ring his mobile after I rang Sab on the off chance, but he had switched it off. I can understand because he is involved with fact finding now, unearthing all sorts of things that we found out that day at the library. Now that Joe has arrived on the scene, well who knows?'

Roger and Sabrina stayed for twenty minutes. When they had gone, the three of them sat down to enjoy a typical Jamaican meal, and Cudjoe opened a bottle of champagne.

'To my good friends.' He raised his glass, his gold watch glinting in the candlelight. 'So, we meet again.' Cudjoe beamed with pleasure and Mark raised his glass in response.

'To be perfectly honest, we'd given up hope of even seeing you again after that day. Cass and I were totally bewildered.'

'Yes, and I am sorry for leaving you that way. I am only glad of the chance to explain. You folks were so nice, and I felt terrible leaving you so suddenly, but I had urgent business to attend to.'

Cassie gazed at him. He was as charming as ever. 'How long are you able to stay?' she asked, feeling herself blush. 'I mean, you're welcome to stay as long as you like.'

'Thank you, Cassie; I may well take you up on your offer. I have to spend two days a week in Bath; the department is publishing my latest paper. It will take a couple of years before it's fully accepted but it's a breakthrough for me that they are even taking my subject seriously.'

'What's your subject Joe? We're in the dark about it; we have heard rumours but …'

The phone rang, and Mark went into the kitchen to make coffee. 'Blue Mountain okay, Joe? We still have some left,' he said, looking in the cupboard.

Cassie answered the phone. It was Sabrina.

'Cass? It's okay, don't panic.'

'Sab,' she questioned, 'where are you?'

'At the restaurant. Cass, I had to ring you – something's been playing on my mind.'

'What has?'

'Cudjoe. Cass, I don't trust him. Don't ask me why. I have this feeling about him.'

'Whatever do you mean?'

'I mean, don't take him into your confidence. Let's face it, you said yourself when you came back from Jamaica, you didn't know anything about him. Have you told him about the plot?' Her voice sounded strange.

'No, I haven't.'

'Don't!' It was a command. 'I have this feeling he's working against us, Cass.'

'Sab, what is all this about?' She could hardly contain her irritation. 'I thought you and Joe seemed to be getting along. Anyway, you have no valid reason for making such an outrageous statement and I am more than capable of making character judgements for myself.' She lowered her voice. 'I suggest you go back and concentrate on Roger and your evening together. I'll speak to you soon. Goodnight.' She put the phone down before Sabrina could say anything else.

'What was that all about?' Mark asked from the kitchen.

Cassie shook her head dismissively and went back to join Cudjoe. 'Mark said you were in Bristol over the Christmas period?'

'Yes, I arrived on Christmas Eve. Not a good time, I can tell you. The train station was packed!' He gave a short laugh. 'I stayed with friends in Montpelier.'

'I promise to send some over when I get back to Jamaica,' Cudjoe said, as Mark came back with coffee.

'I'm sure we can get it here. Can't we Cass?' Mark could see that something from her conversation with Sabrina had upset her. 'Cass?'

'Yes, yes, we can. Sorry, Joe, I was miles away.'

Cassie excused herself and went out to find some nibbles. She felt remorseful, she had never spoken to Sabrina in that way before and it was hurting. If she was honest, it disappointed her that she had not bonded with Cudjoe. Why should she think so badly of him?

She went through into the lounge, holding a tray of assorted titbits. Mark must have pursued Cudjoe's thesis at Bath University because she heard him discussing it.

'In Jamaica, it's known as Obeah, not Voodoo,' Cudjoe said. 'But the religion is similar to Haiti's in many ways.' Cudjoe looked over at Mark. 'I would have thought Della would have told you that.'

Cassie placed the tray on a nearby table. 'So, you know Della?' she asked, giving him a napkin.

'No, Cass, not personally. Her husband, Al, told me what happened to Mark on the boat. There are so many superstitions. You have to remember that Port Antonio is very much a closed community. Did Della tell you anything of interest, Cassie?'

She felt him watching her closely, waiting for a response. Sabrina's words echoed in her head. 'No, not really. We were with a party of Americans, so we didn't get chance to discuss anything.'

Mark reached for her hand. 'You okay, Cass?'

'Yes, it's been a long day. I think I'll turn in if you both don't mind. Mark, you can show Joe to his room, can't you?'

'Goodnight, Cass.' Cudjoe got up and kissed her briefly. 'And thank you for making me so welcome.'

She smiled up at him. Damn Sabrina for making me doubt his motives, she thought.

She took a shower, hoping it would help her to sleep but it had the opposite effect. Instead, she drifted in and out of sleep, dreaming that Sab was crying because she had shouted at her. Then, in her subconscious mind, her father appeared, blaming her for his own death and for her mother's. If you have a daughter, I hope she never turns out like you. Bad, bad, bad!

She woke with a start, passing her hand over her stomach. She automatically felt for Mark, but he wasn't there. In the darkness, she could hear the drone of his voice in conversation with Cudjoe, lulling her back into a troubled sleep. Mark kissed her awake. 'Must go, darling. Rog won't be in until later so ...'

'Is Joe still asleep?' she asked, pushing her hair off her face.

'Don't worry yourself. We've already had breakfast. He said he would be back on Thursday. Are you sure you're all right?'

'Just sleepy. I had so many mixed-up dreams.'

'You could have fooled me. You were dead to the world

when I came to bed. What have you got planned for today?'

'I want to ring Felix sometime today and fit in Mrs Lethbridge. I really must put my mind to her décor.' She paused. 'Mark? You do think Joe is genuine, don't you?'

'What's all this nonsense, Cass? Of course I do, silly! Talk to you later,' he said, kissing her again. And I want the low-down on the conversation you had with Sab – it's obviously making you miserable.'

***

Felix rang Cassie just as she parked her car outside Mrs Lethbridge's house on the Downs.

'This won't take long. Cudjoe came up to the university this morning and introduced himself. He said Mark had been singing my praises and he wanted to meet me. He was very interested in the plot, especially when I told him about the Silas Hunt. He became very excited. Cass, are you there?'

'Yes, I'm listening, Felix,' she shook her head, smiling. Sabrina need not have concerned herself about Cudjoe knowing of the plot after all; Felix had already told him.

'Anyway, to get to the point, I've booked a table for all of us at the Oriental Lily for Tuesday of next week at eight. Cudjoe said he would have finished his business by then. I must say I'm impressed. I can see why he's renowned in his field. I am optimistic now.

'Me too. I'm sorry, Felix, but I have to go. I have an appointment,' she said, waving to Mrs Lethbridge at the window.

'So, the day and time suits you and Mark, does it?'

'Perfect. I'll catch you later, Felix.'

She spent the next two hours with Mrs Lethbridge, going from room to room. In the end, she left several pattern books for her to flick through.

***

'Stop, Mark! You're making me giddy!' Cassie had never seen him so happy. He was swinging her round and round, laughing like a small boy.

Later that evening, they sat together, savouring the moment.

'It must have happened in Jamaica.'

'I don't suppose it'll be a bad omen, do you?'

'Cass, darling, don't even think it. This pregnancy is already making you superstitious, what with Joe and now this. You're going to sail through the pregnancy and produce the most gorgeous baby boy that ever drew breath.'

'Who said it's a boy?'

'My boy, Bill,' Mark said, flexing his muscles.

Cassie laughed, desperately needing his reassurance. The niggling doubts stayed with her.

'You still haven't told me what was so important when Sab rang.'

'It's been resolved – it was nothing, Mark, but I'd rather we kept our news to ourselves, for the moment, at least.'

He went into the kitchen and came back with two glasses of orange juice. He handed her a glass. 'To the baby He murmured.

***

The next morning Cass had a text message from Felix the animation in Felix's voice grabbed her attention. She listened intently to the message urging her to contact him as soon as possible. Puzzled, Cassie chewed on her toast and drained the last of her tea, remembering it was good for morning sickness. Whatever it was couldn't wait, so she returned his call.

'What's so important Felix? What have you found out?'

'Too much to tell you over the phone. Can we meet today?'

'Of course, tell me where and when.'

The rendezvous was not at all where Cassie expected Felix to choose; he was more used to urban pubs in side streets.

'This is a surprise,' she said, entering the very modern bistro. 'I would almost think you wanted me to see your feminine side,' she teased, glancing at the large blooms that hung over the bar.

'Oh, ha,' he said, bringing over a cafeteria of hot coffee and two cup-cakes.

Cassie had found a table near the window, marvelling at the views over central Bristol. Felix went to get napkins.

'I like the décor in here,' she said as he pulled out a chair opposite. 'I couldn't have done any better myself,' she added, glancing at the sparse off-white walls offset by cream and green floral displays.

'I'm intrigued, Felix.' Cassie looked at him, biting into her cake. 'What more have you discovered?'

He spread a map on the table. 'This is the oldest map I could find of the area.'

'Where did you get it?'

'This is your plot.' He pointed, ignoring her question. 'It was originally a barn that belonged to a nearby farm, owned by the Faulkes family. Their farm is here.' He indicated to a cluster of small rectangles. 'Now if you follow the map farther down the coast pass your plot, the rock there, which incidentally is not on any other map I have seen.' He tapped the map emphatically. 'Was where the Silas Hunt ran aground?'

Cassie was impressed. 'So, you think the Coromantee slaves seized the opportunity to escape after being freed from their shackles?' she queried.

'Yes, they were possibly convinced the vessel was doomed and they had nothing to lose.' He sipped his coffee, reflecting. 'We've already established that they were brought over to become personal servants to the merchant ventures, or some other subservient role to the hierarchy.'

'Felix, the fact still remains that it doesn't explain the connection to the plot.'

'I was waiting for you to say that.' He pulled out a frail document. 'I had to charm a few people to get this. Read it to me – be careful how you handle it, though.'

'The skeletons of four Coromantee slaves were found in a barn off the Bristol channel coast at Rockpoint Bay. Bounty hunters failed to capture the two other slaves and therefore decided to torch the barn. They are presumed to be from the frigate the Silas Hunt.'

Cass looked up at him. 'That means two escaped. But how?'

'My theory is they found an escape route from the barn. I figured out that the outside cellar that Mark referred to would have been inside the barn, and I bet if we went up to the plot now, we would find a trap door somewhere under the cellar floor that surfaces …'

'Let me guess, in the corner of the bathroom?'

'And before you ask, Cass, yes, it's possible. I spent last night going through all the paperwork we have collected and matched it up. But as we both know it's only one scenario and we don't even know if the escapees were the twins.'

'If they were, are you telling me there are evil forces at large up there? It makes sense of everything that has happened. It still doesn't explain why I feel empathy with the one on the bridge, Felix.'

Felix noticed how pale she had become. 'That, I can't answer for you, Cass. Come on let's get some fresh air. That's enough speculation for one day.' He took her elbow, guiding her to the entrance. And walked her to her car. He kissed her swiftly, looking at his watch. 'Got to go, see you soon, Cass.'

'Only next time, Felix, please, no more maps!' she shouted after him.

Felix laughed as he hopped on a bus. Cudjoe found Cassie arranging carnations in a square vase. He watched her, as he sat on a kitchen stool. He began telling her about his lectures in Bath, and his meeting with Felix. She turned to look at him, holding a carnation stem. She desperately wanted to take him into her confidence and tell him about her own discussion with Felix, but thanks to Sabrina, she felt she could not trust him. Sighing, she said, 'I met Felix myself this morning. He told me he has confirmed a table at the Oriental Lily.'

'I'm looking forward to it, and talking more with your friends, Cass.'

'How did you find Sabrina, Joe?' Cassie question

'Intriguing, very intriguing. Ask me when I know her better. One thing is certain – she is very fond of you, Cass.'

She smiled at him. 'I suppose she told you about our upbringing?'

'Yes and its very commendable how her family took you in at such an early age. No wonder you were very close to Sabrina and her parents.'

'I owe them so much, Joe. Nothing will ever break my bond with Sab – she is everything to me. There!' She stood back, admiring her flowers. 'Now for a cup of tea,' she said with a smile, putting the arrangement in the lounge window. She looked out the window, surprised to see Mark coming up the path, wondering what brought him home. She soon found out.

'Rog and I had a meeting with the construction people; it's all go from next week.' He pulled up a stool next to

Cudjoe. 'It's going to mean a couple of days at their head office at Swindon. Apparently, they want this project finished by Easter.'

Cassie groaned. 'Mark, that's unrealistic, surely?'

'I admit it's pushing it, but I think it's achievable. Oh, by the way, Cass, I have a message from Sab, via Roger. She says to tell you that Abigail can't wait to see Fenena again.'

She saw Cudjoe looking at her. 'It's a pet name we gave each other as children, Joe, almost like a code. Our family used to take us to their favourite opera, 'Nabbuco' by Verdi. Abigail and Fenena were two sisters …' her voice faltered and Cudjoe changed the subject.

Chapter Twenty-Seven

Daffodils, heavy with rain, trailed against Cassie's ankles as she hurried along the path. Hardly daring to look at Mark, she got in the waiting taxi and sat next to him, focusing instead on why he was in such a foul mood.

Roger, it seemed, had insisted on vetting the hotel suite in Swindon ahead of the next crucial meetings with the Americans.

'I really am at a loss as to why he needed to go today – the meetings aren't until next Monday. He knew how much it meant to us. Cudjoe told me this morning he was very much looking forward to discussing the culture of his beloved Jamaica.'

'And we both know how interesting Joe is, going by that informative day in Port Antonio.'

Cassie looked down at her hands. 'I don't think things are going as well as they should be at home. I felt he wanted to talk the other day in your office, but he had second thoughts. Perhaps he wanted a break from Sabrina, you know how full-on she can be.'

'I do indeed,' Mark said his mood lifting.

'Do you have to stay over? It's only forty minutes on the motorway.'

'It's not that simple. There are other considerations as well. The directors are flying in from the parent company in Baltimore. In addition, they'll expect some input socially. It's all about networking, my girl.' He took her hand and squeezed it. 'And how people interact outside the work environment.'

'Is this the company Vern recommended?'

'Yes, we owe a lot to those two guys. I suspect Vern did more than he needed to do. He said he knew the directors personally.'

'Is there anyone they don't know?'

'I certainly seems that way,' Mark responded, peering out the taxi window for the restaurant.

'What time did Rog say Sabrina would be at the restaurant?'

'About eight-thirty,' he said, paying the taxi driver.

'Don't tell me it's due to her workload?'

'Yeah, something like that.'

Under new management, the Oriental Lily had undergone extensive refurbishment, making it warm and welcoming. The ivory walls and hand-painted water lilies were spaced evenly at eye-level, blending with the citrus carpet and matching drapes.

Cassie glanced at her watch. It was eight-thirty and Sabrina and Anne had still not arrived.

Cudjoe, for his part, found the whole dining experience pleasurable. 'I could get used to this fine dining. First Cassie cooked me an excellent meal, and tonight arranged by you, Felix. Thank you.'

'I think we ought to order.' Felix said studying the menu. 'My usual please darling.' Cassie smiled up at Mark. They all made their choices and grabbing a handful of peanuts, Cudjoe followed Mark to the other end of the restaurant to order.

'Did Mark have any thoughts on my theory?'

'Felix, I'm sorry, it completely slipped my mind. What with Mark talking about the new contract they've secured, and the excitement of the evening. Although at the moment all things 'plot' are not on his radar, he's already made a few tentative enquiries about the prospect of putting it on the market.'

Taken aback, Felix stared at her. 'He wouldn't go against your wishes, surely, Cass?

'No he wouldn't…'Cassie said wistfully.

'I've told Cudjoe everything.' He saw her expression. 'I had no choice; just imagine if Anne had talked about Don, which she will, then it could lead to my mate David or Mr Morgan. It would have laid her open to questions she wouldn't be able to answer. Besides, there is another reason. Cudjoe is the only person I know who has the knowledge and understanding on every aspect of this subject, from African slaves to Obeah, and even hex. We need his well-informed judgement Cass.'

Cassie toyed with the peanuts. 'Felix, I want to trust Joe, but Sabrina has warned me against him and …' She stopped, mid-sentence, her attention diverted towards Sabrina and Anne who were making an entrance. Sabrina hugged Cassie. Crying and laughing at the same time, Cassie turned towards Anne, standing meekly beside Sabrina.

'Hello, Anne.' Cassie embraced her, feeling Anne's cold grey skin against her cheek. She watched in horror at the listless way she moved beside Sabrina.

'I hope you don't mind, Sab, we've ordered for you both.' Mark bent to kiss them both and introduced Anne to Cudjoe. She held out a limp hand, staring at him.

'I'm pleased to meet you, Anne. Cassie and Mark talk of you often.' Cudjoe returned her stare, wondering if he had got through to her.

'Our table is over there in the corner, Sab.' Cassie linked arms with her, sharing a joke as they walked over.

'You ladies must be starving. Would you like some salted peanuts, Anne?' Cudjoe offered her the glass dish. Anne reached across to take some but Sabrina, leaving Cassie, caught hold of her wrist.

'We don't want to spoil your appetite, do we, Anne?'

Cudjoe stared at them both, and replaced the glass dish back on the bar.

They took their places and, despite the delay, the aroma of jasmine rice soon reached them.

'I'm sorry Rog couldn't make it, Sab,' Cassie said. 'He's such a workaholic, that husband of yours.'

'Him and me both, Cass.'

The meal was served quickly and consumed even faster. The only exception was Anne, who toyed with her food, pushing it around the plate with her fork, Felix and Mark enjoyed easy banter at one end of the table, while Cudjoe made small talk with Sabrina. She was obviously making an effort to be charming because she glanced over at Cass for approval.

It was at the dessert stage that the tone of the evening changed. Everyone overheard Mark ask Felix if there had been any fresh information on Lorna. At the mention of her name, Anne began to whimper quietly into her lap. Sabrina put an arm around her, and Cassie looked on, disturbed. Felix, noticing that they were attracting unwanted attention from other diners, changed the subject.

'It looks as if the refurbishment has been a success. The lilies look almost real.'

The name 'Lily' caused Anne to lose all control, her whimper turned into an agonised wail, her tiny frame doubled over in anguish, saliva dripped on to the place mat in front of her.

Cassie and Sabrina helped her out of her seat, but she was inconsolable.

Only Cudjoe seemed completely unfazed. He watched with a mixture of surprise and pity. Leaning towards Felix, he said. 'I want you to tell me everything and I mean everything.' He watched Sabrina wiping Anne's mouth as she led her to the exit. 'Particularly from the time Cassie and Mark returned from Jamaica. It doesn't matter how insignificant it might seem to you. I need to know.'

'Then I suggest you come back to my flat.' Felix got up, throwing his used napkin on to the table. 'You can have access to all the maps and information I have collected so far.'

Felix settled the bill, and Cudjoe reassured Cassie he would ring in the morning. Sabrina waved briefly, steering Anne towards Sabrina's car.

***

'Sab did hint on Anne becoming more unstable, but I wouldn't have believed it if I hadn't seen it for myself.' Mark said when they got home Cassie went into the bedroom followed by Mark. 'It should not have got to this stage Cass. The woman is a shell of her former self, and as for that outburst, well; her mind seems to be completely gone. Thank God Sab had the presence of mind to get her out of there.'

'Surely she has someone.'

'Well, you find them, Cass. You saw for yourself at Don's funeral – she has no one. Anyway, it will be in the hands of the specialists soon. It is obvious that counselling is not the answer. I mean, for Christ's sake, what was Sab thinking about, bringing her to the restaurant in that state?'

'Come on, Mark, you can hardly blame Sabrina. How did she know how she would react? I've been trying to think what triggered her.'

'That's something we'll never know.'

'Do you think Joe is staying with Felix indefinitely?' Cassie said, going into the bedroom.'

'I haven't a clue, but it wouldn't surprise me, they have a lot in common. I would feel a lot happier if he stayed here for your security more than anything else. I thought Roger might have got in touch.' He threw his loose change on the dressing table.

'I expect he had a better evening than we did.' She yawned, giving into the tiredness. 'I'm glad Sab and I have settled our differences.'

Brushing his teeth, Mark could hear her talking in that sleepy way of hers. Now was a good time to broach the subject. 'Cass,' he said, walking back into the bedroom, 'the estate agent has someone interested in the plot. I can't get workers to stay for any length of time and if I do, what with the new contract, I won't be able to oversee the work. I hesitate to use the word cursed … Anyway we will find another site to build on, darling.'

'After Felix's theory about the brothers, it might be a good idea, but you'll be wasting your time – it won't let you.'

Babbling again, he thought, smiling down at her. She had taken on a different aura since her pregnancy. He pushed back an auburn tendril of hair that had fallen over her eyes. It was going to be difficult to keep this pregnancy a secret for much longer, especially from Sabrina. Kissing her tenderly, he placed her arm under the duvet.

***

As soon as the party had gone their separate ways, Felix and Cudjoe made straight for Felix's room.

'It's not quite so frantic now that the Easter break is looming,' said Felix, searching for his flat key.

Cudjoe looked around, surprised at the small room. The only window looked out on to a narrow pavement with a streetlight casting dark shadows into the room.

'Perfect for my needs,' Felix justified, guessing Cudjoe's thoughts.

'Very compact,' Cudjoe answered, scanning the books

lining the fitted bookcase.

'It's like a reference library, Felix.' He spun around to face him. 'I am impressed.' He picked one out at random. 'The Other Religion,' he murmured, his eyes resting on the word 'Vodoun.'

'I hope you don't mind the sofa, Joe.'

'No problem.' Cudjoe indicated the bookcase. 'You have a fine collection of books on Voodoo?'

'The more Cass and I researched the plot, the more interested I became and so I bought a few books on the subject,' Felix said, taking the book from him and placing it back on the shelf.

'Have you been there?'

'Where, to the plot? No, I don't think anyone has, except Don, poor man, Cassie and Mark, of course. Oh, and Mr Morgan, the solicitor on the sale.'

'What was the incident there, didn't you mention a curse?'

Felix relayed the story exactly as Elizabeth Morgan had told them that day.

'I've come across this before, Felix, but not in this country.' Cudjoe leant forward, his head in his hands. Leaving him to his thoughts, Felix went into the kitchen and returned with two mugs of coffee.

'Did Cassie and Mark say any more about their visit to the plot?'

'Only what I told you before – Mark being spooked in the building and Cassie's accident in the rockery…'

'The same rockery where the bones were found?'

'Apparently, yes. The garden is on a slope that stretches towards the channel, albeit high up on the coastline. That night was the worst storm anyone can remember, even the old Willow tree began thrashing in the storm.'

'Willow tree? Did you say willow tree?'

'Yes, but what frightened her most was the fact she found herself surrounded by toads from the rockery.'

'What sort of toads?'

'Black ones, according to Cass. She must have inadvertently stumbled into their territory. What's this all about, Joe?'

'Sorry, Felix.' He laughed. 'I did say I wanted every little detail, and I am beginning to build a picture. What do you think happened on the bridge that night?'

'You have to decide for yourself on that one. I've told you everything, from the closure of the suspension bridge, to the police officer that spoke to Mark. And of course, the apparition of the black man that Cassie saw.'

Felix collapsed into a battered armchair. 'And then we have David telling me that Voodoo is practised in Bristol …' He closed his eyes and they fell silent, the quiet broken only by the chime of the clock outside the window.

Cudjoe got up and looked outside, but he didn't see the clock, he only saw Anne's tortured body. 'Felix, I want to tell you something that you might feel is even more incredible.' He paused and took a deep breath. 'What would you say if I told you I think Anne is a zombie?' He turned around to see Felix's reaction. It was as he expected.

Cudjoe moved away from the window and stood in front of Felix's library of books. He picked out the book he looked at earlier and waved it in front of Felix. 'You must have read extracts on this very subject. Zombification is part of the Voodoo religion.'

Felix got up and stood beside him. 'Yes, of course, but are you seriously asking me to believe that the woman I've known for the last few months, and helped bury her husband, is a zombie?' Felix stared at him, his expression incredulous. 'The walking dead? Come on, Joe.'

'Yes, Felix I am.' Cudjoe was equally direct, his dark eyes fixed on Felix.

'Well, I certainly need a drink now.' Felix helped himself to a double brandy from the drink cabinet, drank it straight and then poured out another one for himself and Cudjoe.

They sat opposite each other, not only digesting everything they discussed, but this latest revelation.

'You must have noticed how blue her lips were at the restaurant? And the blank stare?' Cudjoe searched his face. 'For God's sake, Felix, you must have seen how Sabrina fed Anne at one point?'

Felix shuffled uncomfortably. 'Are you saying that Sab is in on this zombification?'

'Not at all,' Cudjoe answered.

'Okay, I'll buy it, but what would be the point of turning Anne into a zombie?'

'Felix, I can only add to what I know and the facts you have given me, as well as what I have seen for myself.' Cudjoe reached over and helped himself to one of Felix cigarettes.

'It has something to do with the fires that happened up there. It all goes back to that but if Anne has never been there …' Cudjoe stood up, letting his thoughts drift.

'Have you heard of a boko?'

'Yes, it's a sorcerer.'

'I think a boko sent for her soul.' He clicked his fingers. 'That's how it happened.'

'The zombie idea is so far-fetched all those awful seventies movies with row after row of zombies, tearing into each other.' He saw his expression. 'Go on, Joe, I'm listening. How does it happen?'

'They simply break the skin of the victim in water. A spirit is called, and then water would be mingled with her blood. Anne, from what I have seen of her, would be aware of her situation but would have certainly been confused. In her dreamlike state of mind, everything is in slow motion and, as you saw, is incapable of rational thoughts. No, my friend,

I'm afraid Anne is now one of the living dead.' Cudjoe held out his glass for a refill. Felix poured the last of the brandy, laughing nervously.

'Christ, are you trying to frighten me, for God's sake? If not, you're taking a brilliant crack at it.'

'However, there's more.' Felix braced himself, deep furrows creasing his brow.

'Tetrodotoxin is a poison from puffer fish or, as in this case, a species of toads. As potent as any modern-day drug and will induce a state of lethargy, as we saw in Anne this evening. Felix, did you notice a faint smell of ammonia around her? That was the tetrodotoxin.

Hence my interest in the toads that frightened Cassie – they were obviously not your normal garden toads.'

Felix had noticed the odour that Joe talked about but had dismissed it in light of Anne's increasing senility.

Cudjoe continued. 'The zombie will lie dormant, not necessarily buried but something similar an underground bunker for instance. Only the boko can revive the zombie. The boko has a strict timetable; it knows the antidote, mainly made from obnoxious plant matter lying around and bones, or sulphur powder, anything.' Cudjoe drained the last of the brandy. 'It could be in the form of body rub or a liquid that is passed under the victim's nostrils, similar to smelling salts, but whatever was used, the antidote would be buried next to the victim, in this case Anne.'

'You're telling me that a zombie is a corpse with no will of its own and totally at the mercy of the evil that controls it?'

Cudjoe nodded. 'It is in a zone or a fog if you like, that separates life from death. Anne moves, hears, eats, but has no knowledge or memory of her condition.'

They both sat back, mulling over the implications. Felix could hardly comprehend it. Changing the subject, he said, 'you mentioned tetrodotoxin? That would make sense;

there is a crude drawing of a puffer fish on the tomb of Ti, a Pharaoh of the fifth dynasty.'

'Really? I didn't know that. Mark told me Egyptology was one of your lectures.'

They began discussing the ancient history of Egypt. It was a welcome relief for Felix, who threw himself into talking about the subject. The university clock chimed three o'clock.

'I think it's telling us to turn in, Felix.' However, Felix was having none of it. 'Going back to the fire, I still say they could never have survived it. If the other four slaves perished, why not the twins?'

'You have got something there,' Cudjoe said, excitedly going through the titles in the bookcase. 'Not unless one or both of them were Loas.' He chose a title and thumbed the index. 'Loa is a supernatural being and has far-reaching powers that fire cannot touch.'

'Joe, the frigate set sail from Africa, not the Caribbean,' he reasoned.

'Makes no difference – actually, it's even more factual. Voodoo has its roots in Africa.'

'But what about Cassie? She's convinced she has empathy with the plot, or someone or something there. To her, the energy she felt is certainly not evil.'

Cudjoe yawned. 'Yes, I know. That is another missing piece of the puzzle.'

'And Anne, surely she would have to be at the plot for all this to happen to her?'

'Felix, I have a professor friend in Liverpool who is experienced on certain aspects of Voodoo, and he might be able to answer your questions. It might be worth my while to take a trip up there and look him up.'

'What about your commitments?' Felix asked, throwing him a duvet.

'Nothing that can't wait until I get back, but I'm afraid I'm going to have to leave you to explain to Cass.'

***

223

Chapter Twenty-Eight

'He could have had the decency to tell us he wasn't coming back.' Mark placed his shirts in his holdall. 'However much I like the guy, I'm disappointed as well.'

Despondent, she watched him pack the last of his small items. First, the incident with Anne at the restaurant, and now she had a question mark whether she could trust Cudjoe. He was charismatic, of that, there was no doubt, and to be honest he had never given her any reason to think otherwise.

'You must think it odd that Joe never made himself known to us over Christmas, Mark?'

'Well, you have a perfect opportunity to ask him when you see him next.' Mark held up his hands. 'Sorry, Cass, I'm busy and stressed. I really had hoped he would be staying here while I was in Swindon. If you feel the slightest unease about the situation, I'll pick up the phone now and arrange for you to stay with Sab.' He glanced at his watch and zipped his holdall.

'No, I don't think I can handle Sabrina for four days. I know from experience how bossy she can be. Anyway, Joe might turn up tomorrow.'

She walked him to the car and Mark put his holdall in the boot. 'Now are you sure you're okay?' Mark asked, kissing her.

'Don't worry about me, I'll be fine,' she whispered, kissing him back.

'And don't forget to keep the mobile charged. I need to be able to contact you at all times,' Mark emphasised.

A feeling of foreboding welled up deep inside her that

had nothing to do with the baby.

The following day was full on, mainly because not only had she neglected her business but also, she had little appetite for it. Nevertheless, she had at last agreed a price with Mrs Lethbridge but even more importantly, a decision had been made on the décor for every room in the house. Now she could start finding the best contacts, at least it would occupy her while Mark was in Swindon.

Exhausted, Cassie let herself into the flat. Treading on a long white envelope, she picked it up and noticed it was hand-written. She read it immediately.

It explained that Cudjoe had to go to Liverpool on urgent business. That was Joe all over, she decided, crushing the letter with one hand; here today and gone tomorrow. She pulled out the Lethbridge castings from her briefcase, barely glancing at the figures, and placed them on the hall table. Kicking off her shoes, she checked her messages; there weren't any. She had hoped for something from Sab, telling her that Anne was getting the treatment she so desperately needed. Tired, she watched television for a while before going into the kitchen to get supper.

Later, she had a shower. Tears flowed as she imagined Anne's emaciated face looking through the steam. The doctor had warned her she would get these high and lows, especially in the early months. Calming herself, she got into bed and let her hand glide gently over her stomach and the small swelling, as she drifted into a deep sleep. Cassie's dark emotions had all but disappeared by the next day. She had gone to see Anne but not finding her in, and reluctant to pursue it, she got back into the car. She was about to pull away when her mobile rang.

'Cass? It's, Felix. Sorry about the note but I didn't have a lot of time yesterday.'

'No need to apologise, I understand you're busy. How's it going?'

Felix ignored her question. 'Cass, I forgot to mention it in the note, but Joe specifically asked that you stay away from the plot.'

'I wasn't intending to go up there, anyway. Mark already has a buyer lined up. He says enough is enough, especially since Anne's visit seems to have had a devastating effect on her.' The connection began breaking up. 'Felix, can you hear me?'

'What did you just say?'

'Mark's selling the plot. It's too much trouble and he can't get planning on it.'

'No, before that, about Anne.'

'She went up to the plot to look for Don's ring, convinced he had lost it there. She's badgered Sab for ages to take her up there but ever since, she's acted strangely, she's almost become introverted. You saw how she was at the restaurant the other night. I am worried about her, Felix … Felix? I can't hear you!'

'When did she go up there?'

'Last week.' She listened to the crackle as the signal died. What was all that about? She thought, driving through Redland. Why would he be interested in Anne's visit to the plot? More significantly, why would Joe warn her not to go there?

'That's rich, he's not even here.' She was tired of all this cloak and dagger stuff between Felix and Cudjoe. She had a right to know what was going on.

It was much later when Mark rang her. 'Is everything okay, darling?'

'Well, yes, sort of.'

'What do you mean, sort of? What's happened now? Is Joe with you?'

'Mark, please. Apparently, he's in Liverpool on business.'

'Liverpool! Whatever for?'

'I don't know, Felix didn't say. Something to do with the university, I expect.'

'Why don't you go and stay with Sab for a few days, Cass? It would make me feel easier, it'll only be until Thursday and then we'll be able to have a long weekend together.'

'I'm fine, really. Besides, Sab's sorting out Anne.'

'What catastrophe has befallen her now?' he said with a hint of sarcasm.

'Nothing, I hope. I went around there this morning, but I couldn't bring myself to go in. It reminded me of the day of the funeral when she was so upset. Sab told me she's got everything in hand.'

'Good. I was going to mention it to Felix but if Sabrina's dealing with it so much the better, she'll have more influence with the health authorities.' He paused. 'Have you told her about the baby yet?'

'No, I want to keep it to myself for a little longer.'

'It'll be out of your hands soon, Mrs Campbell. I have to go, Cass, they're calling for me.'

'Wait, Mark! You haven't told me about the contracts, and how is Roger?' She sighed, and replaced the receiver. Sabrina had not mentioned Roger when they spoke earlier and, going on what she knew, she thought it was better not to broach the subject. Another one to worry about, she concluded, going into the kitchen to make a cup of hot chocolate.

***

If the folic acid tablets were indigestible, the cod liver capsules were worse. Placing the mini torpedo on her tongue, she gulped fresh orange juice and threw back her head. Despite everything that was going on around her, she had had one of the best night's sleeps for a long time.

It was one of those lovely spring days with blue skies full of the promise of early summer. Cassie decided to walk to the town centre. The dewy sun shone down on a window box of parrot tulips, the burgundy colour reminding her of the Victorian chair she was having upholstered for Mrs Lethbridge.

Passing the farmers' market on Corn Street, she decided to go inside the old building that housed the diverse and various antiques. Perusing the bottles of essential oils, a woman inspecting a lamp caught her attention. Beyond her, she saw Sabrina, her head bent, examining jewellery.

Responding to a tap on the shoulder, Sabrina turned and faced her. 'Hi Cass, just the person.' She placed an Art Deco brooch on the lapel of her tailored suit. 'What do you think?'

'Very unusual. This is a surprise – I didn't expect to see you here.'

'A colleague of mine has a birthday and I'm looking for a suitable present, something a bit unusual,' she said, picking up a colourful '40's brooch and pinning it to her suit. 'What do you think?'

'I prefer the first one.'

Sabrina went to pay for her purchase and Cassie began browsing at the other items, trying on rings, and gazing at them.

'Sab, this ring, is the same as Don's! I remember it distinctly. It was the first thing I noticed when you introduced us at your party.'

'It is very similar, I must admit.' Sabrina examined it. 'But I can't be sure, Cass.' She looked at her. 'I hope you're not going to tell me the staff at the hospital sold it for gain, are you?'

'No, of course not.'

'Come on.' Sabrina linked arms with her. 'I have a spare ten minutes. Let's see what else can tempt us.'

***

For Cassie, gardening was a great leveller. Pulling on her gloves, she dug between grape hyacinths, careful not to disturb the royal blue heads in front of her. Uppermost in her mind was the call she took from the land agent Mark had instructed to sell the plot. She now had the task of telling him that the buyer had pulled out, apparently for no reason. She got up and pulled off her gloves, deciding that she was not in the mood for gardening after all.

Mark came home earlier than expected. 'I'm sure Sab is right,' he said when Cassie told him about the ring she saw in the antique market. 'Don's ring was a typical black onyx and still very popular.' He took the mug of coffee Cassie handed him. 'Has the agent been in touch?'

'As a matter of fact, he has, and you're not going to like it.' She told him about their conversation.

'That's impossible,' Mark said, picking up the phone in the hall.

Ten minutes later, he came into the kitchen, looking relieved.

'Well?'

'It seems he is still interested but he won't commit until he gets back from holiday. I've told the agent to keep it open. It's unbelievable, even selling it is proving difficult.' He glanced over at her. 'Cass?'

'I'm not saying anything, Mark; you know how I feel. There is unfinished business up there, for me and …'

Mark had no intention of going down that road, so he said, 'I don't suppose you've heard from Felix?'

'Yes, and that's another thing: he warned me not to go to the plot. He said he was only passing on a message from Joe.'

'Warned you? That's a bit strong, Cass.'

'I think he meant it wasn't a good idea.' She walked over

to him. 'Mark, I'm beginning to wonder who to trust.'

'Well, you can trust me,' he said, holding her. 'All this fretting is no good for the baby, Cass. I do wish you would come back to Swindon with me.' He saw her expression. 'Let me take you to supper then, Mrs Campbell – you can't refuse me that.'

On Sunday afternoon, Cassie tackled the conservatory – she had until now been putting it off. Picking up a cushion, she noticed a new year's card had slipped down the side of a bamboo chair. Turning it over, she smiled at the colourful picture on the front, triggering recent memories of Jamaica. It was from Della. Puzzled, she sat down, knowing in her heart that it was important. She read the optimistic New Year's greeting but became apprehensive as she read on.

'I'm concerned that you haven't answered my faxes, Cassie. What is happening? I have had a visit from one of Beneba's daughters. The old woman isn't at all well; she drifts in and out of consciousness and continually mentions your name. When she is lucid, she insists that her daughters get a message to you. I quote: The time is drawing near. Again, I say trust no one, not even those you think you can rely on. Your enemies are all around. Remember, he needs you. Marassa needs you. Remember to always wear your charm.'

Cassie stared at the note. Della had added for her not to be alarmed as Beneba rambled a lot of the time. She felt for her charm, before handing the card to Mark.

'I see what you mean about trusting people. Della wouldn't have gone to the trouble to send this otherwise.' He turned it over, as if it would offer more information.

'I don't remember seeing this before.'

'It probably got caught up in the Christmas mail. I am worried, Mark.'

'That settles it. You either come with me to Swindon or

stay with Sab. I don't want you to stay on your own, Cass.' He read the message again. 'What is Della talking about? We don't have a fax.'

'I know but Sab has, I gave Della her number as she wanted to send more information on the Voodoo religion.' She took the card, her hand shaking. 'And why didn't Sab give me the faxes?'

'She probably withheld them because she was worried about the effect they might have had and wanted to spare you the ravings of an old woman. She's always been protective of you. Now listen, I'll dig out the suitcase while you make your preparations, my darling. All the Americans want to meet you. Vern and Bob have been telling them what a raving beauty you are. Besides, it's going to be a short week anyway, what with the Easter holidays.'

She laughed. 'I would love to meet them, especially if they're as interesting as those two.' Cassie shook her head. 'I can't Mark; I have a whole lot of appointments with artisans and soft furnishers at Mrs Lethbridge's. She wants me to start immediately after Easter. I can't stall any more. Anyway, I expect Joe will be back sometime this week.' She stopped, confused. Was Joe an enemy? Who could she trust – Felix?

'You okay?' Mark's voice jolted her from her thoughts. She smiled at him, but she had visibly paled. He led her to a chair, concerned.

'A bit tired, that's all. I think I'll go and lie down.'

'It might be a good idea if you let me have that card. I can email Vern to ask Della to fax me direct at the hotel in Swindon, if necessary. What do you think?'

'Good idea. Thanks Mark, I appreciate that.'

He picked up the newspaper, flicking the pages without seeing, trying not to worry.

Chapter Twenty-Nine

Monday morning saw an overnight fax on Sabrina's machine. She yawned, unravelled it, glanced at it briefly, and then left it to curl up on itself. Deciding it was too early to digest, she went to make coffee.

Roger had already left for Swindon. She grimaced, thinking about the row that prompted him to leave much earlier than he intended. Last night for the first time, they acknowledged there was a problem with their marriage. They were discussing their future well into the early hours. Roger had wanted her to give up her job and concentrate on starting a family.

'I want us to be a real family, Sab.'

She glared at him, her eyes flashing. 'Do you think that I don't? It's not my fault that it's not happening.'

'Perhaps if you took more time off, to relax, have a career break. That's what they call it these days, don't they?' he replied sarcastically. 'After all, it's not as if we need the money. The practice is doing well …'

Sabrina rounded on him, shaking with rage. 'So, does that mean you think my job is worthless, Roger? A little role to keep me happy. How dare you patronise me that way?'

He glanced over at the bedside clock. 'It's two-thirty. If I don't get some kip, I'll feel awful tomorrow. Think about it this week, Sabrina, because if you're not prepared to put something into this marriage, there isn't going to be one!' He turned his back to her and snapped off the light.

Sabrina sipped her coffee. She had three days to think it over. It wouldn't be easy; she loved her job. As she bit into her toast, she already had an idea of her decision.

Ready for work, she brushed toast crumbs from her suit and went through into the hall, backtracking when she remembered the fax. Without a glance, she stuffed it into her handbag and slammed the door shut.

***

It had been a frustrating five days for Cudjoe. He had hoped for a meeting with Professor Davies as soon as he arrived in Liverpool but that was not going to happen. He had rung Byron Davies as soon as he arrived at Lime Street, only to hear a recorded message that he would be out of the city until Wednesday. It was his own fault; he should have checked with him before he left Bristol. He rang Felix to let him know he would be delayed.

Cudjoe left the station and crossed the road, marvelling at the imposing façade of St George's Hall. He took a closer look, appreciating that it was possibly one of the best Greek revival buildings ever built, and yet another testament to the wealth created by the transatlantic trade.

He changed direction, walked down the busy Brownhill Road, and entered 'Christ the King.' He followed the outer perimeter, with hidden alcoves capturing the beguiling serenity of the Virgin Mary. The front pews were occupied by worshippers deep in prayer, whilst others lit candles. Cudjoe stood in silence, breathing in the atmosphere, aware that Catholicism and the Vodoun religion share some fundamental beliefs and superstitions. Leaving, he went in search of a hotel.

Byron Davies had seen many changes in Liverpool. Despite his Welsh name, he was a Liverpudlian through and through. He grew up in the Beatles' era and in his youth visited the Cavern Club. Always an avid fan of their music, he still wore his hair brushed forward in true Beatle style, even though it was now grey.

'Professor.' Cudjoe stepped forward and offered his hand.

Byron clasped it in both of his. 'I'm sorry you've been held over unnecessarily,' he said, offering Cudjoe a chair. 'I do apologise.'

Byron sat opposite him, placing his elbows on the desk, his outstretched fingers forming a bridge. 'I imagine it must be something pretty important to keep you in Liverpool for the last week. Apart from our wonderful culture, of course. Did you get to see the Cavern Club?'

Cudjoe shook his head.

'Then allow me to entertain you this evening. It's the least I can do.'

'I want your opinion, Byron. I don't know anyone else, apart from Professor Lister in Jackson, who is as knowledgeable and more importantly, who understands the Vodoun religion.'

Byron grinned at him. 'Give me slightly more credit. I know Lister is renowned on the subject of Vodoun but foremost he's a toxicologist. Anyway, Cudjoe, what can I do for you?'

Cudjoe related everything he had discovered since arriving in Bristol. He even filled Byron in on the Jamaican episode where he first met Cassie and Mark.

'That's a lot to take in on one go,' Byron remarked.

'Yes, I know, Byron, but I would like your impression.' Cudjoe stood up and began pacing. 'Zombies, for instance.' They began discussing what they both knew.

Eventually Byron said, 'there are several ways it can be brought about, as you know, but I agree with your opinion: the most likely way would have been abrasions to the skin and poison rubbed into the wound.'

'And the antidote?'

'You're right, it would need to be administered within fifteen hours, but that's only a small part of zombification.'

Cudjoe looked puzzled.

'You mentioned the victim, Cudjoe,' Byron added, 'but you've told me very little about the character and personality.'

His secretary chose that moment to come in with a tray and wedge the door open with her foot. Byron thanked her and got up to pull down the blinds, blocking out the sun. The temperature began to drop, making the office more comfortable.

'Coffee?'

'Yes, thank you, no sugar. Please go on, I am interested in your theory.'

'It's one that has been proven and, dare I say, lesser people than you and I readily ignore it, but at their cost.' Byron handed Cudjoe coffee. 'Usually, the victim is of vulnerable or weak character, so much so that a Bokor has little difficulty in exploiting them. It manipulates the victim's hopes and needs.' He stirred his coffee slowly. 'Put yourself in that position. You are able to grasp your heart's desire and the only way to keep it is to succumb to that world.' He paused, his gaze on Cudjoe. 'So, you can see that it takes two elements to make zombification work: the poison and the weakness of the victim's own mind. There is an apt saying, 'the brain has the power to kill the body that bears it.'

'Hex,' Cudjoe offered. 'I never looked at it that way which is precisely what happened to Mr Morgan'.

'Excuse me?'

'No matter, Byron. It just explains everything. That's why I needed your opinion.'

'Two heads are better than one, eh?' Byron put a friendly hand on his arm.

'What is this plot like?' he asked, moving on.

'I haven't been there myself so all the events I described are from what others have told me.'

'And Anne?'

'I think you've summed her up very well. Apparently, she had been very vulnerable since her husband's death.'

'Fear governs zombies. Fear of their Bokor, fear of what they dearly want in life and are not able to do anything about it. It goes on, Cudjoe, but it does sound as if she is the perfect target.' Byron rose and moved to the window.

'What do you know about Loas?'

Byron swung round and faced him. 'Ah, my specialist subject. Loa spirits are both positive and negative and act as intermediaries between humans and the Vodoun god. According to their religion, they are beyond reproach. But wait, I will start at the beginning.'

Byron topped up their coffee and perched on the edge of his desk, facing Cudjoe. 'Voodoo or Vodoun, as I prefer to call it, is commonly associated with a trance-inducing dance. It's well known that the chanting that follows induces a feeling of euphoria. During the ritual, the Bokor or witchdoctor as we term him, makes direct contact with the Loa, enters its path and receives the spirit of the Loa into their body.'

'Is it possible that more than one entity can be a Loa?'

Byron looked puzzled. 'Highly unlikely. Why?'

'Let's say, hypothetically, that we are talking about twins.'

'Now that's an interesting scenario because according to the religion, twins have one soul.'

'Exactly. Okay, let's take it a step further. To put it in layman terms, what if one of the brothers didn't want to be part of the religion?'

'An unwilling partner, you mean. Then he would be trapped with his brother. It would then depend on who was the more dominant of the two.'

'And if one was evil?'

'Then unless the other brother was more powerful, he would succumb to his brother's evil will.' Byron stared at Cudjoe over his half-spectacles. Never in all his experience had he actually come across a genuine case of zombification, never mind a scenario like this.

'What makes it so incredible is that according to the belief system, this is feasible – rare but possible. How did you establish they were Loas?'

'I have no hard facts,' Cudjoe replied. 'But like everything of this nature, it's a question of elimination. We've established that the vessel set sail from the Guinea coast, now known as Ghana, for Bristol. The records show that four skeletons were found together in the same area. Felix consolidated the maps with the other ones he had, and it becomes the internal section of the fire-ravaged ruins of the house still remaining.'

He scanned Byron's face, trying to read his reaction as the professor walked over to the window and pulled the blind down further.

'Felix and I strongly believe the brothers manifested themselves at the plot.'

Byron paced the office, staring at the floor, deep in thought before sitting back down.

'Okay, I'll buy it. You're perfectly right: Loas are strong, and fire can't harm them, but I doubt they would have stayed together because of the animosity between them. One of them, for certain, would have established itself to another area of the plot. It would have to be something living, a tree possibly.'

'The willow … of course?' Cudjoe said. Byron nodded knowingly.

'Why does all this strike a chord with me? What was the name of the vessel again?'

'The Silas Hunt.'

Byron clicked his fingers and grabbed his coat from behind the door. 'That's it. I have remembered. Come on Cudjoe, come with me. I want to show you something.'

He led Cudjoe out of the building. Cudjoe had no idea where they were heading as they hopped on to a passing bus. The bus took them along the same route he had tramped days earlier, reminding him how long he had been in the city.

They got off at William Brown Street and it was now clear what Byron had in mind.

The Walker Gallery was an imposing building. Once inside, Cudjoe could see why it was one of the most famous galleries. He had wandered around the Maritime Museum and the Tate at Albert Dock, waiting for Byron's return, but this was something else. It was a grander building with an atmosphere of its own. Lingering in the lofty halls, the great works of the Pre-Raphaelites hung heavy on the walls.

'I suppose there is a point to all this, Byron,' Cudjoe said, as they hurried past canvases of Rubens and his unmistakable cherubs, ripe and overblown, with lips pouting.

Eventually, Byron stopped in a much smaller room. 'This is what I wanted to show you. I had to think for a moment – I wasn't sure if I saw it here or at the Maritime Museum.'

Cudjoe stood behind Byron, looking up at the painting.

'There – I knew I was right. Look at the faces.'

The canvas was roughly a metre square and was very dark; giving the impression the scene had been portrayed at night. The background featured a large ship capsizing in rough seas, tossing broken timbers in mountainous waves. The foreground caught Cudjoe's attention. He peered closer. The scene depicted slaves fleeing the vessel, some scrambling on all fours, clutching at rocks. He shifted his gaze to the faces of the leaders and immediately registered shock.

'Good gracious, the faces are the same – identical twins.'

He studied the likeness. They had different expressions and it occurred to Cudjoe that one seemed furtive while the other one looked frightened.

'I thought you would be impressed.'

'That's an understatement, Byron.'

'Look at the captions underneath.'

'Runaway Slaves, Quao, and Cuffee 1777. Unknown artist. We have names for them now – Thursday and Friday.' Cudjoe could hardly contain himself.

'Of course! They are Coromantee names. I forgot you're a direct descendant,' Byron said, taking a closer look.

'Coromantee named their children after the days of the week. The odd thing is, if they were twins, why the different names?'

'Well, they could hardly be called by the same name,' Byron said dryly.

Deep in thought, Cudjoe stared at the faces. If there was a joke intended on Byron's part, it was lost on him.

'Unless,' Cudjoe said, inspired, 'one was born on or just before midnight on the Thursday, and his brother after midnight into Friday. That has to be it, Byron. There couldn't be any other explanation.' He viewed the canvas from another angle. 'What I can't understand is why it's here in Liverpool.'

He looked at Byron, seeking an answer.

'To me it is obvious. Liverpool had stronger links with the slave trade. It would be natural to assume the scene happened here in this area. The fact that the artist is unknown adds to the mystery. Come on, Cudjoe, would you look at this scene and recognise it as Bristol? Of course, you wouldn't. This painting didn't even occur to me until you told me the legend of the twins. There is another reason I remembered it, and from your point of view the most powerful.'

Cudjoe looked at him, wondering what else he could possibly tell him.

Byron pulled out a magnifying glass from his briefcase. 'Take a look at that broken mast that the slaves are clinging to. Directly behind them, what do you see?'

Cudjoe took the magnifying glass he offered, locating the section. 'The name of the ship unbelievable! '*Silas Hunt*.' Cudjoe stood in front of the canvas, reluctant to tear his eyes away. 'Is there any way we can find out more about the painting, Byron?'

The curator's office was on the first floor.

'Okay, what do you want to know?' he asked, loading a disc. 'As you already know, the artist is unknown, and the only thing of consequence is the fact that the Africans depicted in the paintings …' He stopped, squinting, trying to read the text. 'Ah, now this is interesting.'

Cudjoe and Byron leaned over his shoulder, their eyes following the screen.

'The runaway slaves were from a remote inland village where they were known to be sorcerers and despised by the other villagers who made them outcasts.' The curator sat back in his chair. Apart from that, gentlemen, I can't help you any further,' he said, shutting down his computer.

'You have been a great help.' Cudjoe shook his hand.

They went back to Byron's flat. Cudjoe had intended to dine with him at Byron's club and then go to the Cavern club, but he couldn't settle. These latest revelations began playing on his mind and the differing birth dates added to the melting pot. He had a lot to think about and felt an overwhelming need to get back to Bristol as soon as possible.

Byron read his thoughts because he said, 'we had better find some transport for you, Cudjoe, but I can't say it will be easy. That's something I hadn't thought about.'

'What.'

'Easter. It's going to have to be the coach and that's bound to be full.'

They walked together to the taxi rank. He clapped Byron on the shoulders as they stood facing each other. 'Keep me informed, Cudjoe. Are you sure you don't want me to come to Bristol with you?'

'No – this is something I have to do. Ever since I met Cassie and Mark, I knew I had a part to play in their lives. I feel bonded with this couple, Byron.'

Byron nodded. 'Well, you know where I am if you need me, and you have all my phone numbers.' He hesitated when Cudjoe got into the taxi. 'It sounds as if it's coming to a head. One piece of advice, Cudjoe: keep salt with you at all times and if you can, dissolve it in water. Salt to a zombie is like garlic to a vampire.' Byron shut the door on him. 'And good luck!' he shouted as the taxi pulled away.

Cudjoe eventually caught the evening coach, settling himself into a quiet corner in the back seat. He rested his head against the rough fabric, trying to still his racing mind. He calculated when he would arrive back in Bristol – if he was lucky, it would be before midnight. As for a game plan, he had no idea and could not even begin to think what he would be dealing with. He felt his mobile vibrate in his pocket – it was a missed call from Felix. Returning it, he left an urgent message to ring him as soon as possible. Refusing to think about it anymore, he drifted into an uneasy sleep.

Cudjoe slept deeply, only to be woken by someone brushing past him and bumping him with a sports bag. He looked around, startled, pulling himself up from the slouching position he found himself in.

'Where are we?' he said to no one in particular.

'Birmingham services mate,' said the same man with the sports bag, barging his way down the aisle.

'You've got twenty minutes, people! Please be back here on time. I've had a weather warning and I'm not leaving anything to chance!' The driver pulled his jacket from the overhead compartment and smiled as they all left the coach.

Cudjoe watched his fellow passengers hurry towards the restaurant. The wind whipped through him as he joined them. His mobile rang as he went through the automatic doors.

'Yes?' His tiredness couldn't hide his abruptness. 'Felix?'

'No, it's Byron. Listen, Cudjoe, I've found out more on the brothers being Loas …'

'Hang on a minute, Byron, I'm at the services, that's better,' he said, going back outside. 'Okay, give.'

'You mentioned that the fires that happened on previous occasions took place around this time of year? Well, it got me thinking after you left and I have unearthed a significant piece of information. Cudjoe, listen to me carefully. It's important for the stronger twin to overcome his weaker brother and in order to do this he would have to take another soul this Easter. More importantly, it would be a soul that his brother had chosen, one that he felt a natural empathy towards or an understanding.'

'Cassie.'

'Exactly. If the stronger brother can possess her soul, he destroys his weaker brother and, more importantly, this ensures his presence into the next century and beyond.' Byron inhaled deeply. 'Cudjoe? Are you still there?'

Cudjoe held the mobile at arm's length, alarmed at events he had no control over. 'That's the link we have been looking for. Cassie was right; she always knew there was a powerful reason … I have to go, Byron.'

'Take great care. You're up against it, Cudjoe. Unfortunately, I won't be able to help.'

Cudjoe bought a bottle of water at the vending machine. Clutching it, he battled the wind and went back to the coach. The driver, already seated, had the engine running and the passengers hurriedly found theirs. Exhausted, Cudjoe slumped in the corner, watching people settling down.

What would I give to swap to the normality of a mundane onward journey? He thought feeling weighed down by the gravity of the situation. His mobile rang just as he dozed. 'Joe?'

'Felix! At last! Why didn't you ring earlier? Did you get my message?'

'Yes, I've been away for a couple of days. I only got back this evening. Terrible journey – I didn't think the car was going to make it at one point. This weather is bizarre, Joe. I even had a puncture, and I began to think things were working against me.'

'The signal's not good. Ring me in five minutes when we are on the move.'

'What have you found out?'

'A lot. Speak to you in five minutes.'

Cudjoe looked out of the window at the first of the rain spiking the glass. It really is in the lap of the gods now, he thought. Ten minutes later, Felix rang.

'Thank God, Felix.'

'Okay, what's happening, Joe?'

'Is Mark home yet?'

'Apparently not. They're behind on one of the projects and he and Roger have decided to work over the Easter period. Cassie isn't very happy but …'

'What? Listen, Felix, go over there now. Cassie must not be left on her own. Do you understand? Her life depends on it. I cannot stress this enough – go over and stay with her.'

'I'll ring her first, Joe.'

'No! Get over there! Just do it, Felix!'

'OK, OK. At the same time, I will find out your arrival time then we can drop down and pick you up.'

'Thanks. I didn't mean to sound overbearing, Felix. Remember – don't leave her alone for a second. I will explain when I see you.' Cudjoe ended the call. Now able to settle back and relax, he glanced at the rain-lashed window and wondered which twin would be the first born, good or evil?

He dozed to the sound of the engine. In his troubled mind, it was confused with the beat of Voodoo drumbeats.

Chapter Thirty

Roger studied the distorted view from the bottom of his glass. He juggled the ice, hoping to get a different picture. Realising he was wasting his time he slid the glass towards the barman for a refill.

His phone call to Sabrina further depressed him – she wasn't home or she was refusing to answer the phone. Perhaps it was time to face the truth. Even in his drunken stupor, he had no idea what he would find when he got home. What he did know was that the veiled threats to leave him were all too real.

He smiled at the barman, a bitter expression on his face. Downing the best malt whisky the hotel could offer, he felt the liquid spreading through his body like fire. Trying to rationalise the disintegration of his marriage, he had once thought near perfect, wasn't easy. He wondered if he should blame himself. Sabrina always got her own way. Perhaps if he had been more assertive, she might have had more respect for him. Now they were barely on speaking terms and the conversation about starting a family had brought it all to a head.

Leaning on the bar, he laid his head in his arms, knocking over his glass. He spilled whisky on the cuff of his shirt as he hid from the world.

Mark successfully ended his discussions with the Americans, but success came at a price.

He had to prove the costing would not exceed the budget. Unfortunately, it meant the entire Easter holiday would be locked into going over everything bit by bit.

He excused himself from the table and walked out of the temporary boardroom, his shoulders sagging with tiredness. The exhaustion felt all-consuming. He had been under so much pressure since they arrived, and Roger's lack of concentration had added to the load. His concern for Cassie drained him emotionally and the thought of her in the flat alone disturbed him. She had taken it badly when he broke the news that he would be staying in Swindon over Easter, making all sorts of accusations; telling him he didn't care for her or the baby before abruptly ending the call.

Mark found Roger where he expected to see him – in the bar. Pulling up a stool, he sat next to him.

'I don't suppose it's crossed your mind that we have bitten off more than we can chew?' Slurring his words, Roger fixed Mark with a glassy stare. 'Sabrina has been giving me bloody hell and frankly, Mark, I don't think this contract is worth my marriage. I don't even know if she'll be there when I get back to Bristol.'

'Oh, come on, Rog, of course she will. We're all under a lot of pressure now, and if it's any consolation, I'm in Cassie's bad books as well. Tell you what, let's go up to your room, and talk about it there?' He steered Roger out of the bar and into the lift, relieved that the client wasn't around to witness the scene.

Inside Roger's room, Mark helped him on to his bed, where he collapsed in a heap.

'I hate to see you so unhappy, Rog.' Mark leaned over to loosen his tie and took off his shoes, but Roger was already asleep.

He went over to Roger's mini bar and helped himself to a whisky and soda. He found Sabrina abrasive, even bordering on controlling, but never had he thought that they wouldn't make a go of their marriage.

Mark was annoyed that he let his emotions get the better

of him. After checking on Roger, Mark closed the door behind him, placed a 'do not disturb' sign on the door handle and went back to his own room to shower and dress for dinner.

The Americans' parent company had taken over the entire ground floor of the hotel – it was their way of keeping things informal.

'We thought it would better than a large office somewhere in Swindon, and what with this god-awful weather closing in, we don't have to move anywhere'.

Mark looked over at him, cutting off a piece of Stilton. 'Well, I have to say you made the right choice.'

The evening meal had been a resounding success, and everyone had the opportunity to meet colleagues socially. Mark and Roger were not the only Brits staying at the hotel; a Marketing Consortium from Bath was also present.

'What did you say Roger was suffering from?'

'Migraine. Unfortunately, he does tend to be affected by them,' he said.

He hated lying, but it seemed easier to save face with one. Making small talk with his opposite number, they began to discuss Vern and Bob, with Mark sharing his Jamaican experiences. Interrupted by an announcement of severe weather, the room became quiet.

'Forget coffee and liqueurs on the patio, guys,' someone quipped. 'Apparently, it's bordering on a force-nine, with reports of force-ten, even eleven, by the end of the night,' he continued.

'Jesus!' said one of the American management team. 'This is England, not the Caribbean.'

Mark's opposite number reached for a Havana cigar, rolled it between his fingers and laughed at the prospect of a force-eleven. 'I honestly don't think it would be a force-eleven. That would almost be impossible over here in Europe.'

Even so, Mark thought about the American's throwaway

remark, remembering where it all began on November fifth. The storm that night had been every bit as ferocious. Was there a link? What if this was part of a plan to keep him here in Swindon? For what purpose? Dismissing his thoughts as absurd, his attention focused on a commotion in the foyer.

'Gentlemen, if you could please listen for a moment. It appears the MD has been delayed. His New York flight is grounded in Amsterdam due to the severe weather and I've just been informed that Bristol airport is closed until further notice.'

'Surely it's not that bad?' the executive opposite Mark commented.

'When was the last time you went outside?' his associate fired back.

He was right. They had become insulated inside the hotel and, until it was brought to his attention, no one had given the worsening weather a second thought. It was the signal for everyone to go their separate ways.

Getting up from the table, Mark bumped into the chief executive, Stuart Patton. 'Can I have a word, Stu?' he said, steering him out of earshot. 'It's my wife, she's pregnant. She'll be terrified in this storm, and I feel I should be with her.'

'Don't worry, Mark.' Stu slapped him on the shoulder. 'I've seen this kind of storm in the States, and they soon blow themselves out. Now, if you were talking about a tornado, then I could understand your fears. Look, if we crack on first thing tomorrow, we could tie up all the loose ends by mid-afternoon. How does that sound?' He saw Mark's expression. 'Hey, Mark, come on. Let me buy you a drink. Sure, is a shame about Roger? What did you say was wrong with him?'

'Thanks, Stu, but if you don't mind, I'll give it a miss.'

'Well, if you change your mind, you know where to find me.' Stu turned to the bar and ordered a double scotch and soda.

Mark smiled, pleased to see that Roger had sobered up enough to order room service. He had gone to his room and found him tucking into a chicken curry, Mark pulled up a chair

'Did you get through to Cass?' Roger asked his mouth full.

'She's not answering.'

'Maybe the lines are down.' Roger scraped the last of the rice on to his fork.

'Rog, Cass is pregnant.'

Roger stopped eating. 'Christ, I had no idea! Congratulations mate. When's she due?'

'Not until September.'

'Sabrina never mentioned it.'

'That's because she doesn't know. Cass wanted to tell her in her own time.'

'She's not going to be happy, Mark. Sab feels she should be privy to everything that concerns Cass.' He wiped his mouth with a napkin.

'Yes, I know, and I did tell her. I think she wanted this news for herself. For the first time in her life, she has something that is hers alone.'

'I can understand that, Mark. How was dinner?' Roger asked, changing the subject. 'Was my absence noticed among the great and the good?'

'It was.' Mark laughed. 'I fobbed them off with an excuse that you had a migraine. Oh, and by the way, the MD's flight is grounded in Amsterdam, and Bristol airport is closed until further notice.'

'Jeese, well that's it then, there's no point in staying here, Mark, if he won't be showing. He is the decision-maker after all.'

Roger put his tray on the side table, threw off the duvet, and started taking his suits off the hangers. 'Meanwhile, I have a marriage to try and salvage,' he said, looking for his suitcase.

Mark went back to his room, surprised at Roger's outburst. If only he was as assertive in their business life, he thought, swiping his key card to his door.

Aware of the pulsating red dot on the fax machine, Mark crossed the room and switched on the table light. The fax had spiralled off the edge of the table and made a path along the carpet. Mark's hands trembled as he tore it off.

It was from Della, and obviously meant for Cass.

'Dear God' he whispered trying to make sense of it. The sentences leapt out at him as his brain absorbed the incredible information.

He knew instinctively that he could not ignore the situation any longer. He had to act now. Shaking, he snapped off the light and headed for Rogers room.

Chapter Thirty-One

Cassie had no idea what had woken her so suddenly, but she was relieved anyway. She had been dreaming vividly about Beneba. Her dream had taken her to the mountains of Jamaica. She was standing in front of Beneba's shack, and it was night. The forest began closing in on her in the darkness. Twisted roots protruded from the earth and gripped the shack like a boa constrictor. In her muddled mind, she could not understand why the clearing had become so overgrown, or even if the roots of the trees were protecting the shack or holding it a prisoner.

She moved closer, listening to the inhuman keening coming from the shack, rising in pitch, until she reached the makeshift door. She banged on the door, the keening suddenly stopped. In the terrible silence, she stepped back. It was as if Beneba knew she was outside. A harrowing wail rose up from underneath the door.

'Marassa … Marassa …' She turned to run, her hands covering her ears. Her feet felt like they were encased in cement as she tried desperately to get away.

Cassie stared, wild-eyed, into the darkness, her heart beating against the wall of her chest as the images flashed before her. Rain lashed against the bedroom window, and she realised the storm had influenced her dream.

She switched on the bedside light – her body and pillow were saturated with perspiration. Stripping off her nightdress, she looked at the clock – ten past ten. Still unnerved by the dream, she fumbled with the dials of the shower and turned it on full. Even the force of the water could not drown out the storm. She searched in the airing cupboard for fresh nightwear as she listened to the nightmare outside. If only Mark were here.

Her thoughts dwelled on the arguments that had resulted on her hanging up on him. A gust of wind sent the dustbins crashing against the wall. Feeling vulnerable and frightened, she got back into bed and drifted into an uneasy sleep.

The telephone rang and for a moment, Cassie thought she had returned to her dream. Disorientated, she answered it, convinced it was Mark.

'Darling, I'm sorry.'

'Cass? It's me, Sab.'

'Sab?' Cassie forced herself to concentrate. 'I thought you had gone away for the weekend?'

'I've been trying to call you, but the phone just rang and rang.'

'What's up, Sab? What is so urgent? Is it Anne? Is she with you?'

A flowerpot crashed on the concrete step outside the flat, accompanied by wild moaning at the door. Cassie looked over her shoulder towards the hall, half expecting someone to break in.

'Cass?'

'Yes, Sab. I'm sorry, it's a bit scary, and every little noise is making me jump.'

'Listen, Cass. Mark rang here. Apparently, he couldn't get through to you either. He told me to tell you he's coming home for the weekend after all.'

'That's brilliant! Did he say what time he would be arriving?'

'The thing is Mark wants you to meet him at the plot.'

'What? Tonight? Are you crazy? There's a hell of a storm going on outside and besides, Mark wouldn't suggest anything so stupid, especially with the …'

'With what, Cass?'

'Are you sure he said the plot, Sab?'

'I'm only passing on his message, Cass. His words were that you have to meet him at the plot – he stressed it was important. I did ask him if he had taken leave of his senses, but he cut me off. Look, why don't I come with you? It's barbaric to expect you to go up there on your own and I would never forgive myself if anything happened to you, Cass.'

'Thanks, Sab but there's no point in both of us going out. He had better have a good reason. What about Rog?'

'He's with Mark. Are you sure you don't want me to go with you?'

'No, it's okay, don't worry. I'll talk to you in the morning.'

As soon as she ended the call, Cass immediately rang the hotel. The staff confirmed that Mark and Roger had left over an hour ago.

So, it must be true! Not that she doubted Sabrina, but the whole scenario was too fantastic for words.

The window rattled, unsettling the casement. She closed the window and switched on the radio, more to prepare her mentally, but the station had been completely taken over with the storm. Various experts were giving their opinions on the cause of the phenomenon.

Depressed, she switched it off and went in search of her boots. She left a message on Felix's answer phone, resigning herself to the fact that in all probability, he wouldn't hear it. She took her wax jacket off the hanger, put it on, and stood for a moment, her eyes closed. She would give anything not to go up there. Everything good and optimistic she had felt that day had disappeared, leaving her with negative feelings that threatened to swamp her.

Bracing herself, she picked up the ignition keys and said a silent prayer before heading out into one of the worst storms she had ever known.

***

Cudjoe's coach pulled into an almost-deserted bus station. He wiped the window, already looking for Felix. From his point of view, he was glad to arrive in one piece after the hellish buffeting they had endured. But thanks to a change of driver at Gloucester and careful driving, they had made it – just.

Passengers had already left the bus station by the time Cudjoe had retrieved his bag from the hold. Left on his own, he waited for Felix.

He rummaged in his pocket for the power snack he had bought earlier. 'What a country,' he said, biting into the cereal bar. He thought about his beloved Jamaica, longing to feel the sun on his back and the aquamarine sea lapping against his skin. Flinching at the tap on his shoulder, he turned to see Felix.

'Where's Cassie?' Cudjoe asked as they embraced.

'That, I don't know.' Cudjoe held him at arm's length.

'Hell, Joe, don't look at me like that. After you phoned, I went to her flat, but it was in darkness. I knocked on the door, she obviously wasn't in and anyway, I had to meet you. That's why I'm late.'

'Come on, Felix, let's get out of here.'

They left Marlborough bus station and headed for Felix's beaten-up old Citroen, the weather throwing everything at them as they struggled to reach it. Already soaked, Cudjoe got in, wondering if the lightweight car was up to the storm. He buckled his seatbelt, deciding to keep his thoughts to himself.

Felix looked at him, incredulous, when he told him to drive to the plot.

'Felix, bear with me and I'll tell you my reasons. Let's get out of the city first.'

Cudjoe could hardly look at the suspension bridge as they climbed the hill. Instead, he began telling Felix everything he had found out in Liverpool. He held up his hand. 'I know Felix, and you were right, Voodoo does have its roots in Haiti and almost the same cultures are practised as Obeah as in Jamaica. You're right – all the superstitions and rituals originated from Africa, regardless of which Caribbean island the slaves were shipped to,' Cudjoe reasoned.

Felix took his eyes off the road for a second. He was particularly interested to hear of the painting hanging in the art gallery in Liverpool.

'So, they assumed the Silas Hunt and her crew were part of the Liverpool slave traffic?' Felix gave a low whistle. 'And if you hadn't got involved, Joe, this wouldn't have become known. To have the name of the ship in the painting …'

'Believe me; I studied the painting for a long time. The brothers were identical. The name of the painting sealed it. "Quao and Cuffee".' Felix glanced at him, puzzled.

'Thursday and Friday, Felix. One twin, Quao, would be born before midnight on the Thursday and the other twin, Cuffee, would be born after midnight into Friday. Byron mentioned that the dominant twin would survive into the next century. That's why this Easter is so important. It is the last one of the century.' Cudjoe fell silent, as Felix absorbed the information.

'They are Loa gods, sorcerers who set out from Africa, as you know, and because they are twins, they share one soul. Both brothers need each other's soul to survive into the next century.'

'Good and evil,' Felix said. 'Let me get this straight – you're saying, Joe, that Cassie relates to the good slave, the one she saw on the bridge and at the auction?'

'That's exactly what I'm saying. If the evil twin is the stronger of the two, all he needs is to take Cassie's soul. Once he has that he will, in effect, have his brother's soul and then nothing can stop him going into the next century – and eternal damnation.'

Felix's mind reeled. It would make some kind of sense to all the research he and Cassie had done, but this was way above even his level of reasoning.

Cudjoe began telling him Byron's thoughts on Anne's zombification. Felix then told him about Anne's visit to the plot to look for Don's ring.

'So that's when it happened. Who went with her?'

'No one. Sab dropped her off on the way to one of her offices.'

'Christ, she must have been at the mercy of everything and anything, poor woman. I knew she had been got at,' he said thoughtfully. 'It's Cass I'm worried about in all this, Felix. For the first time, she is in imminent danger. Don't you see? He has left her alone for a reason, but all that has changed now. He needs her soul tonight. I don't know how he enticed her up to the plot yet, but my guess is she is on her way there now. I only hope we can get there first, although I don't hold out much hope.'

***

Felix put his foot down, temporarily losing control of the car. Changing gear, he followed the white line in the middle of the road. As if on cue, thunder rumbled ominously overhead.

'Just concentrate, Felix.'

High winds rocked the car and rain hammered against the windscreen, making it almost impossible to control the vehicle.

'It's worse up here. Where are we?' Cudjoe asked.

'Not sure, it's difficult to tell in this storm.'

As Felix spoke, a thunderbolt split open the sky, lighting

the way ahead. In his peripheral vision, he could see branches pitching eerily towards the car from both sides of the road. 'My God, this is all we need. It's almost as if it wants to prevent us going to the plot.'

'What time is it?' Felix held his watch up as another flash lit the sky.

'Eleven fifty-five.'

'One twin has been invoked,' Cudjoe said. 'What worries me is which one has been born first: Good or Evil?'

'And if it's the evil one?' Felix offered.

'Then at best it has a head start and at worse, it may be too late for Cassie.'

They fell into silence; Cudjoe deep in thought and Felix desperately trying to concentrate.

'If, hypothetically, what you are saying is true, what power on earth would make her go up there? Christ, Joe, it would have to be important.'

'Her Achilles' heel.' Cudjoe stated.

'You mean, Mark? You honestly think he is involved; no, I can't buy that.'

Cudjoe looked over at him. 'Let's face it, what does anybody know about anybody. Take you and me; apart from our shared knowledge on the slave trade I know little about you Felix.' Cudjoe focused his attention on the road ahead.

'Are you sure you know the way? I thought you told me you have never been up there?'

'Did I? Oh, yes, of course I did. Cassie and I did intend to go to the plot the day we visited Elizabeth Morgan, but we ran out of time. Even so, she pointed me in the direction, and I have seen enough maps on the area to last me a lifetime.

'You see, I rest my case.'

'Fuck, Joe, it's hard enough driving in these conditions without you trying to trip me up.'

'You're right, Felix I'm sorry, we're both on edge.'

Cudjoe settled back into his seat, with a niggling doubt in his mind that wouldn't go away.

'And for the record, Joe, I don't think for one minute Mark means Cass any harm.'

'Me neither. Still, we have to have an open mind, mainly because we don't have a clue what is ahead of us.'

They lapsed into an uncomfortable silence as the storm cracked open the sky again.

'Look out, Felix!' Cudjoe shouted when someone stepped out of the woods in front of them.

Felix slammed on the brakes, feeling a dull thud under the car. 'My God, it's a child' he said, squinting in the wing mirror. 'What the hell is a child doing up here?' Crashing the gears, he managed to put the car in reverse.

'I think I've hit it!' Cudjoe lurched forward as Felix hung on to the wheel, steering the car crazily.

Cudjoe heard the click of Felix's seatbelt as he tried to get out.

'No, stay where you are!' Cudjoe held his arm.

'But there's a child out there, for God's sake! Joe, it could be dying!'

Cudjoe tightened his grip. 'Don't be fooled, Felix. Wait for the second twin to be invoked. Remember, Marassa possessions take the form of child spirits. It's a trick, don't you see? Quao will do anything to stop us going to the plot.'

'So, you think Quao is the evil twin?' Felix already had his hand on the door handle.

'Yes. Unfortunately, it looks that way, which is not good for Cassie. Felix, what are you doing?'

'I can hear the child moaning, Joe!' Felix opened the door and rushed into the night.

He called after him. 'Felix! It's not what you think it is – it's not human, don't you understand?' Cudjoe stared out at the storm blasting into the empty chasm left by Felix. He could do nothing more.

He waited. Another flash lit up the sky and Cudjoe looked at his watch: exactly midnight. Anxious, he peered through the back window, trying to see Felix. He noticed the back door on the driver's side swinging carelessly on its hinges. He switched on the radio, willing some normality into the situation, only to hear bizarre crackling.

A cold sensation crept along his neck, causing his skin to tingle. He shivered and turned to check the door, but it had closed. He reached over, struggling to close the driver's door Felix had left open. 'Where the hell is he?'

A curtain of fog cocooned the car, blinding his vision. Cudjoe wound down the window, but it only made things worse. The fog reached into him, sucking the life out of his lungs. Choking, he looked around for an escape route.

Without warning, Felix wrenched open the door, his wet clothes stuck to his skin.

'I thought you were lost! Did you see anything?'

Felix shook his head. 'I almost did, but I got disorientated out there. And where has this fog come from?' he indicated with his hands. He glanced at Cudjoe. 'Joe are you all right?' he said, noticing his hand shaking as Cudjoe buckled the seatbelt.

'Not really, Felix. Because you decided to rush off, it left me isolated and at risk to …'

'Quao?'

'Yes, and I think we had better get a few things straight. First get that polo shirt off and put this on.' Cudjoe handed him a sweatshirt. 'When I tell you not to do something, it's for a reason.'

'You're right, Joe.' Felix pulled on the sweatshirt. 'I'm sorry; my emotions got the better of me.'

'We must have complete trust – I know my subject, Felix, and by going out on a limb you're not only endangering our lives, but stirring up all manner of other spirits. Besides, it's not a good idea to leave the back passenger door open in a freak storm,' he added.

Felix stared at him. 'But I didn't.'

Cudjoe stared ahead and Felix put the car in gear. His main worry was that events were happening too quickly. He needed to trust Felix one hundred per cent. He allowed the tiredness to sweep through his body. Closing his eyes, he left Felix to concentrate on the road, mentally summoning up every sacrificial ritual he could remember. Now, more than ever he wished he'd taken Byron up on his offer to accompany him to Bristol.

'Jeese! Felix yelled, looking in his driving mirror. 'She's here on the back seat!' His voice became hysterical as he stared, mesmerised, at the face of the most beautiful little girl he had ever seen. She gave him the cutest smile, her golden hair curled softly around her heart-shaped face.

'What the fuck?' Cudjoe gripped the sides of his seat as the car swerved. 'Felix, for God's sake, concentrate on the road, not the mirror. If you don't, everything will be lost!'

For a brief moment, Felix's wild eyes bored into his before the mirror drew him again.

Cudjoe braced himself, watching the car veering towards the wood on his left, bumping and grinding on the uneven track. Branches fell in front of them, whipped up by the storm.

'We are going too fast! Look out, Felix – the tree!' Cudjoe pinned himself back in his seat. It was too late … the impact of the crash was lost in the storm.

Chapter Thirty-Two

Frightened by the brief flash of lightning overhead, Cassie gripped the steering wheel. A deafening clap of thunder followed, and the heavens opened up, the wipers fought hard to cope with the onslaught. As on the previous occasion, she found herself on the same desolate stretch of road.

She listened to music but, deciding she was not in the mood, switched it off again. A blurred road sign loomed in front of her, and she turned right abruptly. Her headlights picked up the bungalows on both sides as she drove slowly down the steep approach. Distracted, she found herself zigzagging towards the channel and a dead-end. She screeched to a halt, blaming herself for not concentrating. She rested her head on the steering wheel, and listened to the crash of the waves breaking on to the rocks

'Damn these roads' with their bloody bungalows! They all look the same, feeling the back wheels spin on wet sand that had drifted on to the road. She sat for a moment searching for a tissue. Wiping her eyes, she felt the storm buffeting the car and knew she must get back on to the top road.

Back on the main drag again, she drove slowly. This time not taking any chances, she began searching for the familiar road sign, and took the next right.

Without warning, the bungalows and street lights from all around failed. Her senses reeled at the realisation that she was in complete darkness. She slowed to a crawl, looking for some brightness from somewhere, anywhere, relying now on her car headlights.

'Damn you, Mark, for putting me through this.' Cassie

banged the steering wheel with her fist; her heart pounding. She continued along the road, too scared to reverse and make her way back.

Suddenly she saw it: 'Sandy Way'. Driving with caution she continued down the cul-de-sac that looked exactly like the other one, her panic threatened to swallow her. I am going into the abyss? Her mind began playing tricks. What is the matter with me? I might as well be the last person on earth, she thought Looking around in the darkness, and finding she was alone.

A blood-curdling explosion, worse than anything that had gone before, lit up the sky. Cassie screamed. The channel flashed in front of her. Huge waves pitched and tossed dangerously, carried forward on the incoming tide before crashing on the rocks in front of her, perilously close.

For a reason she didn't understand, she looked up at the sky and prayed for her life and her baby's.

***

Cassie felt weakened by the course of events. Hysteria threatened to take over at the thought of going up the track again in the storm. She thought about her earlier dream of Beneba and the forest holding her prisoner.

Parking well away from the coast, Cassie positioned the headlights towards the narrow lane leading up to the plot. Now almost overgrown, it seemed evil and secretive. She felt for the amulet Beneba had given her, preparing herself mentally.

Reaching over to the glove compartment, she found the torch and thrust it in the pocket of her jacket. It's ironic, she thought – having avoided coming here, she now had no choice. Cassie bit her lip and took a deep breath. Mustering up every ounce of strength, she watched the torrential rain obscuring the windscreen within seconds. She switched off the engine, killing the lights that led the way leaving a void in front of her.

Outside, the full force of the storm hit her, pushing her back against the closed door. Another flash of lightning, followed by a crack of ear-splitting thunder from overhead that momentarily eclipsed the roar of the sea. Without warning, she felt a spasm in her stomach. It felt as if a spring had been coiled and let go, sending shooting pains through every part of her body. Cassie screamed, doubling up with pain. Clutching her stomach, she clung desperately to a lamppost.

Through her pain, she looked towards the channel, the rain plastering her hair to her face.

The tone of the sea changed. The tide began groaning, menacingly sucking at the undercurrents. The thunder was now a far-off rumble. With an effort, she pulled herself upright, her pain quickly turning to anger.

'How dare you, Mark Campbell! How dare you put me in this position! How dare you bring me all the way out here? Just where the bloody hell are you?'

***

'You okay, Joe?' Felix's voice shook.

'Just about, are you?'

' That was a near thing. If I hadn't taken my eyes of the road and looked in the driving mirror …'

'You can't blame yourself, Felix. It's the spirit exerting its power over you.'

'I should have listened to you in the first place.'

'Come on, we need to get the car back on the road.'

They got out and Felix inspected the damage, the storm beating down on him as he checked the axle.

'It doesn't look good!' he shouted. 'I can't even get the boot open.'

'Where do you think we are?' Cudjoe asked, joining him.

'Got to be on the coast road – I can hear the channel in the distance.'

With all the force they could muster, they pushed the car with their shoulders but without success.

'This is no good, Joe. Somehow, we have to get to the plot!' They looked up at the lightning scarring the sky.

'It's impossible; the ditch is filling up as we speak.' Felix felt the mud pulling at his ankles as he tried to get a foothold. 'It's getting worse.'

Cudjoe looked at him, shocked at how pale he had become. The car tilted dramatically towards the ditch and the sky lit the top of trees, which bent towards them in the wake of the storm.

'We have to get it out; one of these trees is going to come down on top of us.' Cudjoe looked at his watch. 'It's two minutes after midnight – into Friday.'

Felix followed his train of thought 'Cuffee?'

'That plank of wood, Felix, over there under that tree. It might be what we need to bridge the gap between the ditch and the car.'

Neither knew how they managed it. Somehow, with strength and ingenuity, they were back on the road and heading towards the plot.

'That went well – I still can't believe how easy it was.' He smiled at Cudjoe, both knowing why.

'Quao and Cuffee have both been invoked and because they share one soul, it will now be a matter of time to see which brother will overpower the other. They have no choice, Felix. They are twins and 'Marassa'.'

'We're almost on the outskirts of the town.'

'Thank God,' Cudjoe said, gathering all his strength.

***

Roger had tried to doze, reasoning that if he could sleep through the journey back to Bristol, it would stop him from thinking. However, the burden of his marriage problems wouldn't go away and every time he rested his head against the car window, his thoughts returned to happier times.

'Goddammit.'

He heard Mark swearing under his breath, fighting to control the car. Roger had become withdrawn ever since Mark came into his room, waving a fax and demanding they leave the hotel and head back to Bristol. When Roger accused him of being a drama queen Mark had become a man possessed and ordered him to get the rest of his clothes in a suitcase and to be ready in five minutes.

He huddled down in his seat, sensing Mark's tension. He tried to conjure up Sabrina's beautiful face as he looked out at the storm. If only she had answered his calls.

Going over the events that had brought him to this point, he had not seen it coming. It had happened around him – how could he not have understood? He felt confused and isolated. He really thought they were happy. It had happened so quickly, and now his wife wanted out.

'What was the number of the last junction?' Mark asked his tone sharp.

'Sorry, I didn't notice. I think we're near the Avonmouth Bridge.'

'We must get to the plot, Cassie needs me.'

Roger glanced over at him. 'Mark, it's still not too late to take me back to Clifton. It'll only be fifteen minutes out of your way, and it will be a nice surprise for Sabrina.'

Mark looked over at his friend with a mixture of disbelief and pity. 'Oh Rog …'

***

It took a mighty effort to climb the steep track. Clinging to strands of yew hedge, Cassie made her way painstakingly towards the plot. The only sound apart from the driving rain came from squelching mud sucking at her boots.

Distant thunder rumbled, reminding her of the storm that at its height had created havoc. She passed a hand over her stomach, relieved that the pain had not returned. She felt calmer now, even the lightning illuminating the roofs of the neighbouring bungalows no longer frightened her.

Staring ahead into the darkness, the path seemed steeper than she remembered. A sudden resurgence in the storm almost forced her back down. She clung on to a branch of wet ivy, and stopped to listen. Above the moan of the wind, she thought she heard a car engine. Was it Mark? Chiding herself for being stupid she realised that of course it wasn't, he was waiting for her at the top. Buoyed on by the thought, she continued.

Cassie felt, rather than saw, the timbered gates that led into the plot. Standing in front of them, she imagined the burnt-out building dark and sinister behind. Her hands began to shake, and she almost dropped her torch, knowing the bungalow would have a different impact on her now. With everything that had happened, she realised something had made the place evil. Worse, her eyes would be drawn to the bathroom where Don had been gored on a shard of glass.

Chapter Thirty-Three

'I'm sure Cass said the track starts at the end of this road.' Felix drove into Sandy Way as he spoke. 'It looks as if the electricity is down here as well. God, it's eerie.' He came down into second gear and peered over the steering wheel, desperately trying to follow the road.

'Careful Felix. There's no way of telling where the road ends and the channel begins,' Cudjoe warned.

'Isn't that her car parked over there?'

Cudjoe looked into the night. 'If it is, it's dangerously near the coastline.'

Felix swung the car and parked farther up the hill. Prolonged thunder rumbled overhead but the roar of the sea on the incoming tide added a new menace.

They got out. Felix flicked on his torch, but it made little impact. An alarm chose the moment to go off and a dog barked in response. They spotted the path and crossed the road. Climbing the track was easy compared to the obstacles they had encountered earlier.

'Joe, I have a question.'

Cudjoe stopped. Felix could just make out his outline against the cliff rising above him. He shook the sleeve of his jacket before wiping his face with his cuff.

'I'm listening,' he said, his voice impatient.

'You talked about Anne being manipulated by her Boko, and now Marassa has been invoked. Who is making this happen?'

'If it is male, it's a Hungan.'

'And if it's female?'

'Then it's a Mambo'

'Which do you think it is?'

Cudjoe loomed large above him, his silhouette outlined by a further flash of lightning. More sinister, Felix thought, were his sardonic features; even in the storm he could feel his eyes boring into his own.

'I don't think you need me to tell you that do you, Felix?'

***

Cassie stepped inside the gate. A blanket of rain added to the intensity of night sweeping the plot relentlessly. She caught hold of the gate for support, rain splashing off the broad laurel leaves near her face, keeping pace with her heartbeat.

Before she even looked around, she knew Mark wasn't there. Closing her eyes and with her back against the fence, she felt the strength she had held together ebb away, leaving her physically and emotionally weak. The rain continued to slam into her, pinning her to the fence. Her legs buckled and she tried to steady herself, feeling the mud beneath her. How easy it would be, she thought, looking down. The voice in her head willed her to let go. Not caring, Cassie listened to it.

There! She felt it! Her baby. She thought it must be her imagination but then she felt it again, the fluttering sensation. She began to laugh hysterically.

'I felt it!' she shouted into the plot. 'I felt my baby! You will not claim me or my baby! We are too strong – do you hear me? I will not be your next victim!'

Her anger grew when she looked at the building – it hadn't been touched. Even with all the numerous builders, nothing had changed. The stench from the charred structure was as strong as ever. Isolated and terrified, she stood, spent, her hands cradling her stomach. She was unable to stop sobbing.

The turbulence at the end of the garden caught her attention and the branches of the willow tree whipped at the storm, almost willing her to react.

'Show me what to do?' The wind caught the strength of her voice, pitching it around the plot.

She thought about her conversation with Sabrina. Did she know Mark wouldn't be here? Seeds of disquiet began to creep into her mind.

A chilling laugh came from the hollow of the building. Cassie held her breath, unnerved. How could she have felt that this was the perfect plot, when now there was only evil? There it was again. This time, the laugh was louder and more sinister. Cassie stared at the derelict building, her fear making her reluctant to move. Instead, she felt for the fence behind her. She was reassured by the texture of the wood. She calculated where the gates were situated.

A continuous blanket of sheet lightning lit the first floor, reminiscent of a stage set. Cassie watched a child bouncing a ball on the steps. She recognised the lovely face that stared out at her from the bonfire on the first visit to the plot. Cassie was now aware of the child manifestation that plagued this plot.

The girl, tired of the game, placed the ball carefully on a stand before looking out into the darkness. With uncanny accuracy, she pinpointed Cassie.

Petrified, Cassie remembered Della's warning about bakas. A blood-curdling howl came from the child, almost as if Cassie's presence threatened her.

'Oh, my dear God.' Visibly shaken, Cassie turned her back on the scene but a blinding light made her turn. Against her will, she became captivated by the angelic child humming a nursery rhyme and weaving a path through the steel girders as if dancing through a maypole. The child's humming turned to an excited giggle, as she appeared to be chasing an imaginary figure.

She started to go through the gate. It was time to leave. The little girl had other plans. Cassie turned and walked toward the girl, noticing the golden curls and beautiful face that was so reminiscent of that November night. She laughed, watching her perform a pirouette, spinning around the girders.

Suddenly, the willow became restless in the distance. Cassie, distracted, looked towards the tree.

'Look at me!' The child stamped her foot in temper, commanding attention. Her heart thundered under her ribs at the girl walked towards her. Terrified, Cassie pushed the gate.

'Fenena'.

'Sab!' she gasped with relief, then paused. 'What are you doing here?' From the corner of her eye, she saw the child scamper out of sight.

'Waiting for you, of course.' Her voice sounded strange.

'Where's Mark?' The silence filled the space between them. 'Sabrina, you're beginning to frighten me. Where is Mark?' She screamed.

A violent wind threw Cassie aside. Shocked, she clutched at the gate to save her from falling. Sabrina screeched a command in a strange tongue and the wind recoiled to the bottom of the garden. Cassie stared at her, unable to comprehend. Her blood ran cold; she opened her mouth but was unable to scream.

'Please tell me this is some kind of nightmare. Speak to me, Sab!'

Sabrina was dressed in a gaudy skirt Cassie had seen the women wear in the Jamaica mountains, with a sleeveless blouse fitted at the waist.

In the dark, a single candle burned, casting a grotesque caricature of Sabrina on the interior wall. A kerchief covered her hair, with a knot tied in the middle, accentuating her high cheekbones. Large gold hoops swung from her ears, glinting in the candlelight as she bent to light more candles, she would never wear jewellery like that.

'Okay, Sab, you win. This is some kind of sick joke that you and Mark have thought up, yeah?'

Sabrina laughed the same unnerving laugh of the child. 'Where do you think Mark is, eh? Swindon of course.' She expelled her breath into the night air. 'With dear Roger,' she spat.

Taken aback by the venom in her voice, she said, 'I don't understand. You rang to tell me he wanted to meet me here?'

'Oh, I think you're beginning understand. How else would I be able to get you up here?' Her laughter jangled Cassie's nerves.

'He's not here then?' She heard the defeat in her own voice, immediately angry for showing weakness.

'Of course not! Do you think I would let anyone spoil this for me now? I have worked years for this.'

Cassie winced as a splinter from the fence pushed into the bed of her nail.

'Bit by bit, I have been patiently biding my time until he is ready to possess me and take us both forward into the next century and time immortal.' She raised her arms towards the sky. A low rumble of thunder shook the building, followed by a flash of light. As she stood at the top of the steps, her face was euphoric, her black skin shiny with rain.

She is completely mad, Cassie thought, looking at the woman who had meant so much to her. Beneba's words came flooding back – trust no one, someone close means you harm. Even with the evidence in front of her, she wondered if she would ever come to terms with it.

She watched Sabrina stalk the width of the building. This is her stage, Cassie thought, looking at Sabrina's silhouette magnified from the back of the building.

'Why here, Sab?' Cassie began to panic, knowing

nothing and nobody could save her now.

Sabrina stopped and stared at her as if she should have known.

'He chose me. I have been aware for years that somewhere on this coastline the Loas had manifested themselves. I couldn't believe it when you told me what happened to you at the plot, Fenena. I knew instantly.'

Cassie started to shake at Sabrina's disclosure. 'Then you knew what happened to Don the day you rang me in Jamaica?' She forced herself to stay calm.

'Poor Don. He had a liking for the ladies, especially Lorna.'

'Lorna? She was here?' Shocked, Cassie could not believe what she was hearing.

'Oh, Fenena, you were always so naïve. Even as children, I could run rings around you. Mirrie used to say that I put you on a pedestal, and perhaps I did, but I was always in control. You were always going to bend to my will eventually.' Sabrina's teeth gleamed from the reflection of the candle she held.

Going farther into the building, she began lighting more candles. 'Lorna must have arranged to meet Don up here. She never knew I was also here, but Don did, and he saw what I was doing. I had to get rid of him, but someone tried to save his life – remember?' She spat the words.

Cassie felt hysteria rising like floodwaters as she remembered Don's reaction when he saw Sabrina leaning over his bed. At the time, everyone had thought he was delirious, but now …

'Did you … did you have anything to do with Mr Morgan's death.

'Of course,' Sabrina said, coming back into view. 'He told me he had been to the plot and found evidence of ritual activity and food offerings hidden away in the shed. He said it was cursed so I found his office and went over there. He was in a worse state by then and needed his medication. I noticed his pillbox in his briefcase and seized it. The box served two purposes Fenena: not only did I have his lifeline but having something personal to him meant he was in my control.'

'Hex?'

'At last, you have got it. Sabrina's mad eyes bored into hers.

'So, you didn't save his life after all?' Cassie screamed sobbing.

'The delaying of the paramedics helped.' Sabrina's vile laugh spilled out into the night.

'My God, Sab, how could you be so heartless? Who are you, I don't recognise you?' Cassie screeched. Weeping not only for Mr Watson but also for the person Sab had become.

The child flashed in front of her and scrambled up the steps. Sabrina leant forward and patted her curls fondly. The girl, rejuvenated, stepped on to the patio, and danced provocatively in front of Cassie. Cassie turned her head away in disgust.

'None of that matters now, Fenena. The most important thing is that you are here at the plot with me.'

'Listen to me, Sab. Why don't I try to get help? The car is at the bottom of the track and even with the lights out, there are bound to be people inside the properties. Please, you and I are sisters, remember?'

'No! I can't let you go now, Fenena.' Her voice seemed different.

'What do you want from me?' Cassie screamed at her.

'Your soul! Quao needs your soul. He has already been invoked. Don't you see? We are their vessels and Marassa will be channelling all their energy through us.' She pointed to the inside of the shell. 'In there is the veve', the symbol of the Loa.' She held her hand. 'Come, Fenena, I won't let you down, we will be together, just as we have always been.'

Cassie followed Sabrina and stood on the first step of the building. The building was cloaked in darkness.

As she turned to her right she could still picture the kitchen ahead. Horrified, she heard the sinister clatter of kitchen utensils that she remembered hung on the wall.

Cassie focused on every positive and every ounce of emotion she had gone through. 'No Sab, I can't do this.' She turned – this time determined to leave.

'Fenena! you don't understand it's our friend, the slave on the bridge. It is He that needs us.' Sabrina waited, watching Cassie walk towards her again, reluctantly taking her hand. All the feeling of sibling love was now evaporating.

With every step she took she looked into Sabrina's eyes – they were cold and scornful.

Following Sabrina's lead, she went up the stairs, further into the dark, to the bathroom. Sabrina's face had become contorted, her blood freezing. She screamed at the contorted features of evil.

'This way, my brother. Your soul belongs to me. I helped you when the '*Silas Hunt*' went down. I saved you when you fought for your life, hunted like the beasts on the plains of Africa. Cuffee, don't deny me now, I am the first-born.' The demonic voice resounded around the hollow building then stopped.

Cassie began to shake, gradually backtracking out of the building and disturbing the crude veve drawings on the floor. and sodden ashes with her feet, she looked down at the embellished Marassa symbols. She stared into the blackened shell, vaguely making out the outline.

'I deny you, brother. I need to be put to rest. Do not resist me,' Cassie replied, completely taken over; her voice sounded strange even to herself.

'We are Loa gods, you and I, we share one soul and I need yours to go forward into the next century.' Sabrina voice ricocheted around the plot.

'To what, Quao? Eternal damnation? No! Let this be the end. Enough damage has been done. I am tired, let us leave this place forever!'

'Never!' Sabrina commanded.

Chapter Thirty-Four

The storm stopped as abruptly as it began, almost as if it had served its purpose. Everywhere had become deadly quiet in the aftermath; even Sabrina had disappeared. The interior of the building was bathed in candlelight. Cassie remembered when Mark had called out to her from this building. Now, as it was then, it was soulless. The misery she felt knowing that she would never see him again began to surface into a high-pitched wail.

'Don't cry, Fenena.' Startled by her sudden appearance, Cassie watched the charismatic figure in front of her; she had changed into a white robe and was carrying a lantern.

'The time has come to truly ride the Loa with me.'

Cassie could barely look at her – the beautiful features she knew so well were contorted with bitterness. Cassie's childhood flashed before her eyes. The happy times with Winston, Mirrie, and everything, they had done together – university, holidays, and the secrets they shared. She looked into Sabrina's frenzied eyes. The betrayal was now complete. She had to accept it.

'You lied to me, Sabrina!' Cassie shouted at her. 'Quao was not on the bridge, it was his twin, Cuffee. You knew that. Your whole life is a lie; you have tainted everyone who meets you, but not me. Cuffee needs me and it is he that guides me.' Cassie screamed, turning towards the willow tree.

'I won't let you go, Fenena.' Sabrina walked towards her menacingly, 'Quao is more important than both of us.'

'Cass, don't move!' It was a command. Alarmed, Cassie looked around for the source. Was she hearing things? Was that Joe's voice? She strained to see in the dark.

'Joe, is that you?'

Sabrina's eyes followed Cassie's and saw Cudjoe's outline against the fence.

'What have I always told you? Don't trust him!' Sabrina screamed at her. 'He is here for one purpose only – to destroy you for his own ends. He is a member of the secret society of sorcerers, the Zobop. Do not listen to him. Whatever your feelings are towards me, Cassandra, it's me who knows what is best for you!' She held out her hand towards Cassie. 'Haven't I always?' She smiled.

Hearing Sabrina use her full name swayed her for a moment. Perhaps it had been a terrible mistake. Perhaps she might have misjudged her. She smiled back at Sabrina, feeling the warmth of her hand as her fingers closed over hers.

'Listen to me carefully, Cassie!' Cudjoe shouted. Aware of Sabrina's strength, he knew he had not got through to her.

Felix caught hold of Cudjoe's sleeve, watching him edge closer to the building.

'Don't cross the line,' Cudjoe demanded. 'This is a Voodoo ceremony and if Sabrina makes you salute the Marassa, Quao will have you as one of the undead.' He paused, trying to gauge if he was getting through to her. 'It's another way to possess you, to gain your soul. Cass, you will not even know it's happening!' Cudjoe could feel Felix breathing down his neck.

'Dear God, its Sabrina. For pity's sake, Joe, what's happening?'

Cudjoe spoke without turning. 'Remember the question you asked me as we came up the track?' He pointed to the building. 'Sabrina is a mambo, the instigator of everything that happens up here, evil or otherwise. The step up to the building where Cassie is standing is her peristyle, the scene of all Voodoo ceremonies. The steel girders form the pivot for ritual dances – it's where the spirits she invokes come.'

'Dear Lord.' Felix looked over his shoulder, trembling.

'I know it's a shock, Felix, but at least it seems Cassie has resisted the first twin's request to share one soul,' he added, his attention on Cassie.

They watched Sabrina preparing offerings for the Marassa, carefully piling the sacrifices with care. She got up and faced Cassie, swaying in front of her, dancing hypnotically, almost as if she heard the music in her head. Cassie stared at her, wondering what she was doing. Sabrina had always hated dancing. Mirrie was always trying to persuade her to go to dancing classes.

'What has happened to her?' Tears rolled down her cheeks as she saw the insanity in every dance step. Was it something in her character? She wondered.

It was suddenly very cold. The dampness from the building wrapped around her, chilling her body.

'Sabrina is now in control of her peristyle. It is her sanctuary and acts as a passage for the spirits that are invoked. Cassie! You must listen. Do you understand?' Cudjoe continued. 'The symbols that Sabrina is preparing represent the Loas of Africa. Marassa, the cult of twins, are more powerful and they are exerting their influence through you both. In your case, Cass, as you already know, it's Cuffee.' He was met with silence.

'Yes, I hear you, Joe.'

'It's important you remember what Beneba said: you must not let Cuffee down. You have to be stronger than his brother Quao, and whatever you do, do not go into the building. When I tell you, I want you to walk backwards towards the fence. Sabrina has gone into the room where the Loa has his altar for sacrifices.'

'Joe, it's the bathroom, where the fires started. It is horrific Joe!'

'Stay focused, Cass, you need to stay focused.'

Coming back into view, Sabrina looked beyond Cassie, towards the garden. She shouted a command and a human shape emerged from the lower garden. It slowly walked to one side of the garden and lit a candelabra where Sabrina had indicated, throwing out an eerie glow, flickering on a light wind. She pointed to the opposite side of the garden and the same figure lit an identical candelabrum, placing it on a stand.

Sabrina's head clicked and spun around at a bizarre angle, checking for the lit candle behind. Her eyes narrowed as she centred on Cassie again. 'That's right, Fenena, the four corners of the compass. Now you can't escape.' She held her arms above her head, her fingers outstretched towards the sky. Cassie closed her eyes, blotting out the vein throbbing in Sabrina's neck.

'Look, Joe!'

'Cudjoe followed Felix's direction. A shrouded outline stood, still and silent in front of the rockery, highlighted by the candles burning brightly from the four corners.

'It's Anne,' Felix gasped. 'You're right, Anne is a zombie. It's one thing talking about it but when you're faced with the reality …'

Cudjoe saw him shaking. 'Felix, whatever you do, don't lose it, not now.'

'Lorna!' Sabrina's chilling voice echoed around the plot, only to be answered by a blood-curdling howl.

'For pity's sake! Felix saw a silhouette rise up from the rockery. Even with the change in her demeanour, there was no mistaking, Lorna.

Cudjoe leant towards him. 'The rockery is their resting place and Lorna's corpse has risen to Sabrina's call.' Anne and Lorna walked side-by-side. 'The walk of the undead,' Cudjoe whispered.

Felix cried out as they came nearer and the zombies

stopped in unison, looking in his direction. Sabrina barked a command in dialect, and they continued towards the building.

'Don't be frightened, Fenena, it's our dear friends, Anne and Lorna. They want to pay their respects to you before you meet Quao.'

Lorna stood on the steps of the peristyle and looked down at Cassie. Her eyes, always hostile, now stared at Cassie with undisguised malice. Her once well-groomed hair hung limply on her shoulders, her black roots forming a grotesque halo around her cheekbones. She hissed in Cassie's direction.

Sabrina spoke sharply and Lorna cowered in a corner. 'I've brought Anne to see you, Fenena.' The kindness in her voice surprised her. 'She wants to thank you for everything you've done for her – don't you, Anne?'

Cassie screamed as Anne appeared at her side and began stroking her hand. She snatched it away, feeling Anne's icy fingers tightening. She fixed herself to look at her, hoping to find a glimpse of the compassionate Anne but the eyes were dead with no recognition at all.

Anne opened her mouth, displaying brown stumps of rotting teeth. Sabrina laughed callously as she drew crude diagrams at the entrance of the bathroom. She beckoned Lorna from out of the shadows. The flame from the candle Lorna held emphasised her grey features and her emaciated frame.

Cassie began to gauge what had become of Lorna and Anne. Lorna, she had no time for, but dear Anne … She watched a child come out of the darkness – the same child she had seen on previous occasions. As with her earlier instincts, she wanted nothing to do with her.

Suddenly animated, Anne put a scrawny arm around the girl's shoulders. The child's laugh was harrowing and spiteful. Disentangling herself from Anne, she stepped carefully over the mud, the glow of the candle soft on her lovely face. She smiled up at Cassie but her smile froze like a mask as she looked at the little girl's expression – it had changed into the most hideous contortion of evil.

'Lily May, come to mummy.' Anne wrung her hands, her voice racked with pain.

Cassie watched in horror. 'She thinks this thing is her own child,' she said, incredulous.

'Let her think it – it's what she wants,' Sabrina responded coldly. She spoke to the child again in dialect and the girl cried and returned to Anne's outstretched arms. Anne whimpered, burying her face in the golden curls.

Cassie watched the scene, her face a mixture of emotions.

'She doesn't need your compassion, Fenena. She just needs!'

The smell of candle grease whipped up again from the bottom of the garden. Cassie turned, expecting to see Anne, the girl and Lorna but they had disappeared into the night.

'She's trying to side-track you, Cass. Don't let her.' Cudjoe edged nearer to the peristyle. He had cut through her fear. Taking comfort from his voice, she listened.

'These are the tricks of the sorcerers, especially the child. Keep your objections in the foremost of your mind. You must release Cuffee and put an end to this reign of evil.' Hearing the wind moaning at the bottom of the garden, he pressed on. 'You have to be strong, Cass – keep Sabrina focused on the past, it's our only hope to get through to her.'

'How, Joe?'

'You have memories, don't you?'

Cassie watched Sabrina pick up a chicken wing and ceremoniously snap it in front of her. Their eyes met, Sabrina's black and wild, She was sucking blood from the broken flesh – the feathers sticking to her mouth.

Cassie began humming their song, the slaves' chorus from the opera 'Nabbuco.' The song had the wrong effect.

The little girl came out from the back of the building, dancing, followed by Anne mimicking her steps. This is absurd, Cassie thought. What am I doing? She stopped humming, watching the bizarre scene.

'Don't stop, Cass. Ignore what you are seeing. Anne is lost now; I'll explain later,' Cudjoe added. Cassie hummed louder.

Sabrina turned and gave her a lovely smile. 'We used to hum that, Cass, remember?'

'I'm pregnant, Sab.' She saw the effect it had on her and knew she should have kept quiet.

'A baby? You're having a baby?' She abandoned the offerings and walked towards Cassie, her white gown flowing behind her.

Cassie felt the unbearable pain gripping her. Bent double, she steadied herself against the demolished patio wall, gasping for breath.

'You even had to do that before me!' She raged.

'My baby!' Cassie screamed, clutching her stomach. 'Please, Sab, not my baby!'

The willow thrashed, the branches beating frantically from all sides, reflecting the menace of Sabrina's anger. Sabrina gave Cassie a scathing look as she watched her from her peristyle.

Cassie held out her arms. it was not meant to be like this. The misery she felt threatened to overwhelm her. Her Sab would have been happy, even discussing names and going shopping … If Cassie ever had any doubts about Sab's feelings towards her, she only had to look at her, and the naked evil staring back into her eyes. She collapsed against a wall, weeping for her lost friend.

Chapter Thirty-Five

Unknown to Cudjoe, Felix was becoming increasingly isolated. The shock of watching almost everyone he had become close friends with over the months disintegrating before him had a devastating effect. He stood beside Cudjoe, watching events unfolding. Then he saw her. He stared, watching her take a ball off a stand and bounce it, laughing as it spun. Felix, captivated once again, smiled at her, just as he had earlier in the car mirror.

The scene had become illuminated, and he realised it was because of the candles Sabrina had lit everywhere in the building. The girl stopped bouncing the ball and tucked it under her arm possessively, looking out into the darkness towards him. Her smile could have only been meant for him. Focusing on her, he walked towards the building. Felix stopped, and turned to look at the willow, wondering what had made it restless.

Cudjoe, who stood passive, watched him intensely. Sabrina and Cass had disappeared from view. Only Anne was in sight. Bending towards her, she kissed the girl's hair.

'Look at me!' the child demanded. 'You are not looking! I have a present especially for you.' The child began throwing the ball in the air, laughing when she caught it.

'Here, catch your present, Uncle Felix!'

Felix's laughter rang out as he went to catch it, willing to play her game. He felt the thud as he caught it. Something was not right. He looked down at his blood-stained hands. Lifting his head, he gave an inhumane cry. The eyes staring up at him belonged to David.

***

Against his better judgement, Mark left Roger in the car. He had become more morose the nearer they got to Bristol and Mark had difficulty snapping him out of his melancholy mood. Concerned to what he would find when he reached the top; Mark began thinking about the fax he received from Della. She had made it clear the plot had lain derelict for centuries and Guede, the spirits of death, had manifested themselves undisturbed for all that time.

Della had suggested that the Mamba, or high priestess, was a close friend of Cassie's and her sole purpose was to protect both the plot and the Loas cult of twins and the Voodoo legacy. She had gone on to say that Cassie must wear the amulet that Beneba had given her for protection. Cassie has been chosen to stop Quao through his twin Cuffee and to cleanse the plot before the Easter of the Millennium – and damnation.

In the fax, there was a reminder that they needed to carry salt water with them. It also added that if a zombie tasted salt, the fog in its brain would be lifted, they would realise their distressing state and turn on the one person that made them zombies in the first place. Their anger would know no bounds and they would have a compulsive desire to kill their master and demolish everything. They would know they were living corpses and would try to find their way back to their graves.

The fax went on: 'Mark, you must keep one step ahead. The Mambo will be too strong; you have to go for the zombies. This will blind-side Sabrina, and she won't see it coming. That is your ace card. Good luck and may God be with you.'

Feeling the weight of Della's words on his shoulders, Mark braced himself as he made his way up to the plot. He stopped at the sound of a harrowing wail from above. His fingers tightened around the flask he held, knowing that the two women that had grown up together with so much love between them were now in conflict against each other.

Cudjoe was beyond devastation. He saw Felix's crumpled body rocking, and he knew he was lost forever.

'You bastard!' He shouted at the empty peristyle 'You fucking bastard.' He jumped at the hand on his shoulder. 'Mark! You're the last person …'

Mark fixed his gaze beyond him, at Felix, trying to comprehend what had happened.

'I was the only person that knew David had been decapitated at Temple Meads station, Felix took me into his confidence the day of Don's funeral I don't think he ever got over it, but I suppose he needed to tell somebody. I never even told Cass. But, to have his head up here …'

'It happens in some African witch-craft ceremonies. If you want to blame anyone, blame her.' Cudjoe pointed a finger at Sabrina, his voice outraged.

Mark followed his gaze handing Cudjoe a torch and a fax, all the time staring at Sabrina. He heard a twig snap and turning, watched Felix disappear farther into the garden.

'Leave him, Mark. I knew he had been got at on the coast road'. Joe said. Della is right; Byron also mentioned salt as an antidote when I left the city.'

Mark looked at Cudjoe. 'But zombies, Joe,'

'Believe me that is what Felix Lorna and Anne have become, and now we know Sabrina is a Mambo, and she is in charge of all she surveys, waiting for the one that possesses her. Look at her, Mark – have you noticed how she's focused towards the channel, watching for him to come in from the shipwreck?'

Cudjoe held up the flask. 'This, my friend, is the most important thing you could have done for Cass. We have to aim this salt water at them, to bring them out of their comatose state if we are going to survive this, and I mean Cassie as well.' He put his arm around Mark's shoulder. 'Sabrina will have to be destroyed by her zombies and this is how we are going to do it.'

Mark stared at him, horrified, as he listened. His voice rose in panic.

'Where is Cass? I can't even see her, Joe!'

'You know the plan, Mark. Let's go.'

Mark edged his way towards the burnt-out shell, softly calling her name. 'Cass? It's me, Mark. Listen, darling, hold the necklace Beneba gave you.' Cudjoe looked at Mark, 'Where is Roger?'

'In the car. He knows nothing, thank God. If he did, it would break him. Funny, he never once asked me why we were returning to Bristol,' Mark said,

'Mark, is that really you?' Her voice filled her with renewed hope – she had no idea how he got there, and she didn't care.

Sabrina went towards her and gripped her wrist. 'What are you doing here, Mark?' She screeched. 'You're not part of my plan!'

'You're wrong, Sabrina. Beneba protects Cassie and ultimately Cuffee. Not you!' His voice was powerful, reverberating through the building.

Sabrina loosened her grip.

'Enough, Abigail, stabbing me in the back to destroy me, your sister Fenena. Remember this, you will always be a slave, and Nabucco knew that,' Cassie said, pushing past her.

'Where are you going, Fenena? Do not leave me, there is unfinished business. Fenena, please.'

Cassie stopped at the sound of her pleading. Turning slowly, she looked up at her on the steps, the lit candle turning her face into a mask of grief. With a heavy heart, she turned back and continued walking down the garden to Mark. They watched Felix fall into step beside Anne as they walked in unison. The child, skipping behind them.

Cassie buried her head into Mark's chest, sobbing. He stared at Felix, unable to come to terms with what he had become.

Cudjoe felt Felix's cold hand as he brushed pass, He caught sight of Lorna as she joined the group. Together they formed a protective circle around Sabrina as she welcomed them.

'My dear Lord.' Cassie watched as they fawned over each other.

'Gede!' Sabrina shouted into the wind. 'Gede! Spirits of the dead!'

Cudjoe reached over behind Cassie. Taking the flask from Mark, they exchanged nervous glances. A second later, Cudjoe lunged towards the group.

***

Lorna and Anne took the full force of the water, their eyes widened, the shock registered on their grey faces. Lorna broke the circle, only serving to increase the confusion as Anne began chattering incoherently. The child looked up at Anne's hysterical face, laughing cruelly.

'Gede!' Sabrina screeched in desperation. Her head lolled from side to side, her eyes rolled in her sockets. Her soul was succumbing to the madness she had created. She looked over at Cassie, trying to focus, and screeched again.

Cassie covered her face, blocking out the harrowing scene.

Felix fixed a gaunt look at Cudjoe. The salt water had barely touched him.

'Felix, I didn't want this to happen, but you wouldn't listen to me.'

At the sound of Cudjoe's voice, Felix walked towards him in the slow rhythm of a zombie and Cudjoe threw the last of the water at him. Felix jerked backwards, his expression changing; he licked the salt from his lips. The recognition lasted a split-second before a vicious grin spread across his face.

Holding each other close, Mark and Cassie distanced themselves from Felix.

'Listen, Mark, the willow is calling me!' With surprising strength, she broke away from him and ran towards the bottom of the garden.

'Cass, come back!'

It was too late. She found herself near the rockery – standing almost in the same spot she had several months earlier.

The weather began to turn again, this time, becoming even more intense and disturbing. She shivered, remembering the toads clambering over her feet on that November night, and worse, the thought of more zombies underneath the stones. She screamed into the wind, the rain whipping her hair into her face as she went deeper into the garden.

The tree was alive, the frenzied branches engulfing her view, dancing to the crashing waves down below. A distant moaning joined the orchestra of evil and she knew without turning the wailing sound of the zombies as they recognised their undead plight.

Cassie never looked behind, but she knew they had turned on Sabrina.

She looked at the tree, it was calm again.

'Oh, my brother, it has to be, I am alone now. No more shall this area be vilified; your spirit has vanished forever.'

Mark's first thought had been to go after his wife. He felt the painful grip as Cudjoe held him back.

'Wait, Mark.'

They looked towards the building. The zombies had begun their onslaught on Sabrina, their long nails tearing at her skin.

With a chilling scream, Roger burst through the gate and threw himself at Sabrina, knocking Lorna and Anne to the ground with such energy that the crack of broken bones could be clearly heard.

'Rog! Don't do it, she's not worth it!'

Yet Roger wasn't listening. His sights were on the pathetic figure of his wife as he covered her body with his own. The wrath of the zombies had taken its toll on her scrawny body. He looked into her eyes, trying to find a connection with her. Wiping away a strand of her hair, he kissed her face. Then, contorted with grief, he leant over, snatched the lantern next to her and set fire to her bloodied gown. The flames caught hold, quickly licking at the folds of the material.

'No!' Mark shouted.

Roger held Sabrina close as the flames engulfed them both.

Cudjoe relaxed his grip on Mark's arm. 'I'm sorry, my friend, but I had a feeling Roger knew what he had to do. He put her on a pedestal but in the end, he couldn't ignore her flaws, especially when he found out she had put Cass in danger.

He looked down the garden. Where is she, Joe?'

'Look down at the willow.' As Cudjoe spoke, the tree burst into light. From the centre, a surge of blue light spiralled like a tornado, the branches falling away as the trunk looked as if it was pulsating before their eyes. The channel roared as if applauding and the waves broke on the rocks beneath.

Cassie, her arms outstretched, looked up at the sky. 'Never again, Quao. This is the end of your reign!' she shouted triumphantly, the elation in her voice unmistakable as it echoed around the garden.

The sky was illuminated with colour. 'Beneba,' she said, dropping to her knees in front of the willow, sobbing. Cassie watched the light spiral upwards towards the sky and beyond. Slowly, she made her way back up the garden. Already it felt different.

She stood before the building and said a silent prayer for Sabrina, Roger, Anne, Don, Felix and Lorna.

It was only Mark who saw the tears streaming down her face as she embraced the amulet that Benenba had given her.

Chapter Thirty-Six

It took several months before Cassie could even begin to come to terms with the loss of Sabrina and the events that led up to it. On the advice of her doctor, Mark took her to a rambling old manor house in deepest Wiltshire to convalesce.

'She must have complete rest,' the doctor stressed. Especially in the vital months leading up to the birth.'

'I feel as though I am abandoning her, Doctor. She has been through so much. I can't even begin to tell you …'

'You have my assurance; your wife will have the best of care, Mr Campbell.'

Mark gazed out at the manicured lawns. How could he possibly understand? He thought, irritated by his glib statement. How can anyone understand?

'Based on the information I have of your wife, she has a lot of guilt trauma that should have been dealt with in her formative years.' The doctor got up from his swivel chair. 'What tends to happen in such cases is that suppressed feelings of guilt are transferred to any trauma that is current at the time … in this case, the horrific death of her close friend.'

The doctor's voice droned on. Mark thought about those closing moments, desperate to get counselling of his own.

'It's possible that she may benefit from regression therapy.' The doctor saw the look of dismay on Mark's face. 'Don't worry; we won't do anything without your consent. If we did, we would certainly wait until after the birth. Now I will leave you to settle your wife.' He moved to the door and opened it. 'Oh, by the way, I think it would be better if we kept visiting to only you, just for the time being anyway.'

Mark stood in the doorway; misery etched on his face. 'I don't think that will be a problem, doctor. There is no one else.'

Driving through Welsh Back and across the city centre towards Cotham was relatively easy. The doctor's chance remark had brought all the raw emotion to the surface. How easy it would be to sink into a well of self-pity. The traffic lights were in his favour, as he turned right into St Michael's Hill.

His thoughts turned to Roger. He would leave a huge hole in his life and the devastation of watching him burn alive would live with him forever. Winding up their business interests had been easier than anticipated – thankfully he had left most of it to the accountants. However, it meant he had to deal with Roger's personal belongings, triggering memories of when they both started the business together in the early days.

Turning into his road, he wondered how Cassie would cope. She hardly noticed him when he kissed her goodbye. Instead, she stared straight through him. Offering her cheek to receive his kiss. He noticed how her once beautiful eyes had a vacant look, making them unusually large.

Mark parked under a hawthorn tree bursting with early leaf. The evenings were already drawing out. Nodding at a passing neighbour, he activated the car alarm and crossed the road. Depressed, he went into the empty flat.

It was two weeks later when Mark met up with Cudjoe and for the first time, he felt able to unburden himself after the incident. Cudjoe had gone back to Liverpool, seeking solace in the wisdom of his friend Byron.

'It's good to see you, my friend,' Mark said, hugging him. 'Your time in Liverpool seems to have agreed with you. We all have to find our own way of dealing with this, Mark.' Mark nodded.

Guiding Cudjoe's arm, he led him into the restaurant. The sombre mood stayed with them over lunch.

'How is Cass?' Cudjoe looked up from playing with his food.

'Not a lot of progress at the moment but in fairness, the doctor did warn me it would take time.'

'Mark, I am sorry. After everything that happened that day, you certainly don't deserve this as well.'

Mark gave him a wry smile. 'She was the one that had been chosen. I have to accept that, Joe. However, I do believe that Beneba's death is having a profound effect on her. I know she bonded with the old woman that day when they all went up into the mountains.'

'What about you, Joe? How are you coping?'

'Meeting up with Byron was a lifesaver, I just to have someone that's on the same wavelength to talk with. Mind you, I have given him more information on Voodoo religion than he has come across in his lifetime. Or so he says,' Cudjoe added, glad of some light relief.

'What has happened with the business?'

'I'm in the process of winding up our partnership. The American contract ended, of course, and I am trying to recuperate monies there.' Mark sighed, shaking his head, and finishing the last of the wine. 'Under the circumstances, it's a small price to pay, Joe.'

Cudjoe signalled for the bill. 'You were right about the doll, by the way. It was an effigy of Don. To have that much body hair and nail clippings, Sabrina must have been alone with him for some time.'

'It could only have been when he was in hospital,' Mark said.

'Where did you say you found it, Mark?'

'Roger's cousin came across it in Sabrina's dressing-table drawer. I was finalising some of Roger's papers and suddenly he came rushing in with this tiny effigy wrapped in a bandage congealed with dry blood.' Mark grimaced.

'Well thanks for handing it over. I've left it with Byron. He's making a study of Voodoo dolls. I remember you saying at the time that he might make a full recovery ... then I saw how venomously Sabrina had stuck the pins in the doll ...' Cudjoe looked at the bill the waiter had brought. 'It's no wonder all his internal organs were shot to hell, poor bastard.'

'Let me pay for this, Joe.'

'I won't hear of it. You can pay next time.' Cudjoe handed over his credit card. 'And we now know the pathologist's death was linked to the plot.'

Mark shivered at the memory of Felix holding David's head.

'And Mr Morgan?'

'My guess is he was hexed. There's no doubt Sabrina had found a nice little outlet to get rid of her evil collections of personal items.'

'How Sab must have hated Cass.'

'In some ways, yes. She must have grown up with a certain amount of jealousy and resentment, although it seems she was able to keep it in check.'

'She certainly did that. Any idea how she got caught up in all this in the first place?'

'No, I haven't. I wouldn't think it would be Bristol, even though Felix thought otherwise. I have heard there is a network in London that she may have been involved with. But going back to what you said just now, my feeling is it was not Cassie that Sabrina hated, but Cuffee. Once she knew that Cassie was a receptacle, from then on, she only saw her as the twin that stopped her going into the twenty-first century.'

They fell silent as they wandered out into the car park, bathed in afternoon sunlight. Blotches of bright-coloured flowers spilled out of flowerpots lining the gravel path, but the scene was lost on the two men.

'Now I know why Cass was never in any real danger. Sabrina must have orchestrated that. Until the millennium. I could never understand the reason why.'

'Oh yes, Sabrina knew how to be patient, my friend.' Cudjoe opened his car door. 'Have you been up to the plot since?'

'No, the previous buyer pulled out, so I left it with the agent. To be honest, Joe, I don't have the appetite. He reported back that everything is burnt to the ground this time and there was no mention of … of the others.' Reaching his car he added, 'it's almost certain we will move. Everything depends on Cass, of course. You'll be about for a while, won't you Joe?'

'Yes, I intend to have a break in Port Antonio as soon as I can, though.'

'Good because Cass is discussing godparents and your name is at the top of the list. You haven't heard that from me, though.'

'I would be honoured. You know that.'

'Joe, before you go, have you heard what happened to Beneba?'

'Yes, she died the moment Sabrina was destroyed. I think she knew she would be able to die in peace.'

Mark was left alone with his thoughts. He watched Cudjoe stir up the gravel; pull out of the car park on to the road. A cloud moved in front of the sun, casting a dull shadow.

Chapter Thirty-Seven

Three months later, Mark had that long-awaited phone call to collect his wife. He had spent the morning in his office. Everything concerning the business had been finalised and all traces of Roger and their hopes for the future was now past.

His heart leapt when he saw her. Gone were the pale shadows under her eyes. She had returned to her former health. Her hair shone against her golden skin after days spent in the sprawling gardens.

It was only four weeks to the birth, and she was positively glowing. Cassie looked over at him and smiled as she relaxed beside him, enjoying the leisurely drive through the Wiltshire lanes.

Cudjoe took Mark's call two days later, and asked him over for lunch. The pleasure of seeing Cassie restored to her vibrant self, delighted him, and the easy atmosphere brought with it the same familiarity they had all experienced in Port Antonio.

'I had a beautiful handmade card from the Americans and Della wrote me a lovely letter,' Cassie said, handing them to Cudjoe. 'Mark and I have invited them over to the baptism, but we will see.'

'You could be in for a surprise, Cass – you know how they embrace every aspect of British culture. A traditional baptism in an English church would be something they would not be able to pass up,' Mark added.

'Well, we have enough of them in this area,' Cassie laughed. Cudjoe helped her out of the chair 'And thanks for agreeing to be a godfather, Joe. It means a lot to us.'

He kissed her, feeling himself welling up.

'She's good, Mark,' Cudjoe said as they walked to the end of the road.

Mark smiled. 'Yes, she is, Joe. Will you be drawing on this case when you get back to Jamaica?'

Cudjoe put his hands on Mark's shoulders, a poignant look in his eyes.

'No. I don't think the world is ready for this, do you, Mark?' They embraced and Mark watched Cudjoe walk towards Redland.

He looked up at the chink of blue sky, transforming an otherwise dull day, the clouds were already lifting.

With a lightness of spirit he hadn't felt for months, he went back into the flat and Cassie.

THE END